Otherwise Engaged

Otherwise Engaged

A M A N D A Q U I C K

G. P. Putnam's Sons
New York

G. P. PUTNAM'S SONS
Publishers Since 1838
Published by the Penguin Group
Penguin Group (USA) LLC
375 Hudson Street
New York, New York 10014

USA • Canada • UK • Ireland • Australia
New Zealand • India • South Africa • China

penguin.com
A Penguin Random House Company

Library of Congress Cataloging-in-Publication Data

Quick, Amanda.
Otherwise engaged / Amanda Quick.
p.   cm.
ISBN 978-0-399-16514-6
1. Women travelers—Fiction.   2. Scientists—Fiction.   3. Spies—Fiction.   I. Title.
PS3561.R44O85   2014   2013042660
813'.54—dc23

Printed in the United States of America
10   9   8   7   6   5   4   3   2   1

Book design by Meighan Cavanaugh

For Frank, my seriously romantic hero

Otherwise
Engaged

One

Are you a passenger traveling on the Northern Star, *by any chance, madam?"*

The voice was male, British, well educated and raw with what sounded like pain and shock. It came from the shadowy entrance of a nearby alley. Amity Doncaster stopped cold.

She had been on her way back to the ship, her notes and sketches of the local island scenes tucked into her satchel.

"Yes, I'm traveling on the *Star*," she said.

She made no attempt to approach the alley. She could not see the speaker concealed in the shadows, but she was quite certain that he was not a fellow passenger. She would have recognized the dark, curiously compelling voice.

"I am in rather urgent need of a favor," he said.

She was quite certain now that the speaker was in great pain. It was as if it took every ounce of strength and will he possessed just to speak to her.

Then, again, she had met some very fine actors in her travels and not all of them had been professional thespians. Some had been very talented con artists and criminals.

Nevertheless, if the man was injured she could not turn her back on him.

She lowered her parasol and unhooked the elegant, specially made Japanese fan from the chatelaine at her waist. The tessen was designed to look like an ordinary lady's fan, but with its pointed steel spikes and metal leaves it was, in truth, a weapon.

Gripping the tessen in the folded position, she went cautiously toward the alley entrance. She had seen enough of the world to be wary of strangers calling out from the shadows. The fact that in this case the man spoke with an upper-class British accent was no guarantee that he was not a member of the criminal class. The Caribbean had once been plagued with pirates and privateers. The Royal Navy and, more recently, the U.S. Navy had eliminated much of the threat from that quarter, but there was no permanent solution to the problem of ordinary thieves and footpads. She had found them to be as ubiquitous as rats everywhere in the world.

When she arrived at the mouth of the alley, she saw at once that she had no cause to fear the man sitting with his back braced against the brick wall. He was in desperate straits. He appeared to be in his early thirties. His night-dark hair, damp with sweat, grew from a sharp widow's peak. He no doubt usually wore it sleeked back behind his ears, but now it hung limply, framing the planes and angles of a hard, intelligent face set in a grim, resolute mask. His light brown eyes were glazed with pain and the beginnings of shock. There was something else in those eyes, as well—a fierce, ironclad will. He was hanging on, quite literally, for dear life.

The front of his hand-tailored, white linen shirt was soaked with fresh blood. He had removed his coat, wadded it up and now clutched it tight against his side. The pressure he was exerting was not enough to stop the slow, steady stream of blood leaking from the wound.

There were bloody fingerprints on the letter he held out to her. His hand shook with the force of the effort required to make even that small gesture.

She reattached the tessen to the chatelaine and rushed toward him.

"Good heavens, sir, what happened? Were you attacked?"

"Shot. The letter. Take it." He sucked in a sharp breath. "Please."

She dropped the satchel and the parasol and crouched beside him. Ignoring the letter.

"Let's have a look," she said.

She infused her voice with the calm authority that her father had always used with his patients. George Doncaster had claimed that the notion that the doctor knew what he was about gave the patient hope and courage.

But this particular patient was not in the mood to be reassured. He had one objective in mind and he pursued it with every ounce of his fading strength.

"No," he said through gritted teeth. His eyes burned with determination to make certain she understood what he was saying. "Too late. Name's Stanbridge. I booked passage on the *Star*. Looks like I'm not going to be making the voyage to New York. Please, a favor, madam. I beg of you. Very important. Take this letter."

He was not going to let her help him until he had made certain that she would deal with the letter.

"Very well." She opened the satchel and dropped the letter inside.

"Promise me that you will see to it that the letter gets to my uncle in London. Cornelius Stanbridge. Ashwick Square."

"I am on my way back to London," she said. "I will deliver your letter. But now we must deal with your wound, sir. Please let me examine you. I have had some experience with this sort of thing."

He fixed her with a riveting gaze. For the briefest flash of time she could have sworn that she saw something that might have been amusement in his eyes.

"I have the impression that you have had a great deal of experience in many things, madam," he said.

"You have no idea, Mr. Stanbridge. I will take excellent care of your letter."

He looked hard at her for a few seconds longer through half-closed eyes.

"Yes," he said. "I believe you will do precisely that."

She unfastened the blood-drenched shirt and eased aside the hand he was using to press the crumpled coat against the wound. A quick look told her what she needed to know. The flesh of his side was ripped and bloody, but she saw no sign of arterial bleeding. She pushed his hand and the coat back into place and got to her feet.

"The bullet passed cleanly through and I don't believe any vital organs were struck," she said. Working quickly, she hiked up the skirts of her traveling dress and tore several lengths of fabric off her petticoats. "But we must control the bleeding before we take you to the ship. There is no modern medical care available on the island. I'm afraid that you are stuck with me."

Stanbridge grunted something unintelligible and closed his eyes.

She fashioned a thick bandage out of one long strip of the petticoat. Once again she eased his clenched hand and the coat away from his side. She pulled the edges of the wound together as best she could, fit the bandage over the gash and then clamped his hand on top to hold the compress in place.

"Press hard," she ordered.

He did not open his eyes but his strong hand clenched tightly around the makeshift bandage.

Swiftly she wound two long strips of petticoat fabric around his waist and tied them securely to hold the bandage in place.

"Where did you learn to do that?" Stanbridge growled. He did not open his eyes.

"My father was a doctor, sir. I was raised in a household where medicine was the chief topic of conversation at every meal. I often assisted him in his work. In addition, I traveled the world with him for a few years while he studied medical practices in various foreign lands."

Stanbridge managed to open his eyes partway. "This is, indeed, my lucky day."

She glanced at the bloody shirt and coat. "I wouldn't go so far as to call it your lucky day, but I do believe that you will survive it. Under the circumstances that is no small thing. Now we must see about getting you aboard the *Star*."

Her father had died a year earlier, but she still carried his medical kit with her on her own journeys abroad. The kit, however, was back in her stateroom on board the ship. Now that she had staunched the worst of the bleeding she had to figure out a way to get Stanbridge to the *Star*.

She rose, went to the entrance of the alley and stopped the first two people she saw, both locals on their way to the market. It was only a matter of a few minutes to get things organized. One glance at Stanbridge in the alley and the men understood what was needed.

With the assistance of two of their friends, both fishermen, they conveyed the barely conscious Stanbridge back to the ship in a make-shift litter fashioned from a fishing net. Amity tipped them quite extravagantly, but they seemed more pleased with her heartfelt grati-tude than with the money.

Members of the *Star*'s crew got the patient into his stateroom and onto the narrow bunk. Amity requested that her medical kit be brought from her own stateroom. When it arrived she set to work cleaning the wound and closing it with several stitches. Stanbridge groaned from time to time, but for the most part he drifted in and out of consciousness.

Amity knew that she was on her own with the patient. There was no longer a doctor on board the *Star*. The ship's physician, a ruddy-faced, overweight man who had been given to smoking and heavy drinking, had succumbed to a heart attack shortly after the ship de-parted from its last port of call. Amity had stepped into the breach as best she could, treating the various shipboard injuries and occasional bouts of fever that occurred among the crew.

There were only a handful of other passengers on the *Star*—British and American for the most part. The *Star* would take on a few more when it stopped at other islands along the way, but it was unlikely that Captain Harris would be able to find another doctor until they arrived in New York.

❧

The fever set in sometime around midnight. Stanbridge's skin was alarmingly hot to the touch. Amity soaked a cloth in the basin of cool water that the cabin attendant had brought to her and draped it across the patient's forehead. His eyes flickered open. He looked at her with a bewildered expression.

"Am I dead?" he asked.

"Far from it," she assured him. "You are safely on board the *Northern Star*. We are on our way to New York."

"You're sure I'm not dead."

"Positive."

"You would not lie to me about a thing like that, would you?"

"No," she said. "I would never lie to you about something that important."

"The letter?"

"Safe in my satchel."

He watched her intently for a long moment. Then he seemed to come to a conclusion.

"You would not lie about that, either," he said.

"No. You and your letter will both arrive in New York, Mr. Stanbridge. You have my word."

"Until then, promise me that you will not tell anyone about the letter."

"Of course I won't tell anyone about it. The letter is your personal business, sir."

"For some reason I think that I can trust you. In any event, it doesn't look as if I've got much choice."

"I will keep your letter safe, Mr. Stanbridge. In return you must promise me that you will recover from your injury."

She couldn't be certain, but she could have sworn that he almost smiled.

"I will do my best," he said.

He closed his eyes again.

She removed the cloth, dampened it and then used it to cool the portions of his overheated chest and shoulders that were not covered by the bandage.

A knock sounded on the stateroom door.

"Come in," she called quietly.

Yates, one of the two stewards, put his head around the door.

"Is there anything else I can do to help, Miss Doncaster? The captain told me you are to have everything you need."

"That will be all for now, Mr. Yates." She smiled. "You have been very helpful. I have cleaned the wound as thoroughly as possible. The stitches have slowed the bleeding. From now on it is up to nature. Fortunately, Mr. Stanbridge appears to be endowed with a strong constitution."

"The captain says that Stanbridge would have died back there on St. Clare if you hadn't found him in that alley, got him to the *Star* and closed up that hole in his side."

"Yes, well, he didn't die so there is no point dwelling on what might have happened."

"No, ma'am. But he's not the only one on board who has cause to be grateful to you. The crew knows that you're the reason Red Ned didn't die of that fever he came down with last week and Mr. Hopkins didn't lose his arm after his injury got infected. The captain is telling everyone he wishes he could keep you here on the *Star*. The crew would be pleased if you stayed and that's a fact."

"Thank you, Mr. Yates. I'm glad I could be of some assistance, but I must return to London."

"Yes, ma'am." Yates bobbed his head. "Ring if you need me."

"I will."

The door closed behind the cabin attendant. Amity reached for another wet cloth.

Near dawn the fever broke. Satisfied that Stanbridge was out of danger, at least for the moment, Amity curled up in the room's only chair and tried to get some sleep.

Sometime later she awoke with a start. An unfamiliar flash of awareness shivered through her, rattling her nerves. She blinked several times, listening closely in an attempt to identify whatever it was that had roused her from her troubled sleep. All she heard was the low rumble of the *Northern Star*'s big steam engines.

She unfolded her legs and sat up somewhat stiffly. Stanbridge watched her from the bunk. That was what had awakened her, she realized. She had sensed his gaze.

She was oddly flustered. To cover the awkward moment she fluffed out the folds of her staid, brown traveling gown.

"You are looking much improved, Mr. Stanbridge," she said.

It was the truth. His eyes were no longer hot with fever, but there was another kind of heat in his expression. It sent a shivery thrill of excitement across the back of her neck.

"I'm glad to know that I appear to have improved." He shifted position a little on the bunk. His face tightened in pain. "Because I certainly feel like hell."

She glanced at the medical kit on the dresser. "I'm afraid there is not a lot that I can do for your pain. I am running low on supplies. I have a little morphine left but the effects are short-lived."

"Save your morphine, thank you. I prefer a clear head. I'm not sure I introduced myself properly. Benedict Stanbridge."

"Captain Harris advised me of your name. A pleasure to meet you, Mr. Stanbridge." She smiled. "Under the circumstances, perhaps not exactly a pleasure but better than the alternative. I am Amity Doncaster."

"Doncaster?" His very interesting face tightened into a frown of concentration. "Why does that name sound familiar?"

She cleared her throat. "I have written several travel pieces for the *Flying Intelligencer*. Perhaps you have read one or two of them?"

"Not likely. I never read that rag."

"I see." She gave him her coldest smile.

He had the grace to look abashed. "Now I've managed to insult you. That is the very last thing I wish to do, believe me."

She got to her feet. "I'll ring for the steward. He can assist you with your personal needs while I go back to my own stateroom to freshen up and get some breakfast."

"Hold on, I know where I've heard your name." Benedict looked pleased with himself. "My sister-in-law mentioned your travel pieces. She is a great fan."

"I'm delighted to hear that," Amity said in the same cool tones.

She yanked hard on the bell pull and reminded herself that Benedict was recovering from a nasty wound and therefore could not be held accountable for his poor manners. But the knowledge did not lessen her irritation.

Benedict looked at the satchel she had placed on the dresser.

"That letter I gave to you for safekeeping," he said. "You still have it?"

"Yes, of course. Shall I get it?"

He considered that question for a few seconds and then shook his head. "No. Leave it there in case—"

"In case of what, Mr. Stanbridge?"

"It's a long way to New York and I might take a turn for the worse," he said.

"Unlikely."

"Nevertheless, I prefer to have a plan in place to deal with such an eventuality."

She smiled. "I take it that you are a man given to planning for all possibilities?"

He touched the bandage on his side and grimaced. "You see what happens when I fail to plan well. As I was saying, if I fail to make it to New York, I would consider it a great favor if you kept your promise to deliver the letter to my uncle."

"Cornelius Stanbridge, Ashwick Square. Never fear, I wrote down the address so I won't forget it. But I assure you it won't be necessary for me to deliver it. You will recover from your wound, sir, and deliver the letter yourself."

"If I recover, there will be no need for me to deliver it."

"I don't understand," she said. "What does that mean?"

"Never mind. Just promise me that you won't let that satchel out of your sight until I feel strong enough to take care of the letter myself."

"I give you my word that I will keep the satchel and the letter with me at all times. But I do feel that, given all that has transpired, I am owed some explanation."

"In return for your promise to guard the letter I give you my word that someday I will explain as much as I can."

And that was all she was going to get by way of a guarantee that she would one day be told the truth, she concluded.

A knock announced the return of Yates. She hoisted the satchel and crossed the small space to open the door.

"I will look in on you again after breakfast, Mr. Stanbridge," she said. "Meanwhile, be sure you do nothing to undo my needlework."

"I'll be careful. One more thing, Miss Doncaster."

"What is that?"

"According to the *Northern Star*'s schedule, we are not due to arrive in New York for another ten days. In addition to the passengers who are already on board, we will no doubt be picking up a few more."

"Yes. What of it?"

He levered himself partway up on one elbow. Pain tightened the corners of his eyes. "Do not tell anyone else about that letter—not any of the other passengers or any members of the crew. It is vitally important that you not trust anyone who is on board now or who may come aboard between here and New York. Is that clear?"

"Quite clear." She gripped the doorknob. "I must say, you are certainly a man of mystery, Mr. Stanbridge."

He sank wearily back down onto the pillows. "Not at all, Miss Doncaster. I'm an engineer."

Two

The storm at sea was far away but the lightning illuminated the clouds in a fiery radiance. The atmosphere was charged and intoxicating. On a night like this a woman could be forgiven if she believed she could fly, Amity thought.

She stood on the promenade deck, her hands braced on the teak railing, and watched the spectacle with wonder and excitement. Not all of the intense, exhilarating emotions were generated by the storm. It was the man standing beside her who was responsible for most of the thrilling sensations, she thought. Somehow they went together, the night and the man.

"You can feel the energy from here," she said, laughing a little with the sheer pleasure of it all.

"Yes, you can," Benedict said.

But he was not watching the storm. He was looking at her.

He rested his hands on the railing, his fingers very close to hers.

His wound had closed with no sign of infection, but he still moved with care. She knew he would be stiff and sore for a while. A few days ago, having concluded that he was going to live, he had requested that she return his letter.

She told herself that she was happy to be relieved of the responsibility. But something about the small act of giving him the letter had left her feeling wistful, even a trifle bereft. The task of concealing the letter—knowing that Benedict entrusted her with it—had created a sense of a bond between them, at least on her side.

Now that frail connection had been severed. He no longer needed her. He was swiftly regaining his strength. Tomorrow the *Northern Star* would dock in New York. Her intuition told her that everything would change in the morning.

"I won't be traveling back to London with you," Benedict said. "As soon as we dock tomorrow I must take the train to California."

She had been prepared for this, she reminded herself. She had known that the interlude on board the ship would end.

"I see," she said. She paused. "California is a long way from New York." And even farther from London, she thought.

"Unfortunately, my business takes me there. If all goes well, I won't be obliged to stay for long."

"Where will you go after you leave California?" she asked.

"Home to London."

She did not know what else to say, so she held her tongue.

"I would like very much to call upon you when I return, if I may," Benedict said.

She could suddenly breathe again. "I would like that. I shall look forward to seeing you again."

"Amity, I owe you more than I can ever repay."

"Please don't say that. I would have done as much for anyone in your situation."

"I know. It is one of the amazing things about you."

She knew she was blushing and was grateful for the cover of night. "I am certain that you would have done the same under similar circumstances."

"You have been forced to take me on faith," Benedict said, very serious now. "I know that can't have been easy. Thank you for trusting me."

She did not respond.

"One day I hope to be able to explain everything to you," he continued. "Please believe me when I say that it's best if I don't tell you the whole story yet."

"It is your story, sir. You may tell whomever you wish to tell."

"You deserve the truth."

"Now that you mention it, I agree with you," she said.

He smiled at her crisp tone. "I wish I was sailing back to London with you."

"Do you?"

He put his hand over hers on the railing. For a heartbeat he did not move. She knew that he was waiting to see if she would pull her fingers free of his grasp. She did not move, either.

He caught her hand and turned her slowly around to face him.

"I'm going to miss you, Amity," he said.

"I will miss you, as well," she whispered.

He drew her to him and took her mouth with his own.

The kiss was everything she had dreamed it would be and so much more—darkly passionate, utterly thrilling. She put her arms around his neck and parted her lips. His scent captivated her. She breathed him in. A sweet, hot hunger uncoiled deep inside. Fearful of causing him pain, she was careful not to lean too heavily against him even though she wanted to do so; oh, how she wanted to lose herself in the wonder of it all.

He dragged his mouth away from hers and kissed her throat. His hands moved to her waist and then slipped up the bodice of her gown until his fingers rested just beneath the weight of her breasts. The heat and fire on the distant horizon was an extraordinarily perfect backdrop to the fierce emotions that threatened to sweep her away. She gripped Benedict's shoulders very tightly, seeking promises but knowing she would not get them—not tonight. Tonight was an ending, not a beginning.

Benedict gave a low groan, shifted his mouth back to hers and deepened the kiss. For a timeless moment the world beyond the *Northern Star* ceased to exist.

Driven by a passion that was unlike anything she had ever experienced, she longed to follow the kiss straight into the heart of the storm, as if there was no tomorrow. But with a low groan, Benedict broke off the embrace, setting her gently but firmly away from him.

"This is not the time or the place," he said.

His voice was as harsh and as heavily freighted with the steel of his ironclad self-control as it had been the day she found him bleeding in the alley.

"Yes, of course, your wound," she said quickly, mortified that in the heat of the moment she had forgotten all about his injury. "Forgive me. Did I hurt you?"

His eyes gleamed with dark amusement. He brushed her cheek with the back of his hand. "My injury is the very last thing on my mind tonight."

He walked her back to her stateroom and said good night at the door.

In the morning the *Northern Star* docked in New York. Benedict escorted her off the ship. A short time later he disappeared into a cab—and from her life. He never even bothered to send so much as a telegram from California.

Three

LONDON

Amity blamed herself for failing to realize until too late that there was a man concealed in the shadows of the cab. It was the rain, she concluded. Under most circumstances she would have been far more observant. Traveling abroad, she made it a point to pay strict attention when she found herself in unfamiliar surroundings. But this was London. One did not expect to be kidnapped straight off the street in broad daylight.

True, she had been distracted when she left the lecture hall. She was still fuming because of the countless inaccuracies in Dr. Potter's lecture on the American West. The man was a benighted fool. He had never so much as set foot outside of England, let alone bothered to read her pieces in the *Flying Intelligencer*. Potter knew nothing of

the West, yet he dared to present himself as an authority on the subject. It had been too much to take sitting down, so of course she had
been forced to stand up and raise some serious objections.

That had not gone over well with Potter or his audience. She had
been escorted out of the lecture hall by two stout attendants. She
had heard the muffled snickers and disapproving sniffs from the
crowd. Respectable ladies did not interrupt noted lecturers with the
goal of correcting them. Luckily, none of those in the audience were
aware of her identity. Really, one had to be so careful in London.

Irritated and eager to escape the dreary summer rain, she had
leaped into the first cab that stopped in the street. That proved to be
a serious mistake.

She barely had time to register the odd, shuttered windows and
the presence of the other occupant before the man wrapped an arm
around her neck and hauled her close against his chest. He pressed
the tip of a very sharp object to her throat. Out of the corner of her
eye she saw that he gripped a scalpel in one gloved hand.

"Silence or I'll slice open your throat before it's time, little whore.
And that would be a pity. I'm so looking forward to photographing
you."

He spoke in a harsh whisper but the accent was unmistakably
upper-class. His face was covered by a mask fashioned out of black
silk. Openings for his eyes, nose and mouth had been cut into the
fabric. He smelled of sweat, spice-scented cigarettes and expensive
cologne. She was vaguely aware of the fine-quality wool of his coat
because of the way he held her pinned against him.

He moved, reaching out and around her to pull the door shut. The
vehicle jolted into motion. She could tell that the carriage was moving at a rapid clip, but with the view through the windows blocked
by the heavy wooden shutters she had little sense of direction.

One thing was evident immediately. Her captor was stronger than she was.

She stopped struggling and allowed her arms to go limp. Her right hand rested on the elegant fan attached to the silver chain at her waist.

"What do you want with me?" she asked, striving for a thoroughly indignant and outraged tone of voice.

But she knew the answer. She had known it from the moment she saw the scalpel. She had fallen into the clutches of the fiend the press had labeled the Bridegroom. She struggled to keep her voice cold and assertive. If there was one thing she had learned in her travels, it was that an air of coolheaded self-control was often the most useful defense in a crisis.

"I'm going to take a lovely wedding portrait of you, my sweet little harlot," the killer crooned.

"You're welcome to my purse but I must warn you that there is very little of value inside."

"You think I want your purse, whore? I have no need of your money."

"Then why are we going through this pointless exercise?" she snapped.

Her insulting tone enraged him.

"Shut your mouth," he rasped. "I will tell you why I have taken you. I am going to make an example of you, just as I have done with the other women who displayed a similar lack of shame. You will learn the price of your deception."

She did not think that it was possible to be any more frightened, but an even more intense wave of terror swept through her at his words. If she did not take some action to free herself, she would not survive the night. And she was quite certain she would only get one chance. She had to plan well.

"I'm afraid you have made a great mistake, sir," she said, trying to project conviction into the words. "I have deceived no one."

"You lie very well, Miss Doncaster, but you may save your breath. I know exactly what you are. You are just like the others. You give the outward appearance of feminine purity but underneath the façade you are tainted goods. The rumors of your shameful behavior while abroad reached my ears this past week. I am aware that you seduced Benedict Stanbridge and convinced him that, as a gentleman, he has no choice but to marry you. I am going to save him from the trap you set for him, just as I saved the other gentlemen who were deceived." The killer traced the blade lightly around her throat, not quite piercing the skin. "Will he be grateful? I wonder."

"You think to protect Mr. Stanbridge from the likes of me?" she asked. "You are wasting your time. I assure you, Benedict Stanbridge is quite capable of taking care of himself."

"You think to trap him into marriage."

"If you feel that strongly about the matter, why don't you wait until he returns to London? You can inform him of your theories concerning my virtue and allow him to draw his own conclusions."

"No, Miss Doncaster. Stanbridge will discover the truth about you soon enough. Meanwhile, the Polite World will learn what you are tomorrow morning. Don't move or I will slit your throat here and now."

She held herself very still. The tip of the scalpel did not waver. She contemplated the possibility of slipping away from the blade and hurling herself to one side of the seat. But such a maneuver, even if successful, would buy her only a few seconds at most. She would find herself trapped in the corner, her tessen against the scalpel.

The Bridegroom was unlikely to murder her inside the carriage, she thought. It would be far too messy, to say the least. Surely there would be a great deal of blood and that would require an explanation to someone, even if only to the coachman. Everything about the killer, from his elegantly knotted tie to the furnishings of his vehicle, indicated that he was the fastidious sort. He would not ruin his fine suit and the velvet cushions if he could avoid it.

She concluded that her best chance would come when he attempted to remove her from the carriage. She gripped the closed tessen and waited.

The killer reached across the seat to a small box that sat on the opposite cushion. When she caught the telltale whiff of chloroform, another current of panic arced through her. She no longer possessed the option of waiting for the carriage to halt. Once she was unconscious she would be helpless.

"This will keep you quiet until we reach our destination," the Bridegroom said. "Never fear, I will wake you when it is time for you to put on your wedding gown and pose for your portrait. Now, then, lean back in the corner. That's a good girl. You will soon learn to obey me."

He prodded her with the scalpel, forcing her to edge toward the corner. She tightened her grip on the fan. The killer glanced down, but he was not alarmed by her small action. She could not see his expression because of the mask but she was quite sure that he was smiling. He no doubt enjoyed the sight of a helpless woman clutching piteously at an attractive bit of frippery attached to her gown.

He readied the chloroform-soaked rag, preparing to clamp it across her nose and mouth.

"Just breathe deeply," he urged her. "It will all be over in a moment."

She did what any delicately bred lady would do under such circumstances. She uttered a deep sigh, raised her eyes toward the heavens and fainted. She took care not to collapse straight onto the blade, sliding sideways along the seat instead. From there she started to tumble off the cushion onto the floor.

"Bloody hell," the Bridegroom grumbled.

He moved instinctively to avoid the weight of her body.

The blade of the scalpel was no longer pointed directly at her throat. As if in answer to her silent prayers, the coachman turned a sharp corner at speed. The vehicle lurched to one side. The Bridegroom automatically sought to steady himself.

It was now or never.

She straightened, twisted and stabbed the sharpened steel ribs of the folded fan into the nearest target, the killer's thigh. The points bit deep through clothing and flesh.

The Bridegroom screamed in surprise and pain. He slashed at her with the scalpel but she already had the tessen open. The steel leaves of the fan deflected the blow.

"Bitch."

Startled and off balance, the killer tried to ready himself for another strike. She snapped the fan closed and stabbed the points deep into his shoulder. The hand holding the scalpel spasmed in a reflexive action. The blade landed on the floor of the vehicle.

She yanked the tessen free and stabbed wildly a third time, heedless of her target. She was in a panic, desperate to free herself from the carriage. The Bridegroom shrieked again and batted at her, trying to ward off the blows. He groped for the fallen scalpel.

She opened the fan again, revealing the elegant garden scene etched into the steel, and slashed at the killer's hand with the edges of the razor-sharp leaves. He jerked back, shrieking in rage.

The carriage slammed to a jarring halt. The coachman had evidently heard the screams.

She clawed at the door and managed to get it open. She closed the tessen and let it dangle from the chatelaine. Seizing handfuls of her skirts and petticoats in one hand to keep the yards of fabric out of the way, she scrambled out of the vehicle.

"What the bloody hell?" The coachman stared at her from the box, rain dripping off the brim of his low-crowned hat. He was clearly stunned by the turn of events. "Here, now, what's this all about? He said you was his lady friend. Said the two of you wanted a bit of privacy."

She did not stop to explain the situation. She dared not trust the coachman. He might be innocent, but he might just as easily be in league with the killer.

A quick glance showed her that the vehicle had come to a halt in a narrow lane. Once again she hiked up her skirts and petticoats. She fled toward the far end where the cross street promised traffic and safety.

She heard the coachman crack his whip behind her. The horse broke into a frenzied gallop, hoofs ringing on the stones. The carriage clattered away in the opposite direction. The anguished, enraged howls from inside the cab grew faint.

She ran for her life.

There was more screaming when she reached the cross street. A woman pushing a baby in a perambulator was the first person to see her rush out of the dark lane. The nanny uttered a high, shrill screech.

Her horrified cry immediately attracted a crowd. Everyone stared, shock and fascinated horror etching their faces. A constable appeared. He hurried toward her, baton in hand.

"You're bleeding, ma'am," he said. "What happened?"

She looked down and saw for the first time that her dress was splashed with blood.

"Not mine," she said quickly.

The constable assumed a forbidding air. "Who did you kill, then, ma'am?"

"The Bridegroom," she said. "I think. The thing is, I'm not certain that he's dead."

The following morning, Amity Doncaster woke up to find herself notorious—for the second time that week.

Four

He came awake again to the same oppressive cloud of pain and confusion that had overwhelmed him on previous occasions. But his head was somewhat clearer this time. There were voices in the mist. He kept his eyes closed and listened hard. Two people were speaking in hushed tones. He knew them both.

"He will live." The doctor's voice was weary and grim. "The wounds are closing properly. There are no signs of infection and it appears that no vital organs were injured."

"Thank you, Doctor. You have surely saved his life."

The woman spoke words of gratitude but her well-bred voice was cold and hollow, as if she was torn between rage and anguish.

"I have done what I can for his body," the doctor said. "But as I have told you before, madam, there is nothing I or any other doctor can do for his mind."

"I was assured that he had been cured. Indeed, he appeared quite well these past few months. Happy. Even-tempered. Enjoying his photography. There was no indication that he was slipping back into madness."

"I would remind you, madam, that there were no indications of insanity prior to the previous occasion, either, if you will recall. As I have tried to explain to you, the medical profession lacks the knowledge required to cure him. If you do not intend to summon the police—"

"Never. You know as well as I do what would happen if I did that. Such an action would not only destroy him, it would devastate the entire family."

The doctor said nothing.

"I will deal with this just as I did the last time," the woman said. Resolve strengthened her voice.

"I anticipated that you would make that decision," the doctor said. He sounded resigned. "I took the liberty of sending word to Dr. Renwick at Cresswell Manor. There are two attendants waiting outside."

"Send them in," the woman said. "Remind them that I expect absolute discretion."

"They are well trained. As I explained on the previous occasion, Dr. Renwick specializes in dealing with situations such as this. He accepts only patients from the best families and he is mindful of his obligations to those who pay his fees."

"In other words, I am buying Dr. Renwick's silence," the woman said bitterly.

"I can assure you that you are not the only one in Society who is doing so. But given the alternative, there is nothing else to be done, is there?"

"No." The woman hesitated. "You are certain that he is fit to travel?"

"Yes."

"In that case, send for the attendants."

"I think it would be safest for all concerned if I administered more chloroform before we prepare the patient to be transported."

"Do what you feel must be done," the woman said. "I will go now. I cannot watch them take him away again."

She was leaving.

Panic flashed like wildfire through the patient. He opened his eyes and tried to rise from the bed, only to discover to his horror that he could not move. Leather straps bound him to the bed rails.

The doctor came toward him with a white cloth in his hand. The sickly sweet smell of chloroform scented the atmosphere. Two burly men in ill-fitting coats came through the door. He recognized them from his previous stay at Cresswell Manor.

"Mother, no, don't let them take me," he pleaded. "You're making a terrible mistake. You must believe me. That lying whore tried to murder me. Don't you see? I'm innocent."

His mother's shoulders stiffened but she did not look back. The door closed behind her.

Dr. Norcott clamped the chloroform-saturated rag over the patient's nose and mouth.

Fury scalded his veins. This was the harlot's fault. Everything had gone wrong because of her. She would pay. He had granted the others a swift death, taking pity on them after they acknowledged their sins. But Amity Doncaster would die slowly.

Five

I do not think that my reputation can withstand any more gossip," Amity announced. She set aside the copy of the *Flying Intelligencer* and reached for her coffee cup. "Three weeks have passed since I was attacked and I still find myself in the newspapers every morning. It was bad enough knowing that silly people in Polite Society were amusing themselves with speculation about my association with Mr. Stanbridge."

"Stanbridge is a very wealthy gentleman from an old, distinguished family," Penny said. "He is also unmarried. In addition, he was involved in a great scandal several years ago when his fiancée stood him up at the altar. That combination makes his private life a matter of considerable interest in certain circles."

Amity blinked. "He was left at the altar? You never mentioned that."

"The young lady ran off with her lover. It's been a few years now but there was a great deal of speculation about the event at the time.

Everyone wondered why the woman would abandon a gentleman of Stanbridge's rank and wealth."

"I see." Amity gave that information some thought. "Perhaps she got tired of having him disappear on her the way he did on me."

"Indeed."

"Yes, well, I knew him as Mr. Stanbridge, an engineer who happened to be traveling in the Caribbean," Amity said. "He never bothered to mention his finances or his social connections. As I was saying, the gossip about our so-called affair on board the *Northern Star* was certainly annoying, but I had hoped it would dissipate before my book was published. Unfortunately, the lurid reports of my escape from the Bridegroom don't show any sign of diminishing. They may prove to be the ruin of my career as a travel guide writer."

"For heaven's sake, Amity, you were very nearly murdered," Penny said. She put down her fork, anxiety and alarm shadowing her eyes. "According to the press, you are the only intended victim of that dreadful monster known to have escaped his clutches. You must expect to find your name in the papers. We can only be grateful that you are alive."

"I am grateful—exceedingly grateful. But I do not enjoy seeing myself pictured on the front covers of the *Illustrated Police News* and the *Graphic*. Both of those magazines portrayed me fleeing from the killer's carriage dressed only in my nightgown."

Penny sighed. "Everyone knows those periodicals are prone to exaggerated, melodramatic illustrations."

"When will it stop?" A sense of foreboding settled on Amity. "I fear that my career as an author of guidebooks for ladies is doomed before my first guidebook even appears. I expect it is only a matter of time before Mr. Galbraith sends word that he has decided not to publish *A Lady's Guide to Globetrotting*."

Penny smiled reassuringly from the other side of the breakfast table. "Perhaps Mr. Galbraith will look upon the uproar in the press as good publicity for your travel guide."

That was Penny for you, Amity thought. Her sister was always a model of grace and serenity, regardless of the disaster at hand. But, then, Penny was a paragon of feminine perfection in all things, including widowhood. Six months ago she had lost her husband after not quite a year of marriage. Amity knew that her sister had been devastated. Nigel had been the love of her life. But Penny concealed her grief behind an air of stoic fortitude.

Fortunately, Penny was riveting in black. But, then, she looked spectacular in virtually any color, Amity thought. Nevertheless, there was no denying that the deep hues of mourning set off Penny's silver-blond hair, porcelain skin and sky-blue eyes, bestowing upon her an ethereal quality. She could have stepped out of a Pre-Raphaelite painting.

Penny was one of those women who drew every eye in the room—male and female—when she entered. She was not only lovely, she possessed a natural charm and a kind heart that endeared her to all she met. What most people failed to realize, Amity thought, was that beneath all the beauty and fine qualities, Penny was also endowed with a decided talent for investing. The ability had stood her in good stead after Nigel had broken his neck in a riding accident. He had left a fortune to his wife.

Unlike Penny, who took after their mother, Amity was well aware that she owed her own dark hair, hazel eyes and decidedly assertive nose to their father's side of the family. Unfortunately, the women of the Doncaster bloodline who had the misfortune to be endowed with those particular characteristics had acquired a certain reputation over the years. Tales were still told of the many-times great-grandmother who had barely escaped hanging as a witch during the 1600s. A century later a spirited aunt had managed to disgrace the family by running off with a highwayman. Then there was the aunt who had vanished on a hot-air balloon ride only to reappear as the mistress of a married earl.

There were other women who had tarnished the Doncaster name over the centuries—and every single one of those who had succeeded in making herself something of a legend had possessed the same witchy coloring and the same nose.

Amity had heard the whispers behind her back from the time she was a young girl. Everyone who knew the Doncaster family history was of the opinion that there was a streak of wild blood in the female line. And while a bit of wildness was often viewed as a positive attribute in males—it certainly tended to make them more interesting to women—it was considered a decided negative in females. At nineteen Amity had learned the hard way not to trust the sort of gentleman who was attracted to her because of her family history.

No one, least of all Amity, understood quite how her disreputable female ancestors had managed to land themselves in so many outrageous situations. Their looks were hardly remarkable—except for the nose, of course. As for their figures, there were limits to what even Penny's talented dressmaker could do with a shape so lacking in feminine curves that when dressed in masculine attire Amity had been able to pass as a young man on more than one occasion while traveling abroad.

She took a long, fortifying swallow of Mrs. Houston's strong coffee and put down the cup with some force.

"I don't think that Mr. Galbraith will consider the kind of publicity I have attracted to be useful when it comes to selling my book," she said. "It's difficult to imagine that people will be induced to purchase a travel guide written for ladies if they discover that the author is in the habit of stumbling into the clutches of terrible killers like the Bridegroom. That incident certainly doesn't make me look like an expert on how a lady may travel the globe in perfect safety."

The stack of newspapers and lurid magazines had been waiting for her on the breakfast table when she had walked into the morning room a short time ago, just as they had been every other morning since her escape from the killer's carriage. Usually there was only one paper on the breakfast table, the *Flying Intelligencer*. But lately Mrs. Houston—a great fan of the lurid penny dreadfuls—had gone out early to collect a wide assortment of morning reading material. As far as Amity had been able to determine, each new report of her encounter with the Bridegroom was more replete with descriptions of bloodcurdling thrills and shuddering horror than the previous one.

It was quite astonishing, she thought, that however shocking the newspapers portrayed the kidnapping and her narrow escape, none of them managed to capture the very real, nerve-icing terror she had experienced. In spite of two stout doses of brandy before bed every night since the near disaster, she had not been sleeping well. Her mind was filled with nightmarish images, not only of her own panic and desperate struggles but of horrid imaginings of what the last moments of the other victims must have been like.

This morning—as with every morning for the past three weeks—most of the fear was replaced by a quiet, seething rage. This morning—like the other mornings—she had come down to breakfast, hoping to discover that the newspapers would be filled with assurances that the police had found the body of the Bridegroom. But once again she had been disappointed. Instead, there was a great deal of speculation about his possible fate. Surely the loss of so much blood would prove deadly, the press insisted. It was only a matter of time before the killer's corpse was discovered.

Amity was not so certain. In the course of her travels abroad with her father she had sewn up the wounds of a number of people who had been injured by a variety of sharp objects, including shears, razor blades, hunting knives and broken glass. Even a small amount of blood could look like a great quantity if it was splashed around in a spectacular manner. It was true her new walking gown had been ruined by the blood of the Bridegroom, but she did not think that she had struck a death blow.

"You must take a positive attitude toward this situation," Penny said. "There is nothing the public loves more than a great sensation involving murder and an interesting lady. Your encounter with the Bridegroom certainly meets both requirements. I'm sure that when all is said and done it will inspire sales of your book. Mr. Galbraith is nothing if not pragmatic when it comes to publishing."

"I can only hope you are correct," Amity said. "There is no denying that you are far more versed in the ways of Society than I am. You have a knack for navigating awkward situations. I am in your hands."

Penny surprised her with a knowing look. "You have hiked in the wilderness of the American West and the jungles of the South Seas. You survived a shipwreck and confronted a would-be thief in a San Francisco hotel room. You have ridden a camel and an elephant. To top it off you are now the only woman in London known to have survived an attack by a criminal who has killed three women thus far. Yet you quail at the very thought of having to deal with the social world."

Amity sighed. "I did not fare well the last time I went into Polite Society, if you will recall."

"That was a long time ago. You were only nineteen and Mama did not protect you properly. You are much older now and, I'm sure, a good deal wiser."

Amity winced at the "much older" and felt the heat rise in her cheeks. She knew she was flushing an unbecoming shade of red, but there was no avoiding the fact that at twenty-five she had crossed the boundary that separated marriageable young ladies from the doomed-to-spinsterhood crowd.

The memories of the Nash Debacle, as she privately termed it, always made her cringe. Her broken heart had healed quite nicely but the dent in her pride was permanent. It pained her to acknowledge how naïve she had been. In the wake of the discovery that Humphrey Nash's intentions were less than honorable, Amity had concluded there was nothing for her in London. The last letter from her father had come from Japan. She had packed her bags and purchased a ticket on a steamship bound for the Far East.

"I am most certainly older now," she conceded. "But I'm starting to wonder if I am cursed when it comes to London. I have been back for only a month and my name is on everyone's lips. What are the odds that I would feature in not one but two scandalous situations. Speaking of which, I fear that it is only a matter of time before Mr. Stanbridge learns that his name is being dragged through the gutter press."

"If and when Mr. Stanbridge discovers that his name has been brought up in connection with an illicit shipboard affair, I'm sure he will understand that it was not your fault," Penny said.

"I'm not at all certain of that," Amity said.

Secretly she hoped that he might at least discover that hers was not the only name featured in the newspapers lately. It might even impel him to send a letter or a telegram informing her that he was less than pleased. A message of any kind would offer her assurance that he was alive and well.

She had heard nothing from Benedict since the *Northern Star* had docked in New York. The following day he had boarded a train to California. To all intents and purposes he had vanished. True, he had said something vague about calling on her when he returned to London, and for a time she had been hopeful that she would someday find him on the doorstep. But a month had passed and there had been no word from him. She did not know whether to be hurt because he had so easily forgotten her or worried that whoever had shot him on St. Clare had tracked him down and made a second—successful—attempt to kill him.

It was Penny who had assured her that if a gentleman of Stanbridge's rank and wealth had been murdered abroad the papers would be filled with the news. Unfortunately, Amity thought, that bit of logic left her with the depressing realization that while Benedict might feel some degree of gratitude toward her—she had saved his life, after all—he had certainly not developed any feelings of a romantic nature toward her.

In spite of that searing kiss on the promenade deck the night before they had docked in New York.

Night after night she told herself that she must put her foolish dreams back on the shelf. But night after night she found herself thinking of that magical time on board the *Northern Star*. As Benedict recovered from his wound, they had walked together on the promenade deck and played cards in the lounge. In the evenings they sat across from each other at the long table where the first-class passengers dined. They had talked of many things long into the night. She had found Benedict to be a man of wide-ranging interests, but it was when the conversation turned to the newest developments in engineering and science that his eyes heated with an enthusiasm that bordered on true passion.

Mrs. Houston bustled in from the kitchen with a fresh pot of coffee. She was a handsome, robust woman of middle years. Her brown hair was lightly streaked with gray. Penny had hired her after moving out of the large, fashionable house that she had entered as Nigel's bride.

Penny had set up her new home in a much smaller town house in a respectable but quiet and not particularly fashionable neighborhood. In the process she had dismissed the entire staff of the mansion. Now there was only Mrs. Houston, who had come from an agency.

Amity sensed there was more to the story. It was true, Penny no longer needed a great many servants. Nevertheless, her household staff had been trimmed to a bare minimum. When Amity had asked why Mrs. Houston was the sole live-in employee, Penny had said something vague about not wanting a lot of people underfoot.

"I'm sure it's only a matter of time before they find the Bridegroom's body," Mrs. Houston declared. "I've read all the accounts in the papers, Miss Amity. The wounds you inflicted were clearly of a grave nature. Surely he cannot survive them. One of these days they'll find him in an alley or the river."

"Those accounts were written by newspaper reporters, none of whom were present at the scene," Amity said. "In my opinion, it is entirely possible that the monster survived, assuming he got medical attention."

"Must you be so negative?" Penny chided.

"Medical attention," Mrs. Houston said. She appeared quite struck by the notion. "If he was badly injured, he would have been forced to seek out the assistance of a doctor. Surely any man of medicine called upon to tend such wounds would be aware that he was treating a violent person. He would report the patient to the police."

"Not if the killer managed to convince the doctor that the wounds had been inflicted by accident or by a footpad," Amity said. "May I have some more coffee, Mrs. Houston? I shall need a great deal of it in order to get through the interview with that man from Scotland Yard who sent a message asking if he could call this morning."

"His name is Inspector Logan," Penny said.

"Yes, well, we can only hope that he is more competent than his predecessor. The inspector who spoke with me after I escaped the killer was less than impressive. I doubt if he could catch the average street thief, let alone a monster like the Bridegroom."

"According to Inspector Logan's message, he is not due to call until eleven o'clock," Penny said. "You do not look as if you slept well. Perhaps you should take a nap after breakfast?"

"I'm fine, Penny." Amity picked up her cup. "I have never been able to nap during the day."

The muffled clang of the door knocker echoed down the hall. Amity and Penny exchanged startled glances.

Mrs. Houston's face set in disapproving lines. "Who on earth would be calling at this hour?"

Amity put down her cup. "I expect that will be Inspector Logan."

"Shall I tell the inspector to come back at a decent hour?"

"Why bother?" Amity said. She crumpled her napkin and set it beside her plate. "I may as well get the conversation over now. No point postponing the inevitable. Perhaps Inspector Logan is early because he has some news."

"Yes, of course," Penny said. "Let us hope they found the body."

Mrs. Houston went down the hall to answer the door.

A hush fell on the room. Amity listened intently as Mrs. Houston greeted the caller. A man's voice—dark, gruff and freighted with impatience and command—responded.

"Where the devil is Miss Doncaster?"

Amity felt as if she had just been struck by a very large ocean wave.

"Oh, dear," she whispered. "That's not Inspector Logan."

In spite of her sleepless nights and too much coffee—or perhaps because of those two factors—frissons of panic and excitement shivered through her. The little icy-hot tingles of awareness splashed across her nerves and caused her pulse to kick up. In all of her travels she had met only one man who had such an effect on her.

"Miss Doncaster is at breakfast, sir," Mrs. Houston announced. "I'll let her know you're asking for her."

"Never mind, I'll find her."

Boot steps echoed in the hall.

Penny looked at Amity across the table, a delicate frown crinkling her brows.

"Who on earth—?" she started to ask.

Before Amity could answer, Benedict swept into the room. His hair was windblown and he was dressed in traveling clothes. He carried a leather case under one arm.

At the sight of him joy and relief flashed through her. He was alive. Her worst nightmare was just that—merely a nightmare.

And then the outrage set in.

"What a surprise, Mr. Stanbridge," she said in her steeliest accents. "We weren't expecting you this morning. Or any other morning, for that matter."

He stopped short, eyes tightening at the corners. Evidently that was not the greeting he had been anticipating.

"Amity," he said.

Predictably, it was Penny who took charge of the volatile situation, doing so with her customary grace and dignity.

"Mr. Stanbridge, allow me to introduce myself, as my sister appears to have forgotten her manners. I'm Penelope Marsden."

For a dash of time Amity did not think that Benedict would allow himself to be distracted by the introduction. Judging by her experience of his company on board the *Northern Star*, he had excellent manners when he chose to use them. For the most part, however, he had little patience for the niceties of Polite Society.

But clearly it dawned on him that he had overstepped the bounds of good manners by invading a lady's morning room at such an early hour, because he turned immediately toward Penny.

"Benedict Stanbridge, at your service." He inclined his head in a surprisingly elegant bow. "I apologize for the intrusion, Mrs. Marsden. My ship docked less than an hour ago. I came straight here because I saw the morning papers. I was concerned, to say the least."

"Perfectly understandable," Penny said. "Won't you join us for breakfast, sir?"

"Thank you," Benedict said. He looked at the silver coffee pot with something approaching lust. "I would be very grateful. I didn't get breakfast, as we docked earlier than anticipated."

Penny looked at Mrs. Houston, who was staring, fascinated, at Benedict. "Would you be so kind as to bring Mr. Stanbridge a plate, Mrs. Houston?"

"Yes, ma'am. Right away, ma'am."

Mrs. Houston quickly regained her professional composure but her eyes sparkled with curiosity. She bustled through the swinging door of the pantry.

Benedict pulled out a chair and sat down. He set the leather case conveniently at hand on the sideboard and examined Amity as though he had her under a microscope.

"You are unhurt?" he asked.

"A few minor bruises, but they have all disappeared, thank you," she said.

Penny frowned in faint disapproval of her icy tones. Amity ignored the look. She had a right to be annoyed with Benedict, she thought.

"According to the press, you did considerable damage to the bastard with that little fan you carry." Benedict nodded once, evidently pleased. "Nice work, by the way."

Amity raised her brows. "Thank you. One does one's best in those circumstances, I assure you."

"Right," Benedict said. He was starting to look wary. "Did they find the body?"

"Not that we know of," Amity said. "But we are expecting news from an Inspector Logan of Scotland Yard later this morning. I am not hopeful that any real progress has been made, however. Logan's predecessor appeared to be in over his head."

"Never a good sign," Benedict said. He reached out to help himself to a slice of toast from the silver toast rack.

A woman could only take so much.

Amity banged her cup down onto the saucer. "Damn it, Benedict, how dare you stroll into this house as if nothing ever happened? The very least you could have done was send a telegram to let me know that you were alive. Was that too much to ask?"

Six

Amity was furious.

Benedict was amazed that she possessed the energy for such a heated emotion considering what she had gone through three weeks ago. But the fire in her amazing eyes was definitely dangerous.

This was not exactly the passionate reunion that he had been dreaming about for the past month, he thought.

He used a knife to slather some butter on the toast while he tried to think of the best way to respond to the outburst. Nothing brilliant came to mind.

"My apologies," he said. "I thought it best to have as little communication as possible until I got back to London."

She gave him a cool smile. "Did you, indeed, sir?"

This was not going well, he decided. He told himself he had to make allowances for her volatile emotional state. If the press had gotten even half the story correct, she was lucky to be alive. Most women would have taken to their beds following such an ordeal. They would have remained in those beds for a month, dining on weak broth and tea and periodically resorting to their vinaigrettes.

Then again most women would not have survived the attack, he thought. Admiration mingled with the overwhelming relief that he had experienced when he had walked through the door of the morning room a short time ago. The papers had stressed that she was alive and unharmed, but he knew that he could not rest until he had seen her with his own eyes.

He should have known that he would find her eating a hearty breakfast.

Amity was the most unique woman he had ever encountered. She never ceased to astonish him. From the first moment he had seen her there in that wretched little alley on St. Clare, he had been mesmerized. She reminded him of a small, sleek, curious little cat. The range of her interests intrigued him deeply. One never knew what subject she would bring up next.

During the course of the passage from St. Clare to New York, Amity had turned up in the most unexpected places on the ship. It was obvious from the start that the crew adored her. On one occasion he had gone searching for her only to find her emerging from a tour of the ship's galley. She was still engaged in deep conversation with the head chef, who had been holding forth at length on the logistics of providing so many meals to passengers and crew over the course of a long voyage. Amity had appeared keenly interested. Her questions were sincere. The chef looked as though he was half in love with her.

And then there was the time he had found her in close conversation with the handsome, young American, Declan Garraway. Benedict had been startled by the sense of possessiveness he had experienced when he had discovered the pair together in the ship's library.

Garraway was fresh out of an East Coast college and in the process of seeing something of the world before he assumed his responsibilities in the family business. He had seemed quite taken with modern theories of psychology, which he had studied in school. He had lectured Amity enthusiastically on the subject. She, in turn, had taken notes and asked a great many questions. Garraway had been enthralled, not only with the field of psychology but also with Amity.

Over the course of the past few weeks Benedict had pondered his own conversations with Amity on board ship. He had no doubt bored her to tears with his descriptions of such exciting inventions as Alexander Graham Bell's design for a wireless communications device called a photophone. She had managed to appear so interested that he had been inspired to move on to other subjects. He had held forth at length on how several renowned scientists and engineers such as the French inventor Augustin Mouchot were predicting that the coal mines of Europe and America would soon be exhausted. If they were proved right, the great steam engines of the modern age that powered everything from ships and locomotives to factories would grind to a halt. The need to find a new source of energy was the focus of all the major powers. And so on and so forth. On one less than memorable occasion he had even gone so far as to regale her with a detailed explanation of how the ancient Greeks and Romans had experimented with solar energy.

What had he been thinking?

He had asked himself that question every night for a month. Amity had been trapped on board the *Northern Star* with him all the way from St. Clare to New York. It had been a golden opportunity to impress her. Instead, he had gone on endlessly about various topics related to his engineering interests. As if any woman actually wanted to hear about his engineering interests.

But at the time Amity had seemed keen to discuss his speculations and theories. Most women he knew, with the glaring exceptions of his mother and his sister-in-law, considered the realms of engineering and invention to be beneath the proper interests of a gentleman. Amity, however, had gone so far as to make notes, just as she had when she chatted with Declan Garraway. Benedict conceded that he had been flattered. Afterward, though, on the long train trip to California, he'd had ample time to consider the very real possibility that she had simply been polite.

When he thought of his time with Amity on the *Northern Star* he much preferred to contemplate their last night together. The memory had heated his dreams while they had been apart.

They had gone for a walk on the promenade deck and stopped to watch the celestial fireworks produced by a distant storm at sea. They had stood together at the railing for nearly an hour, watching the far-off lightning flashes in the night sky. Amity had been captivated by the scene. He, in turn, had been enchanted by her excitement.

That was the night he had taken her into his arms and kissed her for the first and only time. The experience had proved more electrifying than the night storm. It was only a kiss, but for the first time in his life he had understood how passion might cause a man to defy logic and the dictates of common sense.

Mrs. Houston swept through the pantry doorway.

"Here you go, sir," she said. "Enjoy your breakfast."

She set a plate heaped with eggs and sausages in front of him. He inhaled the aromas and was suddenly ravenous.

"Thank you, Mrs. Houston," he said. He unfolded his napkin. "This is just what I need."

She beamed and poured coffee into his cup.

He forked up a bite of eggs and looked at Amity.

"Tell me what happened," he said. "I trust the press has exaggerated somewhat?"

Penny responded before Amity could say a word.

"Unfortunately, the incident occurred very much as the press portrayed it," Penny said.

"Except for the bit about me fleeing the carriage in my nightgown," Amity said grimly. "That was a gross exaggeration. I was fully clothed, I assure you."

Before he could respond to that, Penny continued with the story.

"A vicious killer they call the Bridegroom seized Amity right off the street in broad daylight and tried to overcome her with chloroform," she said.

"Chloroform." Benedict felt his insides turn to ice. If the killer had been able to render Amity unconscious, it was unlikely that she would have escaped. "Damn it to bloody hell."

He realized that Penny and Mrs. Houston were looking at him.

"My apologies for the language," he said.

It occurred to him that he had apologized twice before even finishing breakfast.

Amity raised her brows. He got the impression that she was amused. It was, he reflected, not the first time that she had heard him swear. Nevertheless, he was back in London now. There were rules.

"Fortunately, I was able to employ my fan before the chloroform took effect," Amity said. "I leaped out of the carriage and ran for my life."

He frowned thinking about it. "Who drove the carriage?"

"What?" Amity frowned. "I have no idea. It was a private carriage so I assume the coachman was in the employ of the killer."

He gave that some close thought. "It was a private carriage?"

"Yes. In the rain, I mistook it for a cab." Amity's gaze sharpened. "What are you thinking, sir?"

"That the coachman is either an accomplice or a member of the criminal class who was hired for the occasion and paid to keep his mouth shut. Either way, he will know something that could help identify the killer."

Amity's eyes widened. "An excellent notion. You must mention that to Inspector Logan."

Benedict shrugged and ate a bite of sausage. "It's an obvious avenue of investigation. I'm sure the police are pursuing it."

Amity assumed an ominous expression. "I would not depend upon that, if I were you."

Penny looked thoughtful. "Until Amity's escape no one knew how the other brides were taken. They simply disappeared."

Benedict ate some more eggs while he pondered that. Then he looked at Amity.

"Why you?" he asked.

She frowned. "What?"

"Do you have some notion of why, out of all the women in London, the killer selected you as a victim?"

Amity looked at Penny, who cleared her throat discreetly.

"I assume that you are unaware of the gossip, Mr. Stanbridge," she said.

"Gossip flows through London like the Thames." He picked up his coffee cup. "What gossip in particular are you referring to?"

This time it was Amity who answered.

"The gossip about us, Mr. Stanbridge," she said coldly.

He paused the cup halfway to his mouth and looked at her over the rim. "Us?"

She gave him an icy smile. "There has been a great deal of idle speculation in certain circles about the nature of our association on board the *Northern Star*."

He went quite blank. "What in blazes do you mean? We were fellow passengers on board a ship."

Penny narrowed her eyes. "There have been rumors to the effect that your relationship with Amity was of an intimate nature."

"Well, she did save my life, which could certainly be viewed as an intimate sort of connection." He stopped, aware that Amity and Penny were both looking at him in a decidedly odd manner. Belatedly, comprehension finally arrived.

Thunderstruck, he looked at Amity. "Do you mean to say that there are rumors that you and I were lovers?"

Mrs. Houston snorted and became very busy with the coffee pot. Penny's jaw tightened.

Amity flushed a vivid shade of pink.

"I regret to say that is the case," she said.

He grappled with that for a moment and decided that it would probably be best not to tell her that he wished it were true. He forced himself to focus on the problem at hand.

"What does the gossip have to do with the fact that you were nearly murdered?" he said instead.

Amity took a deep breath and straightened her shoulders. "According to the press, the Bridegroom chooses female victims whose reputations have been tarnished by scandal."

She spoke so quickly—practically mumbling—that he was not certain he heard her correctly.

"Tarnished by scandal?" he repeated to make certain he understood.

"Yes," Amity said, her tone clipped and brusque.

"You're telling me that the rumors about you or, I should say, us somehow reached the killer's ears and that is why he fixed his attentions on you?"

"That appears to be the case," Amity said. She poured a little cream into her coffee. "I fear the gossip has been circulating in certain circles for some time."

"Ever since the Channing ball, to be precise," Penny added. "As far as I can determine, it started the morning after that affair."

Benedict frowned. "Did you two attend?"

"No," Penny said. "But it was not difficult to establish that the rumors began circulating immediately afterward. Polite Society is a small world, as I'm sure you're aware, Mr. Stanbridge."

"True," he said. "And an overheated hothouse when it comes to gossip. I do my best to avoid it."

"I'm not particularly fond of it, myself," Penny said. "But thanks to my late husband, I spent some time in that hothouse and I still have my connections. That is how I learned where and when the rumors began."

"Did you discover who was responsible?" he asked.

"No," Penny admitted. "That sort of thing is more difficult to pin down. Until Amity was attacked our chief concern was that the gossip might cause her publisher to change his mind about publishing her book."

Benedict looked at Amity. "You've finished your travel book for ladies, then?"

"Almost," she said. "I am making one or two small changes but I had hoped to send it to Mr. Galbraith later this month. Unfortunately, what with the rumors about my association with you and now this situation involving a killer, things have become quite complicated."

He considered various possible solutions to the problem while he downed the last of the eggs. Then he sat back to savor the rest of his coffee.

"The problem of ensuring the publication of your book is simple enough to resolve," he said.

Amity and Penny stared at him.

"What, exactly, do you mean by simple, Mr. Stanbridge?" Amity asked. She was clearly wary. "Do you intend to threaten or intimidate Mr. Galbraith? Because I assure you that, while I appreciate the gesture, I really cannot countenance such an approach."

"You would appreciate the gesture?" he asked.

She smiled the first real smile she had bestowed upon him since he had arrived. It was the kind of smile that warmed her eyes and the atmosphere around her; the kind of smile that made him feel very, very good deep inside.

"It is kind of you to offer to intimidate Mr. Galbraith in order to help me get my guidebook published, but I fear that under the circumstances that might be somewhat awkward," she said.

"Well, in that case I will save the option of inducing fear in your publisher as a last resort," Benedict said. "In any event I don't think it will be necessary to take such drastic measures if we apply the simpler, more straightforward solution that I have in mind."

Penny still appeared somewhat bewildered, but a faint gleam of comprehension lit her eyes. "What is that, sir?"

"From what you have told me it is obvious that the easiest way to deal with the question of Amity's reputation is to announce that she and I are engaged to be married," he said.

Pleased with the obvious perfection of his answer to the problem, he drank some more coffee and waited for Amity and Penny to display the appropriate delight and appreciation of the scheme.

Amity stared at him as if he had just declared that the end of the world was near.

But Penny seized upon the solution with profound relief.

"Yes, of course," she said. "It is the ideal answer. I confess that it had actually occurred to me. But I must admit I did not expect you to suggest the notion, Mr. Stanbridge."

"What?" Amity switched her attention to Penny. "Are you mad? How on earth will such an announcement solve anything?"

Penny assumed a knowing air. "I'm sure Mr. Stanbridge has all the answers. Something tells me he concocted the plan before he arrived on our doorstep a short time ago. Is that correct, sir?"

"Yes, as a matter of fact," he said, trying to appear modest.

Amity clutched her napkin very tightly. "Mr. Stanbridge, I would remind you that you were unaware of the gossip about us until you sat down to breakfast at this very table a short time ago. How on earth can you declare that you conceived this harebrained notion on the way from the ship to this house?"

The harebrained notion comment hurt but he reminded himself that Amity had been under considerable stress lately.

"It was the news of the attack on you that convinced me that an engagement is the only alternative," he said.

Penny nodded, satisfied. "Yes, of course."

Amity glared at both of them in turn. "Why is a fake engagement a sound notion?"

"Because it will do two important things," Benedict said. He was trying to be patient but underneath he had to admit he found her lack of enthusiasm for the plan decidedly depressing. "First and foremost it will allow me to be seen regularly in your company. That will make it easier to protect you."

Amity frowned. "Protect me? Do you mean to say that you believe the killer might try to kidnap me a second time?"

"We cannot know the mind of a monster like this creature they call the Bridegroom," he said gently. "Until we are certain that he is dead or in prison I do not think it wise for you to go about by yourself. If he is out there in the shadows, he will have had time for his wounds to heal. You should not leave this house alone under any circumstances. As your fiancé I will be able to escort you wherever you wish to go."

Amity started to speak, stopped and then took a breath and tried again.

"And the second reason you believe this fraudulent arrangement is a good idea?" she asked.

"Isn't it obvious?" he said. "It will put a stop to the gossip. You will no longer need to be concerned that Galbraith will refuse to publish your book because of the damage to your reputation."

Penny looked at Amity. "You must see that an engagement really is a perfect solution to both problems."

"Excuse me," Amity said evenly, "but I'm not at all sure of that."

"Why?" Penny asked.

"Why?" Amity got out in a half-strangled voice. "You have to ask me that? It's a terrible idea. Such an engagement would be a complete fiction. How on earth could we possibly maintain the illusion? Even if Mr. Stanbridge is content to play the part of my fiancé, what of his parents? I'm sure they will raise some objections."

"No, they won't," Benedict said. "You may leave my parents to me. I will deal with them if it becomes necessary."

"How could it not become necessary?" Amity shot back.

"As it happens, they are in Australia at the moment." He brushed the problem of his parents aside. "They will have no notion of what is going on here in London. And while we're on the subject, rest assured that I will deal with my brother and his wife, as well."

Amity's mouth tightened. "I do appreciate your offer, Mr. Stanbridge, however—"

"Kindly stop saying that you appreciate my offers," he said.

He realized how sternly he had spoken only after she fell abruptly silent. She stared at him with an air of astonishment that made him aware that he had never before shown her the edge of his temper.

He suppressed a groan and tried to explain.

"It's the least I can do after what you did for me," he said quietly. "You saved my life on St. Clare. I wouldn't have made it without you. It was that incident that led to the compromising situation which in turn inspired the gossip about our supposed liaison. Now you have been attacked because of that gossip. I am in your debt and I would very much *appreciate* it if you would allow me to try to repay it."

"By pretending to be my fiancé?" she asked in disbelief.

"Until the police find the killer," Benedict said.

"What if they fail?" she asked.

"Then we shall have to do their work for them."

It had been a stab in the dark but he had made it based on what he knew of her personality. She was, above all else, extremely curious and intrigued by the prospect of adventure. It was that spirit that had compelled her to travel the world.

He knew at once his strategy was working. Amity suddenly glowed with excitement.

"*Hmm,*" she said.

Penny eyed him dubiously. "Have you had any experience with criminal investigations, Mr. Stanbridge?"

"No, but I imagine it is like any problem in engineering or mathematics," he said. "One assembles all of the relevant facts in a logical manner and then one solves for the unknown."

"If it were that simple, the police would catch every criminal on the streets," Amity said crisply. She got to her feet. "If you will excuse us, Penny, I would like to show Mr. Stanbridge the garden."

"I was about to ask Mrs. Houston to bring me some more coffee," Benedict said.

Amity looked at him. "A tour of the garden, sir. Now."

Seven

The summer rain had stopped and the sun had emerged, but the garden was still damp. Amity whisked her skirts above her ankles to avoid the wet flowers and shrubs. She made for the little gazebo at the far end, very aware of Benedict following close behind her. The gravel of the path crunched beneath his boots.

She stepped up onto the floor of the gazebo and rounded on him.

"You appear to have recovered quite nicely from your wound," she said.

He touched his right side in the vicinity of his rib cage somewhat gingerly and immediately lowered his hand. "Thanks to your medical skills."

"As I told you at the time, it was my father who taught me some elementary field medicine."

"I will be forever grateful to his memory." Benedict looked at her. "And to you."

She knew she was flushing again. A wistful longing swept through her. It took a firm act of will to suppress the emotion. She did not want his gratitude, she thought.

"Well, sir?" she said. "What of the outcome of your journey to California. Was your mission successful?"

"My mission?"

"You need not be coy. Did you think that I was not aware that you are a spy for the Crown?"

"Damn it, Amity, I'm an engineer, not a spy."

She glanced meaningfully at the black case he was holding. "Very well, I understand that you are not allowed to tell people that you are involved in the Great Game. But can you at least assure me that your venture, whatever it was, ended successfully?"

He braced one hand against a nearby pillar and loomed over her. "The answer is, yes, I was successful."

She smiled, pleased in spite of her irritation. "Excellent. I am delighted to know that I was able to contribute in some small measure to that success—even if I will never know exactly what happened."

He tapped one finger against the pillar while he contemplated that comment. Then he appeared to come to a decision.

"I don't see any reason not to tell you a few facts now that the affair has been concluded. But first, let me be clear, I am not a professional spy. I did a favor for my uncle who happens to have connections in the government. Those connections asked him for his assistance in a certain project and he, in turn, asked me to help because of my knowledge of engineering. The mission, as you call it, was my first and very likely my last experience in that sort of thing. I don't appear to be particularly adept at the business. It nearly got me killed, if you will recall."

"I'm hardly likely to forget." She hesitated. "Do you have any notion of who tried to murder you on St. Clare?"

"No. Presumably the same person who killed the inventor I went to see while I was on the island."

"Good heavens, someone else was murdered on St. Clare? You never mentioned that."

"I found his body in his laboratory," Benedict said. "He had been killed shortly before I arrived."

"Who was he?"

"Alden Cork. He was an eccentric but quite brilliant engineer who was working on a new weapon that certain parties in the government believed would revolutionize battleship armament. According to their sources, the Russians are also very keen to get their hands on the device."

"What is so revolutionary about it?"

"Cork called it a solar cannon. It is designed to be powered by the energy of the sun."

"Fascinating. Mr. Cork set up a laboratory on a Caribbean island?"

"He had a number of reasons for going to the Caribbean," Benedict said. "The first was that he was trying to conceal his activities from the various interested governments until he could perfect his solar cannon. He had intended to sell it to the highest bidder when it was completed. In addition, for obvious reasons, he needed a sunny climate to carry out his experiments. He also required a destination that was on regular steamship routes so that he could obtain the supplies and equipment that he required."

"Yes, of course, a Caribbean island would be an ideal location."

"As I said, someone, presumably an agent in the pay of the Russians, got to Cork before I arrived. The laboratory had been ransacked. There was no sign of the plans relating to the development of the weapon. One of the servants who had assisted Cork from time to time told me that an important notebook containing Cork's drawings and specifications was missing. I think that it was stolen by whoever killed him."

"And that same person then tried to murder you?"

"I assume so." Benedict paused. "I must have been one step behind him. But before I left Cork's laboratory I found a letter."

"The one you entrusted to me in the event you did not survive."

"Yes," Benedict said. "As soon as I read it I knew that it was far more valuable than Cork's design for the weapon."

"Why?"

"It was written to Cork by another inventor working in California, Elijah Foxcroft. When I read it, I immediately realized that the two men had been carrying on a correspondence for some time. It was clear that what made Cork's weapon a potentially devastating battleship gun wasn't the design of the solar cannon itself—that was fairly conventional—but rather the engine by which it was to be powered."

"A solar engine?"

"Yes."

She smiled. "Well, I suppose that does explain why we had so many interesting conversations about the potential of solar energy on board the *Northern Star*."

"The subject was on my mind," he admitted.

Alarm spiked through her. "Wait a minute. You said Cork's plans for the weapon were gone when you arrived. Does that mean that the Russians now possess them?"

"Presumably, for all the good it will do them."

She beetled her brows at him. "Explain, sir."

"The letter made it clear that Cork had been unsuccessful in creating a suitable engine for his cannon. Without a practical system capable of converting sunlight into energy in an efficient manner and a means of storing it for use when needed, his weapon was just another engineering fantasy." Benedict looked out over the sunny garden. "Rather like da Vinci's flying machines and his fantastical weapons."

"But Elijah Foxcroft has designed such a solar engine and storage device?"

"Right. The letter made it plain that Cork believed that it was capable of powering his weapon. He and Foxcroft planned to work together on the project."

She glanced at the leather case again. "You found Foxcroft, I take it?"

"I did." Benedict exhaled deeply. "Sadly, he was near death."

"Good heavens, someone murdered him, too?"

"No. He was ill with cancer. He knew he was dying. He was most anxious that his design for the solar engine and battery not be lost to history. He gave me his notebook."

"You have it in that case that you are carrying?"

"Right. I will deliver it to my uncle today and then my small role in the Great Game will be concluded—not a moment too soon, as far as I am concerned."

"I see." She studied him for a beat. "This is all quite interesting, sir. I understand your need for secrecy on the *Northern Star*."

"At the time I assumed the less you knew, the safer you would be. It was possible that the Russian agent was also on the ship."

"How did you know that I wasn't the agent?"

He looked amused. "You saved my life, if you will recall. It would have been easy enough to let me die there in that alley after I gave you the letter. That was all the proof I required to know that I could trust you."

Well, what had she expected him to say? she wondered. That he had looked into her eyes and somehow known that she would never betray him? The man was an engineer, for heaven's sake. Engineers liked to have proof.

"Well, it is not as if you had a great deal of choice in the matter."

"No," Benedict agreed. "There was some risk involved in giving you the letter, but it soon became apparent that you were not an agent for the Russians. Nevertheless, I did not tell you anything more about my objectives because—"

"Because you did not want to take the risk that I might accidentally let something slip out in casual conversation with the other passengers," she concluded crisply. "I do understand that, sir. You need not belabor the point."

"I was afraid that if there was an agent on board and if you did say something about the solar cannon or the letter you might be in danger."

She drummed her fingers on the railing. "Is that why you never bothered to contact me after we parted in New York?"

"I thought it best to keep my intention to visit Foxcroft a secret, as well." Benedict frowned. "Damn it, Amity, I was attempting to protect you as much as possible."

She gave him a thin smile. "I can assure you that ignorance is not necessarily bliss. As it happens, I was attacked because of my connection to you and I doubt very much that the Bridegroom is a Russian agent."

"I am sorry." Benedict's jaw hardened. "I seem to be apologizing a lot this morning. In attempting to protect you from a Russian spy I put you squarely in the sights of a monster."

She relented. "It's not your fault."

"On the contrary. It is obvious that if we had not been seen together on board the *Star*, the killer would not have singled you out as prey."

Amity realized that she was becoming more irritated by the minute. "Mr. Stanbridge, I refuse to let you take responsibility for what happened to me here in London. You were not even in town at the time."

He ignored her to look toward the kitchen door. "Your housekeeper is trying to gain your attention."

She turned and saw Mrs. Houston waving from the doorway.

"Mrs. Marsden sent me to tell you that the man from Scotland Yard has arrived," Mrs. Houston announced.

Eight

Penny was in the small drawing room with Inspector Logan. She was perched gracefully on the sofa. The skirts of her black gown fell in perfect folds around the soft leather shoes she wore indoors. She was discussing the weather with the tall, broad-shouldered man standing near the window.

It was not the topic of conversation that startled Amity. Everyone talked about the weather. It was the surprisingly animated expression on Penny's face that caught her attention. It would have been going too far to say that Penny looked positively cheerful, but there was a subtle hint of the old, enchanting sparkle that had once character-ized her.

All the evidence indicated that Inspector Logan was responsible for lifting Penny's spirits, and if that was, indeed, true, Amity thought, she was quite prepared to like the man on sight.

"Oh, there you are, Amity," Penny said. "Allow me to introduce you to Inspector Logan of the Yard. Inspector, my sister, and her fiancé, Mr. Stanbridge."

Amity winced at the "fiancé" but Benedict did not even flinch. Then again, he'd had more experience in covert work, she told herself.

Logan turned quickly. He inclined his head toward Amity. "Miss Doncaster. It is a pleasure to see you safe and sound this morning."

Logan was in his early thirties. Blond-haired and almost handsome, he had a boyish innocence about him that was utterly belied by the watchful expression in his cool blue eyes. He spoke with the accent of a respectable, educated man. The quality of his coat and trousers was good but not exceptionally fine or in the first stare of fashion. Amity suspected that he was able to supplement an inspector's pay with a small, independent income. Or maybe, like Penny, Logan had a knack for investments.

His attitude was both respectful and polite but he did not appear either intimidated or impressed with the expensive furnishings in the drawing room.

He gave Benedict a swift, assessing look and seemed satisfied with what he saw. "Mr. Stanbridge, I congratulate you on your engagement."

"Thank you, Inspector," Benedict said. "I am the happiest of men."

Amity closed her eyes briefly at that. When she looked at Logan again, it was obvious he saw nothing unusual about Benedict's statement.

Logan's brows rose. "Would that be Stanbridge of Stanbridge & Company, sir?"

"Yes," Benedict said. "You're familiar with the firm?"

"My father wanted me to study engineering," Logan said. "If he had lived, he would have been severely disappointed by my decision to apply for a position at the Yard."

"It seems to me that your career requires engineering of a somewhat different nature from my own," Benedict said. He smiled. "But we are both engaged in the business of trying to ensure that the trappings of civilization do not collapse beneath us."

Evidently having concluded that Benedict was not going to try to intimidate him, Logan relaxed. He went so far as to smile.

"Indeed, sir," he said. "That is a very insightful observation."

Amity was not surprised by the ease of manner between the two men. She had spent enough time in Benedict's company to know that he did not judge others by their social rank. He respected competence and professionalism in whatever guise it appeared and Inspector Logan gave the impression of possessing both qualities.

Mrs. Houston appeared with a tea tray and set it on the table in front of the sofa. Logan did appear briefly surprised when he was offered a cup but he recovered smoothly.

Amity sat down in a chair and hid a smile. She was well aware that Penny's manners were not what the inspector was accustomed to from women of the upper classes. Policemen—even inspectors—were usually treated like tradesmen and servants by those who moved in the circles that Penny and Nigel had once inhabited. The very wealthy rarely had occasion to speak to the men of the Yard. When they did find it necessary to talk to an inspector, they did not receive him in their drawing rooms. Nor did they offer tea and cakes.

"Thank you for allowing me to call on you today, Miss Doncaster," Logan said. He set his cup and saucer on a nearby table and took out a small notebook and a pencil. "Please accept my sympathies. I have read my predecessor's reports and I have the greatest admiration for you. Your quick thinking and bold action no doubt saved your life and may well lead to the capture of the monster."

"I was fortunate," Amity said.

"Yes." Logan eyed her with a thoughtful expression. "How, exactly, did you manage to escape? The reports I inherited from my predecessor were rather vague."

"That is very likely because your predecessor displayed little interest in the details I tried to supply." She touched the fan that dangled from her chatelaine. "In my travels abroad I have picked up one or two odd skills. An acquaintance of my father's gave me this fan and taught me how to use it in self-defense." She gripped the fan and snapped it open with a sharp, practiced motion to display the elegant painting. "The ribs are made of sharpened steel. The steel leaves can be employed to deflect a blade. The top edges of the leaves are honed. In effect, my fan is a knife."

Logan looked first stunned and then intrigued. "Good lord. I've never seen anything like that. Every woman should carry one."

"It requires some training and considerable practice," she said. "I do not claim to be an expert. Nevertheless, a sharp object of any kind can be extremely useful in the sort of situation that I was forced to deal with."

Logan nodded. "Indeed. But it also requires clearheaded thinking and the will to employ the weapon."

"My sister possesses both qualities," Penny said calmly. "I cannot imagine her panicking under any circumstances. I sincerely doubt that I would be so coolheaded in such a situation."

Amity snapped the fan closed. "I must tell you that although I have traveled around the world, the only place I have ever had to employ this fan in self-defense was here in London."

"London has never been known as a safe place," Benedict observed.

"Certainly not now with that dreadful killer on the loose," Penny said.

"I regret to say that the Yard has not distinguished itself in this case," Logan said. "To be quite honest, we are at a standstill. That is why my superior put me in charge of this investigation. He is hoping that fresh eyes will see clues that have been overlooked."

Benedict lounged against a wall and folded his arms. "What do you know of this killer, Inspector?"

"Over the course of the past year the bodies of four women—all of whom appear to have been murdered by the same individual—have been found dumped in various alleys around the city," Logan said.

Penny stared at him. "But I thought the Bridegroom was believed to have committed only three murders, Inspector."

"Three bodies have been found in the past three months," Logan said. "However, a year ago a woman was murdered in an identical manner. We—I—believe that she was the first victim."

Benedict frowned. "If that is true, there was a considerable gap in time between the first death and the next three murders."

"Approximately eight months," Logan said. "That time factor is one of the many mysteries involved in this case." He looked at Amity. "We are in desperate need of information."

"I will assist you in any way I can," Amity said.

"Can you describe the man who grabbed you off the street?"

"I did not see his face," she said. "He wore a mask made of black silk. I can tell you a few more things about him but I fear they may not be terribly helpful."

"At this point any details would be better than what I have now," Logan said.

"Very well, then, I will give you my impressions. His speech was that of an upper-class gentleman."

Logan appeared quite startled. Benedict, however, took the information in stride. Evidently the notion of a well-bred, aristocratic gentleman who was also a vicious killer did not seem at all extraordinary to him.

"Are you certain of his social rank, Miss Doncaster?" Logan asked.

"It's not the sort of thing that is easy to conceal," she said. "A good actor could affect the speech and mannerisms, I suppose, but I doubt if he could have afforded the expensive interiors of that carriage or the fine clothes that the killer wore."

Logan tapped his pencil against the notebook. He looked at Penny with an odd expression and then just as swiftly shifted his attention back to Amity.

"You are correct," he said. "It is difficult to imitate great wealth. What else, Miss Doncaster?"

She hesitated and then another memory flashed into her head. "He smokes cigarettes scented with some sort of spice. I could smell the stale smoke on him."

Benedict looked at Amity. "Did you see a family crest or some other indication of his identity?"

"No," she said. "He wore gloves—very good leather gloves, I might add. Everything I saw and touched in that carriage was expensive and in the most elegant taste. Except for the thick wooden shutters."

Benedict frowned. "There were shutters on the windows?"

"Heavy wooden ones," Amity said. "They were closed so that no one on the street could see what was happening."

"And perhaps designed so that you could not get out if the door was locked from the outside," Benedict said, very grim now.

Amity shivered. "I think you are correct."

There was a moment of silence while they all considered the implications.

"A private carriage, then," Logan said. He made a note and looked up. "But you did not identify it as such from the outside?"

"No. I assure you, the vehicle looked like any other ordinary cab. There was nothing unusual about the driver, either."

"Yes, of course," Logan said. "The coachman." He made another note. "We must look into that aspect."

Benedict nodded in silent approval.

"Can you tell me anything else about him?" Logan said.

Amity shook her head. "I'm afraid not. The one time he spoke, he sounded exactly as you would expect a cab driver to sound. Working-class. A bit rough around the edges. But he was certainly skilled with the reins. And he made no move to catch me when I escaped."

Logan wrote something down in his notebook and looked up again. "What did the killer say to you?"

Amity glanced at Benedict and then turned back to Logan. She took a breath. "He informed me that he had chosen me because I had deliberately compromised myself with Mr. Stanbridge. He seemed to believe that I had set a trap for Mr. Stanbridge."

Logan glanced at Benedict, who gave him a cool smile.

"Evidently the killer was not aware that Miss Doncaster and I are engaged to be married," Benedict said.

"I see." Logan made another note and looked at Amity. "I must ask you if the killer made any reference to photography."

"Why, yes," Amity said. "I was just about to mention that. He said he intended to take my bridal portrait. How did you know?"

"I asked because there is one significant detail that we have not divulged to the press," Logan said. He lowered his notebook. "Each victim was found in a different alley. Each one had her throat cut by an extremely sharp blade. The wounds appeared almost surgical in nature."

"A scalpel," Amity said suddenly. "He held a scalpel to my throat."

"Did he?" Logan jotted down another note. "That is very interesting. To continue, the victims were all dressed in the clothes in which they had last been seen. And each was wearing a gold wedding ring."

"That much has appeared in the press," Penny said. "The wedding rings are the reason the papers labeled the killer the Bridegroom."

"Yes," Logan said. "But what we have managed to keep out of the papers is the fact that in addition to the rings, the women were all wearing lockets. Inside each locket there was a small bridal portrait of the victim. The photographs are clearly the work of a professional photographer."

Amity frowned. "But none of the women had ever been married."

"No," Logan agreed.

"Dear heaven," Penny whispered. "The man is quite mad."

A chill swept through Amity. "Were the photographs taken before or after the women were murdered?"

Benedict straightened away from the wall and went to stand at the window. "A number of professional photographers make their livings taking pictures of the deceased."

Amity shuddered. "The practice has always struck me as quite macabre."

"It strikes me that way, as well," Penny said.

"The Bridegroom's victims were all alive when they were photographed," Logan said. "Their throats had not yet been cut."

"Why have you kept the business of the lockets a secret from the press?" Penny asked.

"Believe it or not, we at the Yard have discovered that there are some demented souls who will actually come forward to claim responsibility for crimes that have received a great deal of public attention," Logan explained.

Benedict turned around. "In other words, you use the detail of the lockets to separate the wheat from the chaff. Only the real killer will know about the photographs."

"Yes," Logan said.

Penny put down her teacup. "Something has just occurred to me. It probably amounts to nothing—"

"Go on, Mrs. Marsden," Logan said.

"The rumors of what everyone, including the killer, assumed to be an illicit liaison between my sister and Mr. Stanbridge started to circulate following the Channing ball. If the killer does, indeed, move in Polite Society as Amity believes, perhaps he was actually present at the ball. That would certainly explain how he came to hear of the gossip."

Logan looked impressed. "That is a very intriguing observation, Mrs. Marsden."

Amity turned toward Penny. "It's positively brilliant."

"Thank you," Penny said. "But I don't see how the observation can be of much use."

"It gives me a starting point," Logan said. "I told my superior that I suspected that the killer moved in elevated circles because his victims all came from that world. But he was reluctant to accept the notion."

"Probably because he knew such a theory would be extremely difficult to investigate," Benedict said.

He and Logan exchanged glances. Men and their silent methods of communicating, Amity thought. It could be quite annoying. But she had to admit that women were equally inclined to nonverbal exchanges that were probably incomprehensible to the male of the species.

It was a great pity that the two sexes could not communicate so well with each other, she thought.

Logan's expression was grim. "I see you comprehend my predicament, Mr. Stanbridge."

"Of course, Inspector," Benedict said. "You are looking for a killer who moves in wealthy circles, the one strata of Society where it is virtually impossible for a policeman of any rank to go uninvited."

"If I start to ask questions about a well-bred killer who is given to a particularly perverse form of murder, all doors will be closed to me," Logan said.

There was a short silence.

"They will open for me," Benedict said quietly.

Logan studied him for a long moment. Amity noticed that the inspector did not hasten to shut down the notion of accepting assistance from Benedict.

The possibility of doing something—anything—to assist in the capture of the man who had tried to murder her and who had ruthlessly extinguished the lives of four other women elevated her spirits in a remarkable manner.

"Those doors will open for me, as well," she said quickly. "I am, after all, Mr. Stanbridge's fiancée."

Benedict's eyes gleamed with fleeting amusement.

Penny's jaw tightened. She picked up her cup. "They will also open for me, Inspector. I have had quite enough of mourning."

Logan began to look vaguely horrified. "I am grateful to Mr. Stanbridge for whatever help he can provide, but I do not wish to put either of you ladies in danger."

"According to Mr. Stanbridge," Penny said, "my sister may still be in danger. Do you agree, Inspector?"

Logan hesitated and then inclined his head. "It's possible that, having been deprived of his prey, the beast may well make another attempt to seize Miss Doncaster. Assuming that he's alive. I simply don't know."

"Then I insist on doing whatever I can to help in this inquiry," Amity said.

"So do I," Penny added.

Benedict looked at Logan. "It appears you have a team of investigators ready to help, Inspector. Will you allow us to do so?"

Logan studied the three of them for a long moment. Then he made his decision.

"Four women have died thus far," he said. "Now a fifth has barely escaped the same fate. I accept your offer of assistance. But the four of us will keep this to ourselves, is that understood? I am afraid that my associates at the Yard would not approve of allowing civilians to become involved in an investigation."

"Understood," Benedict said. "I know my fiancée can keep a secret. I have no doubt but that Mrs. Marsden can keep one, as well."

"As it happens," Penny said coolly, "I have had some experience in that regard."

The comment struck Amity as odd. She glanced at Penny, but before she could ask any questions Benedict spoke.

"I will arrange to keep an eye on Miss Doncaster when she leaves the house," he said. "But I think it best to have someone watch this residence at night."

Amity stared at him, shocked. "Isn't that going a little too far?"

"No," Benedict said. "It's not."

Logan blew out a breath. "Mr. Stanbridge has a point. Given the Yard's lack of progress to date, and the fact that we have not found the killer's body, it would be a good idea to have the house watched at night. I will make arrangements for a constable to stand guard."

"Thank you," Penny said. "I would feel better knowing that there was a policeman nearby in the evenings. Now, then, where do we start the investigation?"

"I believe we must begin with the guest list for the Channing ball," Logan said. "But I very much doubt that Lady Channing will give it to me."

Penny smiled. "Obtaining the Channing guest list is no problem at all, Inspector. I can tell you exactly how to get it."

Nine

Benedict went down the front steps of Number Five Exton Street filled with an odd mix of exhilaration and dread. Both emotions were directly linked to Amity. For the past few weeks, ever since he had left her in New York, she had been in his head. The sense of anticipation he had experienced on the voyage back to London had been unlike anything he had ever known. Discovering that she had very nearly been murdered and that the killer had become obsessed with her because of her connection to him had shaken him to the center of his being.

And now he was engaged to her. In a manner of speaking. The thought of having an excuse to spend a great deal of time in her company—the thought of kissing her again—thrilled him. But the reason for the enforced intimacy between them made it impossible to savor the exhilaration. He would not sleep well until the killer was found.

He hailed a cab and went home to his town house. It had been a month and a half since he had left, but he had telegraphed the news of his impending arrival to his butler. As always, Hodges and his wife, Mrs. Hodges, the housekeeper, had everything ready and in order. It was as if Benedict had just gone out to meet a friend earlier that morning and had returned somewhat later than usual. As far as Benedict could discern, there was no force on earth that could shatter the aplomb of either of the Hodges.

"I trust your journey was satisfactory," Hodges said.

"Yes, in more ways than one." Benedict handed his hat, coat and gloves to Hodges. "But there were a few unexpected events. In addition to locating the inventor I had hoped to interview, I am happy to announce that I am engaged to be married to Miss Amity Doncaster."

It took a lot to make Hodges blink. He blinked twice. Then something that might have been astonishment lit up his long, stern features.

"Would that be Miss Amity Doncaster, the lady globetrotter who writes travel reports for the *Flying Intelligencer*, sir?" Hodges asked. "The same Miss Doncaster who was very nearly murdered by the fiend called the Bridegroom?"

"One and the same. I see you are aware of Miss Doncaster."

"I expect everyone who reads the papers is aware of her, sir." Hodges cleared his throat. "And also that your name has been linked with hers in a romantic fashion."

No wonder Amity and Penny were so concerned about the rumors that had been circulating, Benedict thought. He was inclined to ignore gossip for the most part, so he sometimes forgot how quickly it could spread and how deep and wide it could reach. Amity was right to worry that her publisher might cancel the publication of *A Lady's Guide to Globetrotting*.

"Of course our names have been linked in a romantic fashion,"

Benedict said. "As I told you, we are engaged. We were waiting to make a formal announcement until I returned to London."

"She sounds like a very interesting lady," Hodges said. "Mrs. Hodges is a great fan of her travel pieces. I do hope Miss Doncaster is recovering well from her recent ordeal."

"I went to see her before I came here. I found her eating a hearty breakfast and reading the morning papers."

"That is quite impressive, sir. A hearty breakfast, you say? I expect that most ladies would be subsisting on tea and toast after such an experience."

"Miss Doncaster is unique, Hodges."

Hodges did not actually smile but approval flickered in his eyes.

"Obviously, sir," he said. "I would not have expected you to become engaged to a lady who was anything less than unique."

"You know me better than I know myself, Hodges."

"Will you be wanting breakfast, sir?"

"No, thank you. I ate it at the home of my fiancée and her sister, Mrs. Marsden."

Hodges elevated his brows a fraction of an inch. "Would that be the Mrs. Marsden who is the widow of Mr. Nigel Marsden, the gentleman who broke his neck going over a fence in the hunt several months ago?"

"I believe so, why?"

"Nothing, sir."

"Damn it, Hodges, what are you not telling me?"

Mrs. Hodges spoke from the doorway. "What Mr. Hodges is trying to say is that Mrs. Marsden is no doubt grieving very deeply. She inherited a tidy fortune from her late husband, yet according to the rumors, the first thing she did after the funeral was let all of the staff go. They say she has retreated from the world."

Benedict studied Mrs. Hodges, who bore a striking resemblance to Mr. Hodges, except for her housedress and apron.

"You are well informed, Mrs. Hodges," he said. "Anything else I ought to know about my future sister-in-law?"

"I don't believe so, sir."

Benedict started up the stairs. "In that case I am going to bathe and change my clothes, after which I must call on my brother and then visit my uncle." He paused midway up the staircase. "I suppose it would be too much to hope that there has not been any recent word from Australia?"

Hodges picked up the silver salver on the console. There was a single envelope on the tray. "As a matter of fact, a telegram arrived this morning."

"Damn and blast. I suppose that is no surprise." Resigned, Benedict changed course and went back down the stairs. "If the gossip about my association with Miss Doncaster is all over London, then naturally it has reached my parents."

"The invention of the telegraph was an amazing thing, sir," Hodges said. "I believe the undersea cable that linked Australia to the rest of the world was laid more than a decade ago."

"I'm aware of that, Hodges." Benedict picked up the envelope, opened it quickly and read the short message.

RUMORS LINKING YOUR NAME TO THAT OF MISS AMITY
DONCASTER HAVE REACHED US STOP YOUR MOTHER WISHES
TO KNOW THE TRUTH OF THE MATTER STOP SHE REMINDS
YOU THAT IT IS TIME YOU GOT MARRIED STOP

Benedict dropped the message on the tray. "It's from my father. I'll draft a reply before I leave the house."

"Yes, sir," Hodges said.

He exchanged a look with Mrs. Hodges, who smiled what Benedict thought was a distinctly smug smile.

An hour later Benedict went up the steps of an elegant little house situated in a quiet, attractive neighborhood. He was shown immediately into the study, where he found Richard seated at the desk.

Richard looked up from the architectural drawings he had been examining.

"It's about time you got here," he said. "I assume you are aware that you are the subject of some very interesting gossip linking your name with that of Miss Amity Doncaster?"

Richard was two years younger and somewhat taller. His red-brown hair and sea-green eyes had come from their mother. Richard had also inherited Elizabeth Stanbridge's warm, outgoing, optimistic personality.

More than one person had remarked that the Stanbridge brothers were as different as night and day. Benedict was well aware that he was the one cast in the role of dour, gloomy night: always ready to point out the drawbacks and the risks of a venture; always assessing the worst case and planning for that eventuality.

Richard, by contrast, was a bright, sunny morning. Although he was a truly gifted architect, his most valuable contribution to the firm of Stanbridge & Company was his ability to charm potential clients. He also had a very good head for business. The combination made him invaluable.

If the task of dealing with the clients were left to him, Benedict thought, Stanbridge & Company would no doubt be bankrupt within six months. He was the first to admit that he had little patience with clients who did not comprehend the importance of sound engineering principles and the need to resist the temptation to cut corners when it came to the quality of materials and craftsmanship. Most clients wanted to be dazzled by spectacular architectural details. They just assumed the bridge or the building or the glass conservatory would not collapse.

"I have just this morning been made aware of the chatter about my relationship with Miss Doncaster," he said. He set the black leather case on the desk and went to stand at the window. "One would think that people would have more important matters to discuss."

"You can hardly expect people to ignore gossip that involves both a hint of scandal and attempted murder," Richard said. He looked amused.

"Huh."

Richard paused and then cleared his throat. "I'm aware that the bit about attempted murder is true. The news in the press has been remarkably consistent, if very likely exaggerated. I don't doubt but that Miss Doncaster barely escaped the clutches of a killer."

"Thanks to her bravery and self-defense skills," Benedict said.

"They do say that travel is educational. What of the romantic aspect of the stories? Ben, tell me the truth. Are you involved in a liaison with Miss Doncaster?"

"Not a liaison." Benedict turned away from the window and met his brother's eyes. "I am engaged to her."

He realized he liked announcing that he was engaged to Amity. It was as if the more frequently he made the statement, the more real it became.

Richard's brows shot skyward. He lounged back in his chair and put his fingertips together. "Well, well, well. Wait until Mother finds out."

"There was a telegram from Australia waiting for me when I walked through my front door today."

"I'm not surprised." Richard chuckled. "I got one yesterday. Mother sends her love, by the way. Evidently her painting has been inspired by the atmosphere of that artists' colony where she and Father are staying."

"And Father is no doubt enjoying his observations of the Australian flora and fauna. Nevertheless, they both apparently have time to keep up with the London gossip."

"You can't be all that astonished. You know as well as I do that after the disaster of your last engagement they have been desperate to see you married."

Benedict started to respond but paused when he saw his sister-in-law in the doorway. Marissa's light brown hair was caught back in a simple knot at the nape of her neck. The style emphasized her warm, gray eyes and pretty features. Benedict had not seen her for a month and a half. He was taken aback at the change in her appearance. The flowing lines of a loose-fitting housedress could not disguise the advanced state of her pregnancy. A quick calculation told him that she was now very nearly due to give birth to her firstborn. It was all he could do not to stare at her. There was a peculiar glow about her, he concluded. The dramatic changes that pregnancy wrought upon a woman were nothing less than terrifying to a mere male.

"Marissa," he managed. "Are you . . . well?"

"I'm in excellent health, thank you very much, Ben." She smiled and gently touched her rounded belly. "Do not look so nervous. I assure you I am not going to deliver this babe here in Richard's study."

"Darling, you must sit down." Richard was on his feet. He hurried across the room to take her arm and guide her to a large chair. "I'll have Mrs. Streeter bring you a cup of tea."

"Mrs. Streeter has been pouring tea down my throat all day," she said. "I'm fine, Richard."

Richard put a hassock under her feet. "Are you sure you shouldn't be in bed?"

"Nonsense." Marissa looked at Benedict. "I couldn't possibly take a nap, at least not until I hear all of the exciting news. You must tell us everything, Ben. What in the world is going on? Are you and Miss Doncaster involved in a scandalous affair?"

"You needn't look so thrilled with the notion, Marissa. As I was explaining to Richard, there has been some confusion regarding the nature of my relationship with Miss Doncaster." Benedict paused for emphasis. "I am engaged to marry her."

"That is wonderful news." Marissa smiled with approval. "Your mother will be thrilled."

"So Richard says."

"You know very well that your poor mother has been anxious to see you wed. As her firstborn son it is high time you gave the Rose Necklace to your bride-to-be."

Benedict wondered somewhat glumly what Amity would say if he were to give her the Stanbridge family necklace. He tried to cheer himself with the thought that most women adore exquisite jewels. But Amity was unpredictable.

It was odd, he thought. As an engineer he abhorred unpredictability. Ever since the fiasco with Eleanor he had been searching for a predictable female, one who possessed all the qualities of a fine clock. She would be reliable and dependable. She would keep his household on schedule and remind him of his appointments. He would wind her up on a regular basis and she, in turn, would not surprise him by running off with a lover. Was that too much to ask?

"I have been reading the papers," Marissa said. "I cannot begin to imagine what Miss Doncaster went through. She is lucky to be alive."

Benedict propped himself on the edge of Richard's desk and folded his arms. "Trust me when I tell you that there is no need to remind me of that fact."

"You met on board ship?" Marissa asked.

"The story is somewhat more complicated," Benedict said.

He gave Marissa and Richard a summary of events.

"Good heavens." Marissa was horrified. "There wasn't supposed to be any danger involved in that excursion to St. Clare. You were simply supposed to meet with that inventor and ascertain whether or not he had designed a truly revolutionary weapon."

Richard's jaw tightened. "You never informed us that you had been shot."

"Why bother?" Benedict said. "There was nothing either of you could do, and as I survived the incident I saw no reason why the news could not wait until I got home."

"So Miss Doncaster saved your life," Marissa said. "That does explain some of the gossip about the two of you. Naturally she would have been seen coming and going from your cabin on board the *Northern Star.*"

Benedict cleared his throat. "We also spent a great deal of time in each other's company after I was back on my feet."

"I see." Marissa's brows puckered. "I wonder why we never heard that you had been shot. One would have thought that fact would have made it back to London."

"Good question," Benedict said. "But you know how it is with gossip. People tend to focus on the scandalous aspects, not the facts."

"Very true," Marissa said. "I must say, her bold actions are precisely what I would have expected from the Miss Doncaster who has been writing the articles on travel that are published in the *Flying Intelligencer*."

Benedict smiled. "I take it you are a fan of her essays?"

"Absolutely," Marissa enthused. "I can certainly understand why you are engaged to marry her. She sounds perfect for you. Indeed, I look forward to meeting her."

"That will be quite soon," Benedict said. "Meanwhile, my chief concern is that she is still in danger from the man who attacked her. I have told her that I do not want her to leave the house unescorted. When I cannot be with her, someone else is to accompany her at all times. At night a constable will watch the house."

Richard frowned. "You think the killer is still alive?"

"I must assume as much until his body is found."

Marissa looked worried. "What if they don't find him? What if he is alive but the police are not successful in capturing him?"

"Amity and her sister and I intend to give the police some assistance with the investigation," Benedict said.

Marissa looked intrigued. "How on earth can you do that?"

"Amity gained several impressions about the killer yesterday," Benedict explained. "Among other things she is convinced that he moves in Society."

This time both Marissa and Richard stared at him, shocked.

Benedict related Amity's description of the Bridegroom.

"Given the timing of events, we believe that he may well have attended the Channing ball a month ago," he concluded. "Or, at the very least, he is acquainted with someone who was present."

Marissa gave him a knowing look. "You will need the guest list."

Benedict smiled. "As a matter of fact, Miss Doncaster's sister has instructed Inspector Logan on how to obtain it."

"You have set yourself an interesting task," Richard said. "Hunting killers is a job for the police. But I take your point. The sort of people who attend balls do not open their doors to inspectors from Scotland Yard. As you are well aware, Marissa and I prefer to ignore the Polite World for the most part, but we do have some connections. If there is anything we can do to help, you must not hesitate to ask."

"Thank you," Benedict said. "I appreciate that. I may be calling on you."

Richard glanced at the black leather case Benedict had set on his desk. "What of the plans for the solar engine and the battery?"

Benedict picked up the case and opened it. He removed the leather binder that contained Elijah Foxcroft's notes.

"After I leave here I will deliver it to Uncle Cornelius. Once that chore is accomplished, my very short career as a spy for the Crown will be concluded."

"And your new profession as a consultant for Scotland Yard will begin," Richard said. He eyed the binder with great interest. "I would very much like to take a look at Foxcroft's notes and drawings."

Benedict put the binder on the desk. "I am going to show them to you."

❧

Sometime later Richard closed the binder and sat back in his chair. There was an air of cool satisfaction in his smile.

"I understand now why you made that trip to California. The Russians very likely have the plans for the solar cannon, but you brought back the design for the engine system that is capable of powering the weapon. The cannon is of no use without it."

"The thing about Foxcroft's solar engine and battery that is so interesting is that they are just that—an engine and a storage device,"

Benedict said. "The system could power anything, not just weapons. One could use it to operate an oven, a vehicle, a ship or a factory—all using the free energy of the sun. The possibilities are unlimited."

Richard grinned. "Better not let the owners of the coal mines hear you say that."

"Mouchot is right, we are going to run out of coal eventually. At the very least it will become increasingly expensive to extract it from the ground. The French and the Russians have been funding solar research and development for the past few years. Several American inventors are working on solar devices. We need to catch up with the rest of the major powers or risk being left in the dust." Benedict tapped the notebook. "Foxcroft's system is our chance to do that."

"I'm not arguing with you. Obviously Uncle Cornelius would not have asked you to go to St. Clare if the Crown was not interested in the potential for solar power."

"My fear is that all the government will see is the potential to create a new kind of weapon with Foxcroft's engine. Uncle Cornelius's associates won't understand the larger implications."

"If anyone can convince them to take solar energy seriously, it will be Uncle Cornelius."

"You're right." Benedict looked at the binder. "Before I deliver Foxcroft's notes and specifications to him, however, I have a favor to ask. I have a plan and I need your help."

Richard smiled. "You always have a plan. What is it this time?"

Benedict told him.

When he was finished Richard nodded, very thoughtful now.

"Yes," he said. "That makes sense."

Ten

"M iss Doncaster, I cannot begin to express the depths of my admiration, not only for you, personally, but for your succinct and insightful writing," Arthur Kelbrook said. "I have read every single one of your essays in the *Flying Intelligencer*. Your descriptions of foreign landscapes are positively brilliant. It is as if I was at your side, viewing the scenes with you. I shall never forget the poetic picture you painted of the sun setting on that island in the South Seas."

"Thank you, Mr. Kelbrook," Amity said. She flushed, unaccustomed to such rapturous praise. "Very kind of you to take the time to read my little pieces in the *Flying Intelligencer*."

The reception hall of the Society for Travel and Exploration was crowded. The guest of honor, Humphrey Nash, had concluded his talk a short time ago and was now holding court at the far end of the room. He was surrounded by admirers and rivals alike. There were, Amity noted, a considerable number of ladies in the group. The Society was one of the few travel and geographical institutions open to women, but Amity knew that was not the only reason there were so many females at the reception. Nash was a tall, handsome, athletically built man endowed with a patrician profile and piercing green eyes. His curly brown hair was cut short in the modern style.

He was also a very fine photographer. His beautiful pictures of temples, exotic gardens, snow-peaked mountains and ancient monuments lined the walls.

Amity tried not to let her gaze stray toward Humphrey but it was difficult. She had been anxious about attending the reception tonight, but a part of her had known that she needed to see Humphrey again to prove to herself that she had recovered from what, at the age of nineteen, she had considered to be heartbreak.

Tonight, watching him as he commanded the audience from the podium, she found herself wondering what she had ever seen in him. He was still the handsome, dashing explorer who had captivated her at nineteen, but she had realized immediately that she was no longer under his spell. She had to admit that walking into the hall on the arm of her so-called fiancé had provided a great deal of satisfaction.

It was probably quite immature to hope that Humphrey had noticed her sitting with Benedict in the audience and had, perhaps, heard that she was engaged. But she told herself that she deserved to savor the moment. After all, Humphrey had caused her no little humiliation when he had taken advantage of her naïveté to try to persuade her into an illicit affair. Her reputation had taken a blow at nineteen that had destroyed her chances of making a respectable marriage.

It was, she often thought, a good thing that she enjoyed foreign travel, because she'd had little option but to leave the country. She smiled at the thought. Setting out to explore the world had been the best thing that had ever happened to her.

Penny was halfway across the room. She looked especially lovely tonight in a dark blue gown that complimented her hair. The blue dress was an audacious choice. According to the social dictates of mourning, a wife was expected to spend a year and a day in black. Amity had been both astonished and delighted when Penny had come downstairs in the gown. True, it was a very dark shade of blue but it was, nevertheless, blue—not black or even gray.

Amity had to admit that she was rather enjoying the knowledge that she herself was dressed in a stylish, fashionable manner. The conversation in the dressmaker's salon came back to her.

"The deep green color will draw attention to your eyes and enhance the drama of your dark hair," Penny said. "I suspect that Mr. Stanbridge is in for a surprise tonight."

"Why on earth would he be surprised by the sight of me in a dress?" Amity asked. She touched the delicious, rich folds of the green fabric. "He has seen me on any number of previous occasions and I assure you, I was in a gown each time. It is not as though I go about in the nude when I am abroad."

The dressmaker lifted her eyes toward the heavens and muttered *"Mon Dieu"* in a very bad French accent.

Penny ignored her to give Amity a severe look. "I expect that on each occasion you were wearing one of those wretched brown or black things you always pack for your travels."

"They don't show wrinkles and stains," Amity said, finding herself on the defensive. "And they launder well."

"I don't care how easily they can be washed and dried and ironed," Penny said. "The colors are not flattering and they don't show your figure to advantage the way this gown will."

The gown was simply, elegantly styled with long, narrow sleeves and a snug bodice that ended in a point just below her waist. The skirt was artfully tailored to create a long, narrow line in front that, nevertheless, allowed for relative ease of movement. In the back, the fabric was draped over a discreet little bustle.

The dressmaker had pronounced herself horrified by Amity's fan. Madame La Fontaine had insisted that it did not enhance the gown. She had suggested, instead, one fashioned of delicate wooden spokes that opened to display an orchid scene. But Amity had held her ground. In that one instance Penny had taken her side. Neither of them had deemed it wise to explain to the dressmaker that the fan was actually a weapon. The poor woman would have been thoroughly shocked at the notion of a lady carrying a blade to a reception. Tonight the tessen was suspended from a silver chatelaine at Amity's waist.

"I would not miss a single one of your travel pieces," Kelbrook said. "I assure you, I am your most faithful reader, Miss Doncaster."

"Thank you," Amity said again.

She took a step back, trying to put more distance between them. But Kelbrook took a step closer. It dawned on her that the glitter in his eyes was excitement, not admiration, and a rather unwholesome excitement at that.

"I was shocked by the news that you were attacked by that dreadful killer the press refers to as the Bridegroom," he continued. "I must ask how you escaped. The accounts in the papers were rather vague about that aspect of the affair."

"Luck had a great deal to do with it," Amity said briskly. She inched back another small step. "That, plus some experience in getting out of tight quarters."

She was not about to demonstrate her fan to him. There was little point carrying a disguised weapon if everyone knew the secret. One did not confide in near strangers, even those who expressed great devotion to one's writings.

Arthur Kelbrook was in his mid-forties. He was pleasant-looking in a bland sort of way, with a receding hairline, pale gray eyes, a soft mouth, broad hands and very little neck. All indications were that he was fated to expand in girth as the years passed. The buttons that fastened his expensively tailored coat were pulled taut across his midsection.

He was certainly not the handsomest or the most distinguished-looking man in the room, Amity reflected, but his earnest, sincere manner at the start of their conversation had been charming, even endearing. Kelbrook was the only one she had met that evening who seemed genuinely interested in her travel adventures. Everyone else was transfixed with Humphrey Nash.

Which was not to say that she had failed to attract the attentions of several other men in the room, she thought. From time to time she caught a number of males casting quick, speculative glances in her direction. She knew they were wondering if a woman who dared to go abroad on her own was reckless in other ways, as well. It was not the first time she had encountered so-called gentlemen who presumed far too much.

"I hear the police have not yet discovered the body of the Bridegroom," Kelbrook said.

"No." She did not add that there might not be a body to discover.

Kelbrook lowered his voice and edged closer. "There was, I understand, a great deal of blood at the scene."

Whatever charm Arthur Kelbrook had exhibited a short time ago had worn off. She was starting to become more than impatient. A deep unease was stirring inside her.

"Quite true," she said. She kept her tone vague and pretended to search the room. "I wonder where my fiancé is."

There was no sign of Benedict. Just when you need a man he disappears, she thought.

"You must have struggled valiantly," Kelbrook said. "But what could a gentle, delicate lady like yourself do to defend herself against a great, rutting beast of a man?"

Kelbrook's intensity was increasing. So was the feverish look in his eyes.

A chill iced Amity's neck. She tried to step around Kelbrook but he was somehow in her path.

"I assure you the matter was resolved in mere minutes," she said briskly. "I simply jumped out of the carriage."

"I can only imagine how it must have been for you, pinned beneath that brute, his hands on your maidenly body, your nightgown tumbled about your waist, his trousers no doubt open."

"Good heavens, sir, I do believe that you are as mad as a hatter."

Amity whirled on her heel intending to depart the scene. She collided with a large, immovable object.

"Benedict." Jolted, she stopped short. The little green cap that was angled over her left brow came free of its pins. "Oh, for pity's sake." She managed to grab the cap before it landed on the floor. "I didn't see you standing there, sir. Must you sneak around like that?"

"Who was he?" Benedict asked.

The low-voiced question was laden with a dark, fierce, decidedly dangerous threat.

Amity popped the cap back on top of her head and peered up at Benedict. He was not looking at her. His attention was fixed on the crowd behind her. She glanced over her shoulder and saw Arthur Kelbrook disappearing into the throng.

"Mr. Kelbrook?" She shuddered in disgust and turned back to face Benedict. "A very unpleasant man with a decidedly warped imagination."

"In that case, why the devil were you talking to him alone in this alcove?"

She was startled by his tone. Surely Benedict was not jealous? No, of course not. His only concern was for her safety. She should be grateful. And she was grateful. Very grateful.

"I assure you, he was properly introduced and our initial conversation was quite harmless," she said. "Mr. Kelbrook expressed a deep interest in my travel articles. But then he started to ask for details of my encounter with the killer. When I declined to provide them, he resorted to inventing a few outrageous particulars."

Benedict yanked his attention away from Kelbrook and pinned her with a feral gaze. "What the hell do you mean by invent?"

She cleared her throat. "I believe he was nurturing some dark fantasy that involved me being assaulted by the Bridegroom."

"You were assaulted."

"Mr. Kelbrook was enthralled by the notion that I had been assaulted in a more intimate fashion, if you comprehend me."

For a split second Benedict looked confused. Then cold rage lit his eyes. "He imagined you were raped? He wanted you to describe such a scene to him?"

"Something along those lines, yes."

"That son of a bitch," Benedict said much too softly.

The icy fury in his gaze alarmed her.

"I assured him that there had been no time for that sort of thing," she said quickly. "I told him that I had escaped unharmed. I had just informed Mr. Kelbrook that he was as mad as a hatter and I was about to leave his company when you arrived."

"I will deal with him," Benedict vowed in that same too-quiet voice.

In spite of her alarm, Amity experienced a rush of warmth. Benedict really was determined to protect her. She was so accustomed to being on her own and obliged to take care of herself that she was not entirely certain how to respond.

"I appreciate the offer, sir," she said. "But it is entirely unnecessary for you to take any further action."

"It was not an offer," Benedict said.

"Benedict," she said very firmly, "you must not do anything rash. Do you understand?"

"Mad," Benedict said, going abruptly thoughtful.

She frowned. "Eccentric, certainly, and cursed with an unwholesome imagination, but I'm not sure one can label Mr. Kelbrook mad. He is not the killer if that is what you are thinking."

"You're certain?"

"Absolutely. Everything about him was different—his hands, his physical stature, his voice—everything."

"You said that he was as mad as a hatter."

"It was a figure of speech."

"Logan and the press are convinced that the Bridegroom is quite mad," Benedict pointed out.

"Well, surely no sane man would go about murdering women. What are you getting at, sir?"

"It just occurred to me that we might be overlooking a rather obvious clue. If the killer is truly mad, it is quite likely that someone who knows him well—a member of his family, perhaps—is aware of his unnatural behavior."

She considered that briefly. "You may be right. But you know how it is when there is a streak of insanity in the family. People will go to great lengths to conceal it. Rumors of madness in the bloodline can destroy a high-ranking family. The other members of their social circle will refuse to allow their sons and daughters to take the risk of marrying into a clan that is perceived to be tainted by madness."

"On the other hand," Benedict said evenly, "a host of eccentricities and extremely odd behaviors can be overlooked."

"Well, there is no doubt but that what some might call madness has been passed off as merely eccentric behavior," she said. "A tendency toward cold-blooded murder, however, can hardly be labeled an eccentricity."

"Such a tendency cannot be called insanity, either."

"What would you call it?"

"Evil."

Memories of her brief moments in the carriage with the human predator swept through Amity's mind. She was aware of a tightness in her chest. She reminded herself to breathe. Instinctively she touched the tessen. She could take care of herself. Damn it, she *had* taken care of herself. She was safe now.

Except that the monster was still out there in the shadows.

"Yes," she whispered. "Whatever the doctors might say about the state of his mental faculties, there is no doubt but that at his core the Bridegroom is evil."

"The bastard will go on killing until he is stopped. It is the nature of the beast." Benedict paused, frowning. "Is your sister trying to signal us, by any chance?"

Amity glanced around and saw that Humphrey Nash had joined the small group of women that included Penny. At that moment Penny caught her eye and tipped her chin ever so slightly.

Amity took a deep breath and braced herself.

"Yes," she said. "I do believe Penny is trying to gain our attention."

"Nash is with her."

"So he is."

Humphrey followed Penny's gaze and smiled his charming smile when he saw Amity. She summoned up a polite smile in return.

"I think Nash is angling for an introduction to you," Benedict said.

"There is no need for that," Amity said. "Mr. Nash and I are already acquainted."

Benedict looked as if he had more to say on the subject but he held his tongue. Taking a firm, proprietary grip on her arm, he escorted her across the room. When they reached the small group, Penny manipulated the niceties with her customary grace.

"There you are, Amity," Penny said. She blinked. "What on earth happened to your hat?"

"My hat?" Amity reached up to touch the clever little cap. "It's still there."

"It has come unfastened. Never mind, we'll deal with it later." Penny reached up and plucked the cap from Amity's hair. "I believe you know Mr. Nash?"

"We've met," Amity said. She was proud of the cool manner in which the words came out of her mouth. Benedict's hand tightened on her arm as if he was prepared to pull her out of Humphrey's reach should it become necessary to do so.

"Amity, what a pleasure to see you again," Humphrey said. His eyes warmed. "What has it been? Six years?"

"Time flies, doesn't it?" Amity said. She gave him a serene smile. "Are you acquainted with my fiancé, Mr. Stanbridge?"

"I'm afraid not." Some of the warmth evaporated from Humphrey's eyes. He gave Benedict a short, assessing look. "Stanbridge."

"Nash," Benedict said.

Humphrey immediately switched his attention back to Amity. "I have enjoyed your occasional pieces in the *Flying Intelligencer*."

"Thank you," she said. "I must say, your photographs are quite brilliant, as always."

"I am delighted to know that you approve of them, especially since you have actually visited some of the locations and subjects that I have photographed," Humphrey said. "You are in an excellent position to judge the quality of the images."

"They are spectacular," she said. It was the truth, she thought. "You have a talent for capturing the particular essence of each scene—the beauty of a desert setting, the artistic elements of a temple, the glory of the view from a mountaintop. Indeed, sir, your work goes far beyond a mere recording of images. You are an artist with your camera."

"Thank you," Humphrey said. "I would very much enjoy discussing some of our mutual observations. Perhaps I might call on you sometime in the near future?"

"Sorry to interrupt," Benedict said. He took out his pocket watch and flipped open the gold lid. "But I do believe it's time for us to take our leave, Amity. We have another appointment this evening."

Amity glanced at him, frowning. "What appointment is that, sir?"

"Perhaps I neglected to mention it earlier," he said smoothly. "It is with an aging uncle. I want you to meet him. I will give you the details when we are in the carriage. Mrs. Marsden, are you ready to leave?"

"Yes, of course," Penny said. She looked amused.

Benedict took Amity's arm and paused long enough to give Humphrey one last look. "Interesting photographs, Nash. What type of camera do you use?"

"The latest model Presswood," Humphrey said shortly. "It was especially modified by the manufacturer to suit my requirements. Are you a photographer, sir?"

"The subject holds some interest for me," Benedict said. He turned to Amity and Penny. "If you ladies are ready?"

"Certainly," Penny said.

Amity inclined her head toward Humphrey. "Good evening, sir."

"Good evening," Humphrey said. Once again his eyes heated a little.

Benedict escorted Amity and Penny away before anyone could say anything else. Amity was quite sure that Penny was struggling to suppress a smile, but she was too annoyed at Benedict to ask her sister what she found so humorous.

When they reached the entrance of the hall, Amity and Penny collected their cloaks. The three of them went out onto the front steps. There was a slight chill in the summer night but at least it was not raining, Amity thought.

Benedict spoke briefly to the porter, who sent a runner to summon the carriage.

There was a short pause while they waited for the vehicle. Amity looked at Benedict. In the glary light of the gaslight his face was shadowed in a grim chiaroscuro.

"Do not, for one minute, try to tell me that you think Mr. Nash might be the killer," she said.

"He's a professional photographer," Benedict said.

"Trust me, I would know if Mr. Nash was the one who kidnapped me," Amity said crisply.

"My sister is correct," Penny said in low tones. "She would have recognized Mr. Nash as the killer if he were the man who tried to abduct her."

Benedict contemplated Amity with an unreadable expression. "You know Nash well, then?"

"We encountered each other here in London when I was nineteen," Amity said briskly. "But shortly afterward he set out to photograph the monuments of Egypt. I have not met up with him in the past six years. For all that our careers take both of us around the world we never seem to be in the same location at the same time."

"That is no longer the case, is it?" Benedict said. "By some astonishing coincidence you both happen to be here in London at the moment."

She glared at him. "What on earth do you mean?"

"Nash sought you out in the crowd tonight because he wants something from you."

"Yes, I know. You heard him. He wants to discuss our mutual observations on the places we have traveled."

"No," Benedict said. "That is an excuse, I'm sure of it."

Penny smiled coolly. "Do you two think that you might continue this charming conversation at some other time? Perhaps when you are alone? While I will admit that it is entertaining on some level, it is one of those discussions best conducted in private."

Amity suppressed a sigh. "Good heavens, Mr. Stanbridge and I were arguing over an utterly insignificant matter. I do apologize, Penny."

"And so do I," Benedict said. "Not like we haven't got more important things to deal with."

"I agree," Penny said. "Ah, here comes the carriage."

"About time," Benedict said. "We are going to be late as it is. The traffic is rather heavy tonight."

Amity raised her brows. "You mean we actually do have an appointment? You didn't invent it as an excuse for leaving early?"

"A short time ago I received a message from my uncle," Benedict said. "He wants to interview both of us this evening."

"Us?" A flicker of excitement flashed through Amity. "Does that mean you intend for both Penny and me to accompany you?"

"No, only you need go with me. We shall take Penny home first."

"But why does your uncle wish to see me?" Amity asked.

"I don't know yet but I suspect that he wants to interview you in depth concerning our experiences on St. Clare and on board the *Northern Star*. I confess that my own memories of the first few days of the voyage to New York are rather hazy. In addition, I was confined to my cabin for some time. Even if you are not aware of it, you may have information to give him about events that I don't possess."

"I see," Amity said. "I imagine he is trying to identify the person who shot you."

"He very much wishes to learn the identity of the Russian spy who murdered Alden Cork on St. Clare. I wouldn't mind meeting up with that particular agent myself."

"I doubt if I can assist your uncle but I will certainly do my best," Amity said.

"Excellent," Benedict said. He looked at Penny. "We will take you home, Mrs. Marsden. Then Amity and I will continue on to my uncle's house."

"Very well," Penny said. "But I trust that neither of you will continue to quarrel about the nature of Mr. Nash's intentions."

Amity smiled what she hoped was an airy, unconcerned smile. "There will be no further arguing about that little matter because there is nothing to argue about."

"Nash wants something," Benedict said. "Mark my words."

Penny sighed. "I fear it will be a long trip back to Exton Street."

Astonishingly, peace reigned inside the cab until the vehicle stopped in front of Penny's front door. Amity was surprised to see a hansom waiting in the street. She could just make out the shadowy form of the passenger. An uneasy tingle of alarm whispered through her.

"Someone is here," she said. "I cannot imagine who would be calling at this hour of the night."

"Neither can I," Penny said.

Benedict already had the door open. He stepped down to the pavement. Amity was astounded to see him take a gun out from under his coat. She wanted to ask him when he had started carrying a firearm but there was no opportunity.

"I will deal with whoever is in that hansom," he said. "Go on into the house, both of you, and lock the door."

"Benedict, please do not confront whoever is in that cab on your own. There is supposed to be a constable keeping watch tonight. Let him handle this."

"The house," Benedict repeated. "I would take it as a great favor if you would move with some speed, Amity."

"He's right," Penny announced.

She led the way out of the carriage and started up the steps. Amity followed but she reached beneath her cloak and unhooked the tessen from the chatelaine.

All three of them watched in astonishment as a man emerged from the cab of the hansom and descended to the pavement.

"Inspector Logan," Penny said. She smiled, her relief plain. "How nice to see you again."

"Good evening, Mrs. Marsden." Logan nodded at Amity. "Miss

Doncaster." He glanced at the gun in Benedict's hand. "You won't be needing that tonight, Mr. Stanbridge. Constable Wiggins is standing guard in the park across the street."

"What the devil are you doing here at this hour?" Benedict made the gun disappear inside his coat. "Have you some news?"

Logan reached inside his own coat and withdrew an envelope. "What I have is the guest list for the Channing ball." He smiled at Penny. "You were right, Mrs. Marsden. I was able to obtain it from the reporter at the *Flying Intelligencer* who covers the social news. He was a veritable font of information. I shall keep that in mind for future investigations."

In the lamplight Amity could not be certain but she thought Penny actually blushed.

"I'm glad I could be of service, Inspector," Penny said. "Won't you come inside? We can go over it together tonight. My sister and Mr. Stanbridge have another appointment this evening. Isn't that right, Amity?"

Amity hastily collected herself. "Yes, indeed." She smiled at Inspector Logan. "I am to be introduced to one of Mr. Stanbridge's elderly relations."

"Uncle Cornelius keeps odd hours," Benedict added.

"I will see you later, then, Amity," Penny said.

She went up the steps and took out her key. Logan followed her into the dimly lit front hall. The door closed.

Amity looked at Benedict. "Since when do inspectors from Scotland Yard call on witnesses at ten o'clock in the evening?"

Benedict contemplated the closed front door. "I have no idea."

Eleven

"D o you suppose Penny and Inspector Logan will find some suspects on that guest list?" Amity asked.

Benedict assisted her into the carriage. He liked the feel of her delicate, elegantly gloved fingers resting trustfully in his hand, he realized.

"There is no knowing the answer to that question yet," he said. "As Logan pointed out, that list is merely a starting point. The sooner we conclude this visit to my uncle, the sooner we can come back here and see what your sister and Logan have discovered."

Amity stepped quickly into the shadowed interior. When she twitched the cloak and the green skirts of her gown out of the way, he caught a glimpse of her dainty high-heeled boots. The prospect of being alone with her in the intimate confines of the carriage heated his blood.

With an effort he suppressed the stirring hunger and spoke to the driver.

"Ashwick Square, please."

"Aye, sir."

Benedict climbed up into the cab, sat down across from Amity and pulled the door closed. The lamps were turned down low. The soft light gleamed on Amity's hair and created inviting shadows. He wondered if she knew how tantalizing she looked sitting there in the warm darkness. It was, he reflected, extremely unfortunate that they were on the way to Ashwick Square and what would no doubt be a lengthy interview. He would have preferred some other destination tonight—any other destination—provided it would give him some privacy with Amity. Also a bed, he thought. A bed would certainly be nice.

It had been far too long since that kiss on board the *Northern Star*. The memory of the embrace had sustained him for the past few weeks. But now that he was with her again memories were no longer sufficient to quell the urgent, reckless need that she aroused in him.

"Did you miss me these past weeks, Amity?" he asked.

Because he had to know, he thought. He had to know that their time together had been important to her, not just a passing flirtation. He realized that everything inside him had gone still waiting for the answer.

She looked at him, flustered. He knew he had caught her off guard.

"I was naturally concerned about your well-being," she said.

"I missed you."

She stared at him. In the shadows it was impossible to read her expression.

"Did you?" she asked.

Her voice was as unreadable as her eyes.

"While I was away from you I frequently thought about our time together on the ship," he said. "I enjoyed it very much." He paused. "Well, perhaps not those first few days when I was recovering from a gunshot wound. But aside from that—"

"I found our time together quite pleasant, as well," she said quickly. "After I was assured that your wound would not become infected, of course."

"I recovered from my wound because of you. I will never forget that."

She clasped her gloved hands together very tightly and gave him a sharp, decidedly cross look.

"I do wish you would stop saying that," she said. "Really, sir, things are bad enough as they are. If it's all the same to you, I would prefer that you don't add your sense of gratitude to the list of things I have to worry about. I've got enough on my plate as it is."

Her flash of anger stunned him.

"You fault me for feeling grateful?" he asked.

"Yes. No. Oh, never mind." She unlinked her fingers and waved the entire matter aside with a single, sweeping motion of one hand. "There is no point trying to explain things. At the moment we are caught up together in this tangle and we must contrive to get through it." She sighed. "We do seem to be making a habit of jumping from one complicated situation to another, don't we?"

"Yes."

She cleared her throat. "I do apologize for sticking you with this temporary engagement of ours. It was quite generous of you to suggest it, to say nothing of your determination to protect me from the Bridegroom. If you feel that you owe me anything at all for my assistance on St. Clare—which you don't, I hasten to add—then rest assured you have repaid the debt. Assuming there was a debt. Which there was not."

Anger slammed through him. A chill gripped his insides. He leaned forward and flattened both hands on the seat cushion behind her head, caging her.

"Let me make one thing very clear," he said. "I do not want your gratitude, just as you aren't keen on mine."

There was a short, startled silence. But she made no move to escape him. Instead, she watched him closely for a moment and then she gave him a misty smile.

"I suppose we had better cease thanking each other for past and current favors or we shall both grow increasingly irritable and out of sorts," she said. "That would not be helpful for our investigation. Strong emotions always cloud one's thinking."

He suddenly felt warm again.

"We are agreed, on that one point," he said. "There will be no more expressions of gratitude. But I'm not so sure that I can promise not to experience some strong emotions when it comes to you. Every time I remember that kiss the last night on board, for example, I am unable to focus on anything else."

"Benedict," she whispered. She sounded breathless.

"Please tell me that you remember it, too."

Her lips parted. For a moment she appeared bereft of speech. But he was not surprised when she recovered with relative speed. This was Amity, after all. She was never at a loss for words for long.

"I think of it often," she assured him. "But I was not certain that you would also contemplate it from time to time."

"I have relived that kiss every day and every night for the past month and a half. And every time I recall it, I want nothing more than to repeat the experience."

Her eyes were as warm and sultry as the tropical nights in the Caribbean. She did not move.

"I have absolutely no objection to a second kiss," she said.

"I cannot tell you how I have longed to hear you say that."

With his hands still planted on either side of her head he leaned forward and brushed his mouth across hers. She parted her lips a little.

"Benedict," she whispered.

He took his hands away from the seat cushion and shifted to sit beside her. Very deliberately he pulled her into his arms.

She came to him with a tiny, half-stifled gasp and a sweet enthusiasm that was more than gratifying—it reassured him as no words could have done. Her heated response made it clear that she had not forgotten the passion that had flared between them that last night.

"I was so worried about you these past weeks," she said against his mouth.

He groaned. "As it turns out, I am the one who had cause to worry. All that time away from you I told myself that at least you were safe here in London. Little did I know."

He took her mouth, savoring the warmth and softness he found there. She was shivering ever so slightly. He knew it was not because she was cold. An answering shudder of need swept through him. The world and the night narrowed until all that mattered was what was happening in the intimate sphere of reality that existed inside the carriage. But he was also aware that his time with Amity tonight was limited. They would arrive at their destination too soon.

"I wish we were back on the *Northern Star*," he said against her throat. "I would give anything to have the entire night with you."

"I dearly miss the freedom I know when I travel abroad," she said. She speared her fingers through his hair. "I vow, London is worse than any corset. It constricts and binds and confines until it is difficult to breathe."

"You were meant to be out in the world, not trapped in the prison that is London Society."

"Yes," she said. She sounded pleased that he understood. "I am, indeed, a woman of the world. I cannot live my life by Society's rules."

He breathed in her unique, intoxicating scent and then took her earlobe gently between his teeth. She gripped his shoulders and kissed his throat. The low-burning fire that had been smoldering inside him for weeks flashed into flames.

He took her mouth again, savoring the taste of her, and slipped one hand inside her cloak. He wrapped his fingers around her sleek rib cage and edged upward, seeking the soft weight of her breast. But all he could feel was the rigid armor of the stays that shaped the bodice of her gown.

"Damnation," he muttered. "You did not wear clothes like this when you were on board the ship."

"Of course not." She laughed and pressed her face against his shoulder. "When I travel I wear practical gowns. However, my sister's dressmaker insisted on the stays in this dress."

"She may as well have appointed herself your invisible chaperone."

"Dressmakers can be astonishingly tyrannical, especially those who are known for being fashionable. They have reputations to uphold and Penny tells me one defies them at one's peril."

"I admit a man's tailor can be equally dictatorial." He cupped her face in his hands. "I do not think that either of us was intended to live by Society's rules."

The sweet laughter faded from her eyes.

"Nevertheless, we seem to be bound by them," she said. "It is because of those rules that you find yourself engaged to me."

He smiled slowly. "The thing about rules is that they are made to be broken. And very often they even provide a means to do just that."

"You are starting to sound like an engineer again."

"It strikes me that the very rule that has made it necessary for us to announce our engagement is the same one that allows us certain liberties that we would not otherwise enjoy—at least not without paying a price."

She started to smile again. "For example?"

"For example, you could not be alone with me in this carriage without enduring severe damage to your reputation if it were not for the fact that we are engaged to be married."

"Ah, yes, I understand."

In the shadowy light she had the look of a woman capable of casting a spell on a man. He touched the corner of her mouth with his thumb.

"I think that you have put one on me," he said. The words sounded hoarse.

"Put what on you?"

He traced the outline of her lips with the pad of his thumb. "An enchantment, a spell."

Amusement gleamed in her eyes. "You are a man of the modern age, Mr. Stanbridge, an engineer. I'm sure you are well aware that there is no such thing as magic. All can be explained with science and mathematics."

"Before I met you I would have agreed with that statement. But no longer."

He kissed her again before she could say anything else. The swaying of the carriage caused her to lean more heavily into him. Desire fired his senses. He let the flames burn until he could think of nothing else except the need to claim Amity in the most elemental way.

He had just found the first concealed hook at the front of her gown when the cab rattled to a halt. Reality reasserted itself with electrifying force. He eased aside the nearest curtain and stifled a groan.

"It appears we have arrived," he said. Far too soon, he thought.

"Good heavens." Amity straightened away from him as if scorched by his touch. "Whatever were we thinking? We are on very important business tonight. We should not have allowed ourselves to be distracted."

He watched, bemused, as she attempted to put herself to rights. She looked adorable, he thought. Her clothing was delightfully tousled and a few tendrils of hair had slipped free of the pins. There was an enticing fullness about her just-kissed lips. He liked the look, he concluded. But most of all he liked knowing that he was the man who had put that expression on her face.

"How is my hair?" she asked. She raised one hand and found the stray locks. Hastily she attempted to re-anchor them. "Oh, dear, what will your uncle think?"

"Knowing Uncle Cornelius, he is unlikely to take any notice of the state of your hair. He is concerned only with the matter of finding the Russian spy."

Benedict opened the door to reveal a street that was rapidly filling with fog. The lamps at the front door of Cornelius's small town house glared in the mist, but they did little to illuminate the surroundings.

He got out of the cab and turned to assist Amity. She took his hand, collected her skirts, and allowed him to help her down from the carriage. She pulled up the hood of her cloak and surveyed the unlit windows. "It does not appear that there is anyone at home."

"Cornelius lives alone except for his old butler, Palmer," Benedict explained. "My uncle never married. As I said, he is completely dedicated to his work for the Crown."

"You told me that he is elderly. Perhaps he fell asleep."

"I doubt it. He sleeps very little and even less since this affair of the solar weapon began. In any event, he is expecting us. If he has nodded off, he will not mind if we awaken him. In fact, he will be annoyed if we leave without speaking to him."

The fog muffled the quiet neighborhood that had long ago settled down for the night. An uneasy sensation feathered the back of Benedict's neck. He looked around, searching the mist to make certain that there was no one else about. There were no mysterious footfalls in the shadows. An eerie silence gripped the scene. Nevertheless—or perhaps for that very reason—he reached inside his coat and took out the revolver.

He looked at the coachman.

"Wait for us, please."

"Aye, sir." The coachman hunkered down on his box and removed a flask from his coat pocket.

Amity glanced down at the gun in Benedict's hand. "You did not have a weapon with you on St. Clare."

"Let's just say I learned my lesson on that damned island. I picked this up in California."

He guided Amity up the front steps and raised the door knocker. He rapped twice.

But there were no footsteps in the hall. The lights did not come up in the transom window over the door.

He banged the knocker again, harder.

Amity looked at him. In the glary light her hooded face was etched with concern. "There is something amiss, isn't there?"

"Things are not as usual, that is certain."

Without a word she reached inside her cloak. When her hand reappeared Benedict saw that she gripped the tessen.

He tried the knob. It did not turn.

"Palmer is always very careful when it comes to locking up the house for the night," Benedict said. "But Cornelius gave me a key a few years ago."

He took the key ring out of the pocket of his coat.

"Perhaps you should summon a constable before you go inside," Amity said.

"Believe me when I tell you that my uncle will not appreciate it if we draw that sort of attention to this house," Benedict said.

He inserted the key into the lock and opened the door. The front hall was filled with shadows. Nothing and no one stirred in the darkness.

Gun at the ready, Benedict moved into the hall and turned up the lamps. There was no pounding drumbeat of fleeing footsteps. No one leaped out of the shadows. No one challenged them from the top of the stairs.

He led the way along the hall, turning up lamps as he moved toward the room at the far end.

Cornelius was in the study, lying motionless on the carpet. The door of the large, heavy safe in the corner stood open.

"Cornelius," Benedict said.

He went down on one knee beside the old man and felt for a pulse. Relief washed through him when he found one.

Twelve

"Whoever he is, the bastard has the notebook." Cornelius gingerly touched the bandage Amity had just finished placing on his head. He winced. "My apologies for the ungentlemanly language, Miss Doncaster. I fear I am not at my best at the moment."

"I assure you, I have heard far worse language in my travels," Amity said. "And as for your condition, we can only be grateful that the intruder did not murder you. Fortunately, the injury looks quite shallow, although I imagine it does not feel that way. As for all the blood, I'm afraid head wounds tend to bleed profusely but you will heal. The carpet may be beyond repair, however."

She surveyed her handiwork, satisfied that she had done her best to clean and disinfect the wound given the limited resources in the household. A bowl of blood-stained water sat on the small table next to Cornelius's chair. She had bathed the injury thoroughly and then doused it with what she suspected was some very expensive brandy that Benedict had discovered in a nearby decanter.

She and Cornelius were alone in the study. Benedict had disappeared outside into the garden to take a look around. The cluttered room was redolent of old pipe smoke and leather-bound books.

"Thank you for the doctoring, my dear," Cornelius said.

"You are entirely welcome." She smiled. "The bandage will do for now but you might want to summon a real doctor to take a look at the injury in the morning, I trust you know a skilled physician, one who holds modern views on the importance of cleanliness. Meanwhile, you must stay quiet for the next few days. I am more concerned about a concussion than I am about the cut in your scalp."

"I doubt that I will feel like going anywhere for some time," Cornelius said. He peered up at Amity. "So you're the lady globetrotter who saved my nephew's life on that island in the Caribbean."

"I happened to be in the vicinity so of course I did what I could."

"I am in your debt, my dear."

"Don't be ridiculous, sir. You don't owe me anything."

"Yes, I do. It was my fault Benedict was on that damned island in the first place. I knew he wasn't experienced in that sort of work. He's an engineer, not a professional spy."

Amity smiled. "So he keeps reminding me."

"Thing is, he was the only person I knew whom I trusted and who was capable of judging the true value of Alden Cork's invention. And it's a damn good thing I did send Ben because I very much doubt that any of my so-called professional agents would have understood that the real secret of the weapon is Foxcroft's solar engine and battery system."

"But now Foxcroft's notebook has disappeared. Benedict risked his life for nothing."

"*Hmm.* Yes. Interesting, eh?"

Amity glared at him. "How can you be so casual about the theft, sir?"

The kitchen door opened and closed. Benedict walked back into the study. He slipped his gun into the pocket of his coat.

"The intruder evidently has a talent for picking locks," he said. "There is barely a scratch on the door. It appears he left the same way he entered—through the kitchen."

"He must have been watching the house," Cornelius said. "He knew that I was alone. This is Palmer's day and night off. He always goes to see his daughter and her family on Wednesdays. He takes the train and does not return until Thursday morning."

"If the spy is aware of this house, then we must assume he knows a great deal, not only about the solar cannon and Foxcroft's engine and battery but also about your government connections," Benedict said.

"The intruder must be the same person who stole Cork's drawings for the weapon and tried to murder you on St. Clare," Amity said. "Now he has Foxcroft's notebook. This is terrible."

There was a short, tense silence. Cornelius and Benedict exchanged glances. Neither man appeared unduly alarmed. If anything, they seemed remarkably satisfied.

She planted her hands on her hips and narrowed her eyes. "What is going on here? I have the distinct impression that neither of you is sufficiently concerned about this turn of events."

Benedict raised his brows. "Well, sir? You did request my fiancée's assistance in this matter. It seems to me that she cannot be helpful unless you tell her more about the situation."

Cornelius hesitated and then grunted. "Quite right. Miss Doncaster, the reason we are not overly concerned about the loss of the notebook is because Benedict wisely thought to remove the most crucial pages—the ones that provide the specifications and materials required to construct the engine and the battery."

Amity absorbed that news. "Very clever. But won't the spy realize that the important pages are missing?"

"With luck, no," Benedict said. "My brother is a very good architect. He possesses a great deal of talent when it comes to drawing. The plans he produces for Stanbridge & Company are works of art."

"Oh, I see." Amity beetled her brows. "Do you mean to say that you forged some pages of the notebook?"

Benedict smiled approvingly.

"Foxcroft kept his notes in a binder. We simply removed the important pages and inserted new ones." Benedict looked at Cornelius. "I told you that she is very sharp."

Cornelius chuckled and then winced in pain and gingerly touched his head. "I believe you."

Benedict turned back to Amity. "Between the two of us, Richard and I were able to forge two pages of specifications and notes for Foxcroft's engine. We used some of the unused pages in the binder."

Amity caught her breath. "That was a very clever plan."

Cornelius snorted. "Ben always has a plan."

"I thought it best to take the added precautions because Uncle Cornelius believes that there is a well-placed traitor involved in this affair," Benedict said.

"Obviously you are right," Amity said.

Out of curiosity, she moved closer to the safe and leaned down to peer into the dark interior. The only thing left inside was an envelope.

"My plan did not involve you being injured in the process," Benedict said to Cornelius. "I assumed that if someone made an attempt to steal the notebook it would happen when you and Palmer were away from home."

"Don't blame yourself, Ben," Cornelius said. "The important thing is that you predicted that someone might try to steal the notebook and you were correct. Whoever our spy is, we now know for certain that he possesses considerable talent for his profession. The lock on that safe is the most modern model available."

Amity looked over her shoulder at Cornelius. "How do you plan to catch the thief?"

"You misunderstand, Miss Doncaster. I have no intention of arresting the spy. I merely wish to identify him. Once I know who he is, I can make use of him."

"By feeding him false information to give to the Russians," Benedict explained.

"Well, that makes sense, I suppose," Amity said. "But how will you identify him?"

"I have a short list of suspects, Miss Doncaster," Cornelius said, his voice turning grim. "They are all being watched very closely at the moment. When one of them makes a move to give the notebook to the Russians, I will know about it."

Benedict studied him. "What if you are watching the wrong people? You told me that none of your suspects was absent from London at the time I was shot on St. Clare."

Cornelius fumbled with his spectacles and squinted at Amity. "I am hoping that Miss Doncaster will be able to assist me in that regard. But I am not at my best at the moment. I can't even recall all the questions I had intended to ask you, my dear. The interview must wait until I can think more clearly."

"I will be happy to tell you what little I know whenever you are ready, sir," Amity said. "But what of the letter inside the safe?"

Cornelius scowled. "I never put any letter in there."

Amity removed the envelope from the safe, straightened and studied the name on the front. "It is addressed to you, sir."

"Let me see that," Cornelius snapped.

Amity handed the letter to him. "I suspect that your safecracker left you a message."

Cornelius yanked the letter out of the envelope and peered at it for a moment. "Damn and blast, I can't read a thing. My vision is somewhat blurred and my head hurts." He thrust the letter toward Benedict. "Read it, Ben."

Benedict unfolded the single sheet of paper and read it in silence. He looked up.

"It appears our burglar is not particularly loyal to any government," Benedict said. "He has his own best interests at heart. He's looking to turn a profit on this night's work."

"How?" Amity asked.

Benedict tapped the letter. "He states that he is willing to sell it back to us. For a price."

"Bloody hell," Cornelius growled. "And just what the devil is the price?"

Benedict glanced at the note in his hand. "It does not say. It only states that you will be contacted in the near future, at which time details will be provided."

In spite of all he had been through that night, Cornelius appeared suddenly cheerful.

"Well, now," he said sounding quite pleased. "That makes things so much simpler, doesn't it?"

"Does it?" Amity asked.

"There is no way the spy can conduct a transaction without coming at least partway out of the shadows," Cornelius said. "And when he does, we will be ready."

Thirteen

What will happen next?" Amity asked.

"You heard my uncle. He will assign his regular agents to handle the investigation from now on, although I'm sure Cornelius will still want to question you," Benedict said. "But for now I think he is entirely focused on setting a trap to catch our mystery thief. There is nothing more that either of us can do to assist him. That, in turn, leaves us free to concentrate on helping Logan catch the Bridegroom."

The carriage clattered to a halt in front of the little town house in Exton Street. Amity looked out the window and saw that the lights were still on inside.

"Penny is waiting up for me," she said. "She is no doubt curious to hear about my interview with your uncle."

"There is no need to keep secrets from her," Benedict said. "She already knows as much about this espionage affair as we do." He looked out the carriage window in the opposite direction and appeared satisfied. "There's the constable that Logan promised. Good. I'll see you inside and then we must both get some sleep."

He opened the carriage door and got out. Amity gathered the folds of her cloak and skirts and stepped down from the cab. The door of the house opened just as she and Benedict started up the steps. Mrs. Houston appeared. Amity was surprised to see that she was not in her nightgown and robe. Mrs. Houston beamed, looking quite pleased.

"I heard the carriage and thought it must be you coming home, Miss Amity," she said.

"It was kind of you to wait up for me, Mrs. Houston," Amity said. "But, really, there was no need."

"Nonsense. It's not as if I could go to bed, what with a stranger in the house and all."

"What?" Startled, Amity peered through the doorway into the hall. "Who on earth would come calling at this hour of the night?"

"I wouldn't call it a social call." Mrs. Houston chuckled. She stepped back, holding the door wide. "It's that nice Inspector Logan. He's in the study with Mrs. Marsden."

"Logan is still here?" Benedict asked, moving into the hall. "How convenient. I'll have a word with him."

"How odd," Amity said, but she was speaking to herself.

She gave her cloak and gloves to Mrs. Houston. Benedict did not bother to take off his coat.

"I won't be staying long," he said to Mrs. Houston.

Amity hurried along the hall toward the study, aware that Benedict was hard on her heels. When she walked into the room, she saw Penny seated behind the desk. Logan was sprawled in a decidedly comfortable, relaxed manner in a chair. His tie was loosened around his neck. He had a glass of brandy in his hand. He set aside the glass and rose politely when he saw Amity.

"I'm glad to see you, Miss Doncaster," he said. He nodded at Benedict. "Mr. Stanbridge. We have been wondering what kept you."

"Amity," Penny said. "I was starting to get worried. You were gone so long."

"Things did not go as anticipated," Benedict said. He glanced at the sheet of paper in front of Penny. "Any luck with the Channing ball guest list?"

"Inspector Logan and I came up with the names of a few gentlemen who might warrant further investigation because, in a rough way, they match the description that Amity provided," Penny said. "But I must admit there were no obvious madmen on the list."

Logan looked grim. "As I told Mrs. Marsden, the kind of man we are hunting does not stand out in a crowd. He possesses the ability to blend in with his surroundings."

"A wolf in sheep's clothing," Benedict said.

Logan nodded. "That is precisely what makes him so dangerous."

"I was afraid catching him would not be as simple as perusing a guest list," Benedict said. He looked at Logan. "Saw your man keeping watch from the park."

"Constable Wiggins," Logan said. "Quite reliable. He'll be there until dawn. Mrs. Houston was kind enough to send coffee and a muffin out to him earlier."

Amity noticed that there was a low fire burning on the hearth. In addition to the unfinished brandy that Logan had just set aside, there was another half-empty glass on Penny's desk. It was all very cozy, very comfortable, very interesting.

Penny frowned in sudden concern. "Was there a problem?"

"It is a long story, Penny," Amity said. "I promise I will tell you everything."

Logan glanced at the clock. "It's past time I took myself off. I will notify all of you at once if there is any news." He smiled at Penny. "Good night, Mrs. Marsden. Thank you for the brandy."

"You are welcome, sir," Penny said. "Thank you for the company."

Benedict stirred in the doorway. "I have a cab waiting in the street, Logan. I'll be happy to give you a ride to your address."

Surprise came and went on Logan's face. "That is kind of you, Mr. Stanbridge, but unnecessary. I'm sure I will find a hansom within a few blocks."

"It's no trouble at all," Benedict said. "We can discuss the names on that guest list."

Logan appeared satisfied that the offer of a cab ride would result in a discussion of the case. He relaxed. "Very well, then. I accept. Thank you."

Benedict turned to Penny and Amity. "Good night, ladies. I will call tomorrow."

The two men disappeared down the hall. A moment later Amity heard the front door close.

Penny peered intently at Amity. "What in the world happened tonight?"

"The notebook that Benedict—Mr. Stanbridge—brought back from California was stolen from his uncle's safe sometime this evening," Amity said. "The intruder bashed poor Cornelius Stanbridge over the head."

She went to the small table where the brandy decanter stood and poured herself a healthy glass of spirits. She sank down into the chair that Logan had just vacated, propped her heels on the hassock and swallowed some of the brandy.

She gave Penny a quick summary of events.

"In short the intruder intends to sell the notebook back to Cornelius Stanbridge," she concluded. "Stanbridge hopes to set a trap for the thief."

"I see." Penny looked at her across the width of the desk. "This affair of the solar cannon and the engine system is causing no end of trouble."

"Fortunately, it is Cornelius Stanbridge's problem now. When he is feeling better I will provide him with what few observations I can offer concerning the passengers on board the *Northern Star*, but I really don't think there is anything else I can do to assist him. He has the passenger list. It will be up to him to research the individuals on board, always assuming the spy was on the *Star*, which is problematic, to say the least. A number of ships stop at St. Clare."

"How odd that in both cases we are examining lists of names," Penny said.

"Yes." Amity took another sip of the brandy, savoring the warmth. "But I suppose that is what any type of criminal investigation comes down to—a list of names of possible suspects." She held her brandy glass to the firelight and studied the way the flames turned the spirits to liquid gold. "Is that what you and Inspector Logan were discussing when Benedict and I arrived a few minutes ago? Suspects from the Channing guest list?"

Penny went very still. "In part, yes. But Inspector Logan was mostly interested in the scandals surrounding the other victims of the Bridegroom. I was able to provide some information."

"Did you come up with anything helpful?"

"I was able to confirm what he already knew—that all four of the women who were murdered came from high-ranking families that moved in polite circles and that each young lady had been tainted by a scandal of a romantic nature." Penny hesitated. "The discussion did make me aware of one very important thing, however."

Amity paused the brandy glass halfway to her mouth. "Really? What was that?"

"You would not have been thrust into that rarified world if it had not been for my marriage to Nigel Marsden."

Amity set the brandy glass down abruptly. "For heaven's sake, Penny, you must not say things like that."

"Why not?" Penny got to her feet and went to stand in front of the fireplace. "It is the truth. Your association with Mr. Stanbridge would have gone unremarked in Society had it not been for your connection to me and the Marsden name."

"Good heavens, it is not your fault that I came to the attention of the Bridegroom. It was a combination of my essays in the *Flying Intelligencer* and someone's gossiping tongue that made the killer aware of me."

"Perhaps, but if you had not been connected to the Marsden family through your relationship to me that dreadful monster would not have taken any notice of you."

"We have absolutely no idea if that is true." Amity rose quickly and went to stand next to Penny in front of the fire. "I will not allow you to blame yourself for what has happened. We are dealing with a madman. Such creatures follow their own twisted logic. He must have seen my name in the papers any number of times. When rumors about me started after the Channing ball, he seized on that information as an excuse to focus his attention on me. There is nothing more to it than that."

"I wish I could believe that."

Amity grasped Penny's shoulders, turned her around and hugged her. "You must believe it because it is the truth. I will not see you cast back into that dark pit of depression in which I found you when I arrived a few weeks ago. It was so good to see you surfacing from your grief. I know how much you loved your handsome Nigel. But you are my sister and I love you, too. I want you to be happy again and I know Nigel would have wanted that as well."

"Do you think so?" Penny asked in an odd tone of voice.

Startled, Amity gently pushed Penny a short distance away and searched her face.

"Nigel loved you deeply," Amity said gently. "He would not have wanted you to spend the rest of your life pining away for him. For heaven's sake, Penny. You are still young and lovely and—I know this sounds crass, but it matters—you are financially secure. Widowhood gives you great freedom. You should enjoy life."

"How can I enjoy life when I know there is a killer hunting for you?" Penny asked.

Amity was touched. "Oh, yes, well, I do appreciate your concerns, but I am sure Mr. Stanbridge and that very nice man from the Yard—"

"Inspector Logan," Penny said deliberately. "His name is Inspector Logan."

"Right. Inspector Logan. He seems very competent."

"Indeed."

The tone of her sister's voice told Amity that something more was required by way of description.

"And intelligent," Amity said.

"Quite. He is a great fan of the theater, you know."

Amity took a flying leap in the dark.

"He is also quite attractive," she added. She held her breath.

Penny blinked a couple of times and looked into the fire. "Do you really think so?"

"Yes," Amity said. "Not in the same manner as Mr. Stanbridge, of course, but in his own way the inspector is a fine-looking man."

Penny smiled wistfully. "Do you find Mr. Stanbridge handsome?"

Amity hesitated, groping for the right words to explain Benedict's appeal. "Mr. Stanbridge is perhaps better described as a force of nature. But that is hardly the point. What I am trying to say is that I'm quite sure that with both Mr. Stanbridge and Inspector Logan involved it is only a matter of time before the killer is caught."

"I hope you are correct."

Penny slipped away from Amity's grasp.

Amity watched her for a moment.

"Penny, are you concerned because you find Inspector Logan attractive?" she asked.

Penny did not reply. But she raised one hand to wipe tears away from her eyes.

"Dear heaven." Amity touched her sister's shoulder. "Why are you crying? I cannot believe that it is because you feel that Mr. Logan is beneath you socially. I realize that most people in so-called Polite Society would think so, but I know you. You do not judge people based on the accident of their birth."

"It's not that," Penny said. She sniffed and blinked rapidly to suppress more tears. "I'm certain Mr. Logan is uncomfortably aware of the difference in our financial and social stations, so I doubt that he would even dream of approaching me in anything other than a respectful, professional manner."

Amity thought about the cozy little scene she and Benedict had interrupted a short time ago. "Something tells me that Inspector Logan might be persuaded to consider a more personal association with you if he was given the right encouragement."

Penny shook her head, very certain. "No, I'm sure he would never presume anything of the sort. His manner and demeanor are all that is proper."

"*Hmm.*" Amity summoned a mental image of Logan and could not recall seeing a ring on his left hand. "Please don't tell me that he is married."

"No," Penny said. "He told me that he was engaged at one time but his fiancée and her family concluded she could do better than to wed a policeman."

"Well, in that case, I see absolutely no reason why you should not feel free to explore any romantic feelings that might develop between yourself and the inspector."

A wary hope flickered to life in Penny's eyes. It vanished almost at once. "I have only been in mourning for six months. Society—not to mention my in-laws—would be horrified if I abandoned my widow's weeds so soon."

"Do you really care for Society's opinion?"

"At one time I did, yes." Penny clenched one hand into a small fist. "But no longer."

"And as for your in-laws, forgive me, but I got the impression that you are not overly fond of them—nor they of you."

"They never approved of the marriage. They wanted Nigel to marry someone who could bring more money into the family. There is certainly no love lost between us. I think, in a way, that they blame me for Nigel's death."

"That is ridiculous," Amity said. "Nigel broke his neck going over a fence. How could anyone possibly blame you for that?"

Penny's mouth curved in a rueful smile. "You don't know my in-laws."

"I suspect that what really annoys them is that you wound up with so much money from Nigel's estate."

"You're right, of course."

"As I recall, there are two other sons, a daughter and a vast fortune. They should not begrudge you the money and the house that you inherited from your husband."

"I appreciate your support more than you can ever know," Penny said. "It has been very lonely here with you out of the country for weeks and months at a time."

"I can only imagine how much you must miss your dear Nigel."

Penny took a deep breath and exhaled slowly. "No, actually, I don't miss him a bit. I hope the bastard is burning in hell."

Amity stared at her. "Sorry, I think I missed something. What did you say?"

Penny looked at her. "I thought he was the love of my life. But Nigel Marsden proved to be a monster."

"What?"

"I was plotting to leave him when he very conveniently broke his neck."

"Good heavens, Penny. I . . . don't know what to say. I'm stunned."

Penny closed her eyes for a moment. When she opened them again, Amity could see remembered pain, fear and rage.

"At first I believed him to be merely overprotective," Penny said. Her voice was low and even, almost detached. "It was rather charming for the first few months. I told myself that he loved me so much he wanted to take great care of me. But gradually he took away every piece of my life—my friends, my little pleasures such as the theater and walks in the countryside."

Amity was aghast. "You never gave me so much as a hint in your letters."

"Of course not. He insisted on reading every letter I wrote to you before it was mailed. He hated you. He said you were a bad influence on me. He said that about all of my friends, too. There was always something he did not like about everyone with whom I was accustomed to associate. Within three months the only visitors I was allowed to receive were his dreadful mother and his sister. He beat me if another man so much as spoke to me. He claimed that I was trying to seduce his male acquaintances."

"I do not know what to say," Amity whispered. "I am beyond horrified. Father would have been so angry."

"It was not long before I found myself alone in the household all day and most nights with only the servants. I could not trust any of them. I knew Nigel asked them what I did while he was gone and whether I had left the house or received any callers."

"I would kill him if he were not already dead."

"I seriously considered poisoning him but I was afraid I might fail in the attempt. If that happened I knew that he would very likely murder me instead. I intended to disappear. He gave me no money, of course, but there were valuables everywhere in the house. I was going to take some, pawn them and buy a ticket on a passenger ship to New York. I planned to telegraph you as soon as I was free and beg you to meet me."

"Why didn't you send for me? I would have come at once."

"I was afraid of what he might do to you if you actually came to stay with us. I told you, he hated you. I think, deep down, he saw you as a threat. But knowing that you were out there in the world— free—is what kept me from sinking into the abyss. I told myself that if I could just escape the house and disappear, I would be able to find you."

Tears blurred Amity's vision. "Penny, my beautiful little sister. When I think of what you must have gone through. So alone. No wonder you sold the big house and dismissed all the servants. Hah. I imagine that came as a shock to that lot. I do hope you turned them out without any references."

"I did precisely that." Penny gave her a misty smile. "I will admit I took some pleasure in telling them that their services were no longer required."

"I can certainly understand why you are not on good terms with Nigel's family."

"In fairness, I'm not sure they knew exactly what was going on. Nigel always put on a great show of being an attentive husband whenever his mother was around. So much so that I think his mother was actually jealous of me. She made a few attempts to convince me to let her solicitor manage my finances after Nigel died."

"But you knew you could not trust her to look after your best interests."

"Definitely not," Penny said. "One of the first things I did after the will was read was dismiss Nigel's solicitor and hire Mr. Burton to oversee my business affairs."

"Burton handled Papa's affairs and now he handles mine. You can trust him. He's getting on in years and is semiretired, but his son is taking over the business and doing a fine job."

"I admit I don't find it easy to trust anyone except you these days."

"You have taken back your life," Amity said. "I am in awe of your strength and bravery. You are an inspiration, Penny, a fine example of the modern, independent woman."

"Bah, I am no shining example. I was a fool for allowing myself to believe in a fairy-tale kind of love. You are the one who set out to see the world and now you are going to publish a travel guide for other adventurous ladies. *You* are the shining example of modern woman-hood, not me."

"I disagree," Amity said gently. "What I have done requires no particular strength of character, just a deeply ingrained streak of curiosity. But let us not quarrel over which of us is the more modern woman. I am just so very sorry that I did not know what you were going through in your marriage."

"You did not know because I could not risk telling you. I feared that if Nigel found out that I had confided in you, he might actually murder me and possibly you, as well, when you showed up to save me." Penny smiled. "Which I knew you would do, of course."

Amity shuddered and wrapped her arms around Penny. "It infuriates me to know that if he had killed you, he likely would have gotten away with murder. I expect that there would have been a story about how you came to fall down a flight of steps or some such nonsense."

"And his wealthy family would have protected him from any police inquiry that you might have tried to launch."

Amity thought about that for a moment.

"Just as someone in Society is very likely concealing the identity of the Bridegroom," she said.

Fourteen

I t's that famous travel photographer to see you, Miss Amity."
Mrs. Houston hovered in the doorway of the study. She was
flushed a bright pink. "Mr. Nash, the gentleman who journeys
around the world taking pictures of strange monuments and ele-
phants and the like."

"Mr. Nash is here to see me?" Amity set aside the list of names she
had been studying. She had heard the low murmur of voices from the
front hall a moment ago, but she had assumed that the caller was Inspector Logan. She was not sure how to take the news that it was
Humphrey instead. She looked at Penny. "He did say he wanted to
speak with me in private, but I never dreamed he might pay us a visit."

Penny set her pen back in the stand. A troubled expression crossed
her face. "I wonder what he wants?"

"You heard him last night at the reception." Amity rose quickly.
"He wishes to discuss our mutual impressions of various destinations
we have both visited."

Mrs. Houston lowered her voice to a conspiratorial tone. "I must say, he is a very handsome gentleman."

"I thought so at one time myself, Mrs. Houston," Amity said. "Please show him into the drawing room. I will be along in a moment."

"Yes, Miss Amity."

Mrs. Houston went back down the hallway. Amity hurried to the gilt mirror that hung on the wall and pinned up a few stray strands of hair.

"I am so glad I decided to put on one of my new day gowns this morning," she said.

Penny studied the multi-striped dress with a considering eye. "It is very becoming. But I was under the impression that you chose that dress this morning because we are expecting Mr. Stanbridge."

"True," Amity admitted. "Not that Mr. Stanbridge is in the habit of taking any notice of a lady's gown."

"Do not be too sure of that."

Amity turned, smiling ruefully. "Mr. Stanbridge possesses many sterling qualities, but in my experience he is rather oblivious to fashion. Will you join Mr. Nash and me in the parlor?"

Penny studied her with a shrewd expression. "Do you want me to join you?"

Amity considered the question for a moment. "He will likely be more honest about his reasons for calling on me if there are just the two of us."

"I agree. I cannot help but remember what Mr. Stanbridge said last night. He is convinced that Humphrey Nash wants something from you."

"The thing is, I can't imagine what I have that Humphrey might want."

"Perhaps he will tell you that he made a mistake all those years ago when he left you behind to travel the world."

"I must admit that would be rather gratifying," Amity said. She smiled. "Not that I'm the vengeful sort."

Penny laughed. "Of course not." She paused, her amusement fading. "Perhaps I should accompany you."

"I appreciate your concern but there is no need to worry about me. One thing is certain. Mr. Nash cannot break my heart again— assuming that is what happened when I was nineteen. I have recovered quite nicely, I believe."

"I am aware of that," Penny said. "But you are the only family I have left in the world. It is only natural that I wish to protect you."

Amity went back across the room and touched Penny's hand. "And you are all the family that I possess. We will take care of each other. I will never leave you alone again, Penny. I swear it."

"That is very kind of you, but you were born for a life of travel and adventure. I would not dream of tying you to London."

Amity shook her head. "I meant it. I will not leave you alone. But we will discuss our future some other time. Now I must see if Mr. Nash does, indeed, want anything more from me than a lively discussion of ancient monuments and foreign landscapes."

She whisked up her skirts and went along the hall to the door of the drawing room. Humphrey was standing at the window looking out at the small park across the street. He turned when he heard her approach. His smile was warm and friendly. So were his eyes. He was, Amity reflected, just as handsome and just as charming today as he had been last night.

He crossed the room and bowed low over her hand.

"Amity, thank you so much for seeing me today."

"I must say I am rather surprised by this visit." She retrieved her hand and indicated a chair. "Please, won't you sit down?"

"Thank you."

Humphrey lowered himself into one of the formal chairs. Mrs. Houston appeared with the tea tray. She set it on the table.

"Shall I pour, Miss Amity?" she asked.

"I will take care of the tea," Amity said coolly. She decided that it was not the time to inform Mrs. Houston that tea had not been ordered. The housekeeper was only doing what was expected of her.

Mrs. Houston retreated but she left the door open. Amity picked up the pot, poured a cup of tea and handed the cup and saucer to Humphrey. He took it with well-bred grace.

"Before we begin I must ask if the police have made any progress in finding the monster that attacked you," Humphrey said.

"I am told that they are searching for him day and night," Amity said.

"The fact that his body has not turned up is a rather ominous sign, don't you think?" Humphrey swallowed some tea and lowered the cup. "It indicates he may have survived."

Amity wondered if the conversation was destined to take the same unpleasant turn that it had taken with Arthur Kelbrook. She did not intend to regale Humphrey with the details of her escape from the killer's carriage.

"That is a distinct possibility," she said. "But I am sure it is only a matter of time before the police find him or his body."

"I certainly hope so. It is a sad day when a respectable lady who has traveled safely to the far corners of the globe cannot walk the streets of London in the middle of the day without being assaulted."

"Indeed."

Humphrey smiled approvingly. "But the Bridegroom certainly picked the wrong victim when he attacked you. I congratulate you on your amazing escape, my dear."

The "my dear" made her grit her teeth. He had no business speaking to her in such a familiar fashion. But she was not about to kick him out of the house until she knew why he had come to see her.

"Thank you," she said instead. "I was rather pleased myself that I managed to escape, especially considering the alternative. Now, if you don't mind, sir, I would rather discuss another subject—any other subject."

Humphrey looked chagrined. "How very insensitive of me. I swear I did not mean to focus on such a disturbing topic. I merely intended to convey my great admiration for your daring and bravery. The truth, however, is that I came here today for an entirely different reason."

"Last night you indicated that you wanted to compare our observations on various foreign locales."

"Actually, I wanted to do more than compare notes." Humphrey picked up one of the small tea cakes on the tray and took a bite. "I believe I mentioned my admiration for your writing talent. The essays you pen for the *Flying Intelligencer* are quite remarkable. I am told that readers await each piece with the same eagerness that they await the next installment of whatever sensation novel the paper happens to be publishing."

Amity blushed. "I am very pleased that my little essays have attracted an audience."

"Quite a large audience, I understand. My own talents, whatever they may be, are confined to the field of photography."

His uncharacteristic modesty amused her.

"You are quite brilliant with a camera, sir," she said briskly. "As no doubt you are well aware. I would also add that you are a very entertaining speaker. So many of those who lecture on the subject of exploration and travel have a gift for putting the audience to sleep. But last night the crowd hung on your every word."

"Thank you." A determined glint appeared in Humphrey's eyes. "Our talents appear to complement each other very well, wouldn't you say?"

Now they were getting to the heart of the matter, Amity thought.

"Well, I had not thought about it in quite those terms," she said, "but I suppose one could say that was true. Your photographs certainly speak volumes."

"But it is your writing that speaks to the wider audience because your observations are in print for all to read. I will come straight to the point. I recently paid a visit to the gentleman who is going to publish your book."

Alarm flashed through her. She had allowed herself to be influenced by Benedict and Penny, she thought. Nevertheless, her own intuition was finally rising to the occasion.

"You saw Mr. Galbraith?" She felt as if she were walking across quicksand now.

"Yes." Humphrey's eyes lit with determined enthusiasm. "He told me a great deal about your travel guide for ladies. He seems to think it will sell very well."

"Mr. Galbraith has been very encouraging." Amity picked up the teapot. "I am putting the final touches on the manuscript now."

"It occurred to me that the book would sell to a much broader audience if you and I engaged in a collaboration."

A hansom rolled to a halt in the street. Automatically Amity glanced out the window. She saw Benedict emerge from the cab.

Distracted, she set the teapot down so sharply the china rang on the silver tray. She considered the possibility that she had not heard Humphrey correctly.

"I'm sorry, what did you just say?" she asked carefully.

He gave her a winning smile. "I am merely suggesting that you and I collaborate on your travel guide."

She went quite blank. "I don't understand. I have almost completed the manuscript. There is nothing left to collaborate on, if you see what I mean."

"That is wonderful news. It means that all that is necessary is to add my name to the title page."

"Your name?" She stared at him. "Sir, it's a guide for ladies going abroad. Not gentlemen."

"I realize that. But only consider how much more authoritative your guide will appear if my name is also on the cover."

Anger crackled through Amity. "I am well aware that your name carries a great deal of weight in certain quarters, but you did not write the book, Mr. Nash. I wrote it."

Benedict was on the top step now. He banged the knocker. Amity watched Mrs. Houston hurry past the open door of the drawing room on her way to respond to the summons.

"You saw how many ladies were in the audience last night," Humphrey said. There was an edge of urgency in his tone. "I don't want to sound vain, but I do have a way with women. Just imagine if I were to give a series of travel lectures like that one with the goal of publicizing *A Lady's Guide to Globetrotting*. We could make the book available for purchase at the door along with my photographs. I'm sure the lectures would dramatically increase sales. Together we could make a great deal of money, Amity."

Mrs. Houston opened the front door.

"Mr. Stanbridge," she said cheerfully. "How nice to see you again, sir."

Amity shot to her feet. "I am not interested in your proposition, Mr. Nash. Indeed, I have nothing further to say to you. I suggest that you take your leave immediately."

Benedict strode into the room. His eyes were as heartless as those of a hellhound.

"Exactly what sort of proposition are you making to my fiancée, Nash?" he asked.

Alarmed, Humphrey jumped to his feet. "Not the sort you are clearly imagining, sir. It was a business proposition, nothing more."

"You call that a business proposition?" Amity demanded. "How dare you?"

Benedict did not take his eyes off Humphrey.

Humphrey moved toward the door, showing a fine turn of speed. Benedict stepped into his path. Penny appeared in the doorway. Her hand went to her throat. There was near panic in her eyes.

Belatedly Amity realized that the situation was escalating out of control.

"It's all right, Benedict," she said firmly. "Please allow Mr. Nash to leave. I assure you I have dealt with the matter. There is no need for violence. Indeed, I will not allow any fisticuffs in this household. Do I make myself clear?"

Benedict did not move for a moment. Amity held her breath.

Reluctantly Benedict shifted out of Humphrey's path. Humphrey hurried out into the hall, where Mrs. Houston handed him his coat and gloves. A few seconds later the front door closed.

Penny stared at Amity, stricken. "What happened?"

"Evidently Nash just made your sister a business proposition," Benedict said grimly.

"He wouldn't dare," Penny whispered. "He knows she is engaged to you."

"I will speak with him in private," Benedict said.

"No, you will not," Amity said. "I told you, I took care of the matter."

"He insulted you with his proposition," Benedict said, his eyes still burning with icy rage.

Amity wrinkled her nose. "I suppose, viewed in the proper light, it was actually something of a compliment."

"How can you say that?" Penny whispered. "Mr. Stanbridge is right. Fifty years ago, such an insult could have meant pistols at dawn."

"These days such matters can be settled in other ways," Benedict said.

Amity threw her hands wide. "Oh, for heaven's sake, there is no need for such high drama. Mr. Nash's proposition was definitely of a business nature. He wanted me to agree to put his name on my book as a coauthor. Indeed, although he did not come straight out and say it, I suspect that he intended for his name to go first."

Penny blinked. Understanding and something that might have been amusement lit her eyes. "Oh my. The poor man had no notion of what he was getting into, did he?"

Amity clasped her hands behind her back and paced the room in a tight circular pattern. "He seemed to think that my book would sell more briskly if the public thought that he'd had a hand in writing it."

Benedict frowned. "That was his proposition? He wanted you to give him credit as a coauthor?"

"Exactly." Amity stopped. "You see now why I was so annoyed."

"Certainly," Penny said. "He did, indeed, want to take advantage of you. Financial advantage."

"He may be an excellent photographer and an entertaining speaker, but I suspect he cannot string two or more interesting sentences together," Amity said. She exhaled a small sigh. "I must admit you were right, Benedict. Mr. Nash did have ulterior motives for wanting to call on me today."

Fifteen

I am very impressed with your investigative talents, Mrs. Marsden." Inspector Logan lowered the sheaf of notes he had been perusing and looked at Penny. "I wish I had more people like you on my staff."

Amity smiled proudly. "You are brilliant, Penny. You managed to provide some information on every single gentleman who was present at the Channing ball who comes close to my description of the killer. You even found out which ones smoke cigarettes."

They were gathered in the drawing room. Logan had arrived shortly after Benedict. The two men had immediately set themselves to studying Penny's annotated list of guests.

"Excellent work, Mrs. Marsden," Benedict said. He got to his feet and went to stand at the window. "That list should help narrow our search. I will ask my brother, Richard, and Uncle Cornelius to make further inquiries in their clubs. You have saved us a great deal of time."

Penny blushed and made a gracious gesture with one hand. "I had considerable assistance from Mrs. Houston and the members of her family who are also in service. We pooled our resources and worked our way through the list."

Logan smiled at the housekeeper. "I owe you my thanks, as well, Mrs. Houston. Obviously we should be hiring women at the Yard."

Mrs. Houston blushed. "Pleased to be of service, sir. It was very interesting work. I wouldn't mind doing that sort of thing again. Makes a nice change of pace."

Logan gave her a knowing look. "There is something about the hunt."

Amity saw Penny cast a quick, curious glance at Logan. Nothing was said but Amity got the impression that Penny had gained a deeper understanding of the inspector and admired what she saw. Logan was good for Penny, Amity thought. But the last thing Penny needed now was a broken heart.

Benedict picked up the list and examined it again. "One of the men here is of particular interest—Arthur Kelbrook. He is the man who exhibited an unwholesome curiosity about Amity's experience at the hands of the Bridegroom. Kelbrook was present at both the Society for Travel and Exploration reception and the Channing ball."

Amity frowned. "But I told you, I am quite certain that he is not the man who attacked me."

"I understand," Benedict said. "Nevertheless, his curiosity about you concerns me."

"In my experience there is a certain type of individual who is prone to develop a macabre curiosity in crimes of this nature," Logan said. "Kelbrook is obviously one of that sort. If Miss Doncaster is convinced that he is not the killer, however, we must look elsewhere. We cannot afford to waste time on a suspect who does not match her description."

Benedict nodded reluctantly. "You're right, of course, Inspector. We must stay focused."

"I would feel so much more positive about the outcome of our inquiries if we knew for certain that the killer actually did attend the Channing ball," Penny said. "We are operating on pure conjecture here."

"Not entirely," Logan said. "I think our original assumption has merit. As far as we can tell, your sister came to the notice of the Polite World the morning after that ball."

"Many of the people who attended the Channing affair will also be at the Gilmore ball tomorrow evening," Penny said. "As we have noted, Polite Society is a small world. The guest lists for the various events are often nearly identical."

Amity and the others looked at her.

"What of it?" Amity asked.

Penny cleared her throat. "It occurred to me that it might be interesting for you to attend, Amity—with Mr. Stanbridge, of course."

Amity stared at her. *"Me?"*

"And Mr. Stanbridge," Penny repeated. She looked at Benedict. "I'm quite certain you could obtain an invitation, sir. In fact, I wouldn't be surprised if you have already received one. You are no doubt on the guest list of every hostess in town."

"It's possible," Benedict admitted. "Invitations are always arriving at my house. I usually toss them away."

"You receive such invitations because you are considered a highly eligible bachelor," Penny said dryly.

Benedict frowned. "You don't think it's because of my charming personality and my witty conversation?"

They all looked at him for a moment. And then Amity giggled.

"Without a doubt," she said.

Benedict smiled, his eyes warming. "You reassure me." He turned back to Penny. "Do you really think it might be useful for Amity and me to attend the Gilmore affair?"

"She's got a point," Logan said. "If it's true that at least some of our suspects will be there—"

"I might be able to identify the killer," Amity concluded. Enthusiasm splashed through her. "Brilliant, Penny."

Logan smiled at Penny. "Yes, quite brilliant."

Penny blushed. "I admit, the odds of identifying the killer at the ball are probably not very good."

"But at the very least it would allow us to remove some of the suspects from our list," Amity said. "The plan will only work if Mr. Stanbridge received an invitation, though."

"If I did not get one, I know someone who can obtain it for us," Benedict said. "As I may have mentioned, my uncle is very well connected in certain circles."

◦⌘◦

Twenty minutes later Benedict and Logan left the house—Benedict to secure an invitation to the Gilmore ball, Logan to continue with his inquiries.

The moment the door closed behind the two men, Penny looked at Amity.

"There is something I wish to discuss with you now that Benedict and Inspector Logan are gone," Penny said quietly.

Amity wrinkled her nose. "I suppose this is about a gown for the ball? I'm sure we can rely on your dressmaker to see that I am properly attired for the occasion."

"I'm not concerned with the dress. Madame La Fontaine will take care of that aspect of things. What I want to tell you is that, in addition to some of the suspects on our list, there is another person who will very likely attend the ball. Lady Penhurst."

Amity frowned. "Who is she?"

"Her name was once linked with Benedict's in a romantic fashion."

Amity sighed. "I see. This isn't the same woman who left him at the altar, is it?"

"No, this is Leona, Lady Penhurst. She was Mrs. Featherton at the time she was involved with Benedict. She was the widow of an elderly, high-ranking gentleman who did not leave her nearly as much money as she had anticipated receiving. She set her cap at Benedict. When that did not work out as she had hoped, she married Lord Penhurst instead."

"I see."

"Penhurst is a widower twice over," Penny explained. "Leona is some forty years younger than him. It was widely assumed that she married Penhurst because she believed that he had one foot in the grave and could be relied upon to insert the other foot in the near future. But thus far she has been disappointed. Penhurst is in his dotage and going senile but he shows no signs of moving on to the next world."

Amity clasped her hands behind her back and went to the window. "You're trying to warn me that she might create a scene."

Penny came to stand behind her. "I'm not sure what to expect from her. But I did not want you to be taken by surprise tomorrow evening. It is said that Lady Penhurst was furious when it became clear that Benedict had no intention of giving her the Stanbridge necklace."

"I don't understand. She wanted a family necklace?"

"It's known as the Rose Necklace," Penny said. "It's worth a fortune. According to the family tradition, the eldest Stanbridge heir—Benedict in this case—gives it to his bride-to-be when he asks her to marry him. I'm sure there was never any possibility that Benedict would have married Leona, but everyone knows she was furious when he ended their association. She is reputed to be a vindictive woman. If Leona believes that there is some way to take her revenge on Benedict, she might be inclined to do so."

"You think she might try to use me to avenge herself? I don't see how that is possible."

"Neither do I," Penny said. "But Lady Penhurst's reputation is such that you must promise me that you will be very, very careful if you encounter her."

Amity smiled ruefully. "I shall be sure to take my tessen to the ball."

Sixteen

I must say, the news of your engagement came as something of a surprise, Ben." Leona, Lady Penhurst, smiled at Benedict, managing to ignore Amity, who was standing beside him. "Can we assume that the wedding will take place in the near future? Or do you plan an extended engagement?"

Leona was a beautiful woman, tall, willowy and regal. Her profile was classically molded. Her dark hair gleamed in the light of the chandeliers that hung from the ballroom ceiling. Diamonds and emeralds decorated her ears and dipped low into the deep décolletage of her garnet-colored satin and lace gown. But all the glitter and charm could not conceal the frustration and bitterness in her brown eyes.

Leona had been blessed with any number of attractive attributes, Amity thought, but she had been cursed in marriage. Lord Penhurst was, as Penny had said, slipping rapidly into senility, but he appeared to be in remarkably good health for a man his age. Amity suspected that a good deal of Leona's venom was directly attributable to the fact that her husband was still hanging around.

"My fiancée and I intend to marry as soon as possible," Benedict said. He looked around the room, clearly bored with the conversation.

Amity winced inwardly. She could not blame Benedict, she thought. He probably had no notion of how he had just added a little more fuel to the fires of anger that burned deep inside Leona.

Leona seized on the opening. She focused rather pointedly on Amity's midsection.

"I understand the need for a hasty marriage," Leona said with sugary sympathy. "I thought I detected that special glow about you, Miss Doncaster. But not to worry, your gown appears to be designed to conceal any small . . . mistakes. I congratulate you both. Now, if you will excuse me, I do believe my husband is indicating that he wishes to leave."

Leona floated away on a foaming tide of elegantly draped skirts. Benedict pulled his attention from the crowd long enough to scowl at Leona's departing figure.

"What the devil did she mean by that comment about your gown?" he asked. "I think the dress looks very nice on you."

"She was implying that the reason we are planning a hasty wedding is that I am pregnant," Amity said.

Benedict's jaw tightened. "Leona is an extremely irritating female."

Amity fiddled absently with her tessen while she watched the crowd. "I am told that you knew her rather well at one time."

Benedict glanced down at the lethal fan. A smile edged the corner of his mouth and a dark amusement lit his eyes.

"I think I can guess who may have mentioned that supremely unimportant fact," he said.

"My sister thought it best to forewarn me."

"I admit that there was a period in my life when Leona and I passed some time in each other's company. For a while I was under the impression that she found me . . . interesting." Benedict shrugged. "But when I discovered that in reality she considered me to be a great bore we parted ways."

"May I ask how you came to make that discovery?"

Benedict surprised her with one of his rare, quick, grins. "She made the mistake of telling one of her friends, who told her husband. He, in turn, mentioned it at his club. Word got back to me."

"I see." Amity peered at him. "You don't appear to have had your heart broken by the incident."

"To be honest, it was something of a relief when the end came," Benedict said. "I had become aware of the fact that it was all she could do not to yawn in my presence." He paused and then asked coolly, "What about you and Nash? Did he break your heart?"

"I certainly thought so at the time. But, then, I was only nineteen. In hindsight, I consider that I had a very narrow escape. Marriage to Humphrey Nash would have been a nightmare. I very much doubt that he is capable of loving anyone except himself. He does hold a great deal of admiration for his own accomplishments."

"I don't suppose there is any possibility that he might be the Bridegroom?"

The hopefulness in Benedict's voice would have been amusing under other circumstances, Amity thought. He obviously yearned for an excuse to do something drastic to Humphrey.

"No," she said firmly. "He is not the Bridegroom. Furthermore, I regret to report that none of the other men I have met here tonight fit my memories of the killer."

"Damn. We need to get beyond the names on that guest list."

"How do you propose to do that?"

Benedict contemplated the crowd in silence for a long moment. Amity knew that he was silently envisioning possibilities and probabilities.

"Well?" she prompted after a time.

"Connections," he said very quietly.

"What?"

"There must be links and connections to the killer. We need to find the right one."

"I don't understand," Amity said.

"We can't talk in here. Let's take a walk in the gardens."

"Certainly."

Benedict took her arm and steered her through the crowd and out onto the broad terrace. The extensive gardens behind the mansion were drenched in shadows. Here and there lanterns bobbed like fairy lights in the night. On one side of the grounds a glass-walled conservatory glittered obsidian dark in the moonlight. At the far end Amity could see the looming outline of a large structure that resembled an Italian villa. She had been told that it was the handsome stables that Gilmore had built to house his impressive collection of horses.

For the first time since they had arrived at the Gilmore ball, Amity allowed herself to take a deep breath. She had not realized how tense she had been all evening until now. It was as if she and Benedict had been on stage from the moment they had arrived. All eyes had turned toward them when they had entered the ballroom—and just as quickly turned away again. But then the whispers had begun. They had ebbed and flowed through the crowd. More than once Amity had caught snatches of the conversations.

"I see that she is not wearing the family necklace."

"I wouldn't put too much stock in the engagement. Obviously he hasn't given her the Rose Necklace."

It was a relief to escape the ballroom, Amity thought.

"I am not cut out for this sort of thing," she said.

"Neither am I," Benedict said.

It occurred to her that they did not need to explain the meaning of those statements to each other. They both understood.

The evening air was pleasantly cool and refreshing after the over-heated atmosphere of the ballroom. Amity noticed that she and Benedict were not alone on the terrace. A handful of other couples stood in the shadows around them. Low murmurs and soft laughter drifted on the night air.

Benedict paused only briefly. Then, evidently not satisfied with the degree of privacy that the terrace afforded, he drew Amity down the steps into the deeper darkness beyond.

A summer moon shone down, spilling silver and shadow across the elegantly manicured gardens. Amity was reminded of the nights on board the *Northern Star*. She was overcome with a sense of wistful longing. Fate in the form of a killer had brought Benedict back to her, but she might only have him for a short time. That knowledge filled her with a sense of urgency. She must savor every moment with him, she thought.

They walked along the graveled path until it ended at the entrance to the elegant stables. There they halted. Amity folded her arms around herself to ward off the small chill that drifted through her. She examined the stables.

"The Gilmore horses live in quarters that are much grander than those of most of the people in London," she observed.

"Everyone knows Gilmore is obsessed with his bloodstock." Benedict looked at her. "Are you cold?"

"The night has turned rather crisp, don't you think?"

Without a word he took off his coat and draped it around her bare shoulders. Just as he had done that last night on board ship, she thought; just before he had kissed her.

"Better?" he asked.

"Much better." The coat felt oddly heavy. She realized there was an object in one of the pockets. The heat of Benedict's body and his very masculine, acutely invigorating scent clung to the fine wool. Surreptitiously, she breathed in the faint essence of the man. "What did you mean when you said there are always connections?"

Benedict lounged against the wall of the conservatory and looked back toward the brilliantly illuminated mansion. "Earlier we considered the possibility that the killer did not attend the Channing ball himself but that someone he knew well was present that evening."

"You are thinking that is the connection that we need to discover, the guest with whom the killer is closely acquainted. That task will be far more difficult."

"If we are no longer looking for the killer but rather someone who knew him fairly well, we must return to the original guest list."

"Benedict, I must tell you that I am very concerned that the guest list is a dead end. We may be wasting a great deal of time."

"I know. But as Logan keeps reminding us, it is a starting point. Tonight we managed to eliminate a number of men from our list."

"If Penny is right, the person who is connected to the killer may also be here at the Gilmore ball this evening. But how can we possibly identify that individual?"

Benedict wrapped an arm around her shoulders and pulled her close. "There is one other fact that we have which we should not forget."

"What is that?"

"The gap in time between the first murder and the next three. If we could account for that delay we might be able to narrow the list of suspects."

"But there could be any number of reasons why so much time passed between the first murder and the others," Amity said. "Maybe the killer was simply not in London. Perhaps he was at his estates in the country. Or traveling somewhere in the Far East or America."

"Yes." Benedict tightened his grip on her. "Yes, maybe there is a very good reason why he did not commit any murders for several months. That is a very important piece of the puzzle, one that should not be too difficult to investigate. We are looking for male friends and relatives of the people on the Channing guest list who were out of town for approximately eight months this past year."

"Do you really think we can discover that information?"

"We will need some additional assistance from my uncle and my brother, but it can be done." Benedict turned her in his arms. "We will find the killer, Amity. I will not rest until I know you are safe."

She smiled. "I know." She put her arms around his neck and stood on tiptoe to brush her mouth against his. "I know."

He framed her face with his hands and kissed her with such fierce urgency that she felt as if he had literally stolen her breath away.

Very deliberately he set her aside and tried the door of the stable. Amity was surprised when it opened easily. Warm air flowed out of the opening, carrying the scents of hay and horses. Moonlight poured down through the windows that lined the walls.

"Definitely finer accommodations than many that I have enjoyed in my travels," Amity said.

Benedict laughed.

There was some rustling in the stalls. Several horses put their heads over the top of the half doors and nickered softly. Amity smiled. She stripped off her gloves and went forward to stroke the nose of one of the beasts.

"These are very beautiful animals," she said. "They must have cost Gilmore a fortune."

"He can afford it." Benedict inspected the moonlit scene with evident interest. "He prides himself not only on his horses but also on the architecture of his stables. Very modern in design. I understand this place is heated with hot water pipes embedded in the floor."

She hid a smile. She had been thinking that the elegant stables offered a rather intimate, even romantic setting. Trust an engineer to look at things somewhat differently.

"It is pleasantly warm in here," she said. "It reminds me a bit of St. Clare. Without the waves crashing on the shore, of course."

"Or the damn insects."

She laughed and moved down the row of stalls to pat the next horse in line. "I expect your memories of St. Clare are somewhat affected by the fact that you took a bullet on the island."

Benedict came up behind her and put his hands on her shoulders. He pulled her back against his chest and put his mouth very close to her left ear.

"You may be right," he said, his voice low and excitingly rough around the edges. "All I know is that I don't care if I never step foot on another tropical island. But the prospect of not being able to kiss you again? Now, that would crush my spirits forever."

She shivered but not because she was cold. A delicious heat was stirring deep inside her.

"I would not want to be responsible for flattening anything about you, Mr. Stanbridge, least of all your spirits," she said.

He turned her slowly around to face him. His eyes were darkly brilliant in the moonlit shadows.

"I am very grateful to hear that, Miss Doncaster. More grateful than you can possibly imagine."

He folded her close and kissed her again. He went about it slowly this time, carefully, as if he was afraid of trampling her delicate sensibilities. But she was no stranger to his kisses now and she had been dreaming about them for too long. Curiosity and a rush of recklessness were driving her tonight. From the first moment she had seen him in the alley on St. Clare she had been very certain that she would never meet another man like Benedict Stanbridge. If she did not drink from the sparkling spring of desire with him, she might never taste those forbidden waters.

She put her arms around his waist and gave herself up to the embrace with the sense of exhilaration and excitement she always experienced when he touched her.

He must have felt the heat of the flames that were sweeping through her because his mouth was suddenly, devastatingly hot on hers.

He picked her up in his arms and carried her to the far end of the aisle of horse stalls. There he stood her on her feet. He removed the coat from her shoulders. She watched him take a pristine white handkerchief out of one pocket. Then he took out another object and set it aside. She heard the soft clink of metal and caught a glimpse of moonlight glinting on the barrel of a gun. No wonder the coat had felt so heavy. He spread it across a pile of straw.

She was about to ask him if he needed the handkerchief because he feared the hay might cause him to sneeze, but then he wrapped his arms around her again and kissed her, silencing the question.

She was fascinated and enthralled by the electric currents that swirled and roiled just beneath the surface of the man. They aroused her in ways she had never dreamed possible.

His hands moved on her, following the shape of her from breasts to waist. She felt his fingers searching for the hooks that closed the front of the gown. A moment later the stiff bodice fell open revealing the thin lawn camisole beneath. When he touched her breasts through the light fabric, everything inside her tightened.

"Benedict," she whispered.

He eased the gown downward until it tumbled into a sea of satin and silk around her ankles. He untied the petticoat with its small bustle and let both undergarments fall away. She was left clad in the filmy camisole, stockings and drawers.

"You are so lovely," Benedict said. He drew his hands up her arms until he reached her throat. He framed her face between his palms and kissed her with reverent hunger.

Shaken, she clutched at his shoulders to steady herself. His black bow tie appeared in stark contrast to his crisp white shirt. She fumbled with the tie until she got it undone. The ends trailed around his neck.

She went to work on the fastenings of his shirt. When she finally got it open, she slid her hands inside. Her fingers brushed lightly across his chest. She thrilled to the feel of his sleek muscles and warm skin. She had not touched him so intimately since the days and nights on the ship when she had nursed him through the fever and changed the bloody bandages. It was so good to find him strong and healthy once again, she thought.

But when her questing fingers discovered the raised, scarred skin that marked the now-healed wound, Benedict sucked in a sharp breath.

She flinched and swiftly moved her hand away from the scar. "I hurt you. I'm so sorry."

"No." He caught one of her hands and flattened her palm against his chest again. "No, it's all right. The wound is still a little tender but you did not hurt me. When you touched me there, I was reminded of the night I awoke from the fever to see you curled up in a chair, watching over me. I knew then that you had saved my life."

She smiled. "The first thing you wanted to know after you concluded that you were not dead was if the letter was safe."

"And you assured me that it was still hidden in your satchel."

He drew her down onto the bed of straw. They lay together on his coat. In the moonlight she could see the dark heat of sexual desire in his eyes.

"I am not in the grip of a fever tonight." He rolled onto his back, taking her with him so that she tumbled across his chest. "And the only pain I am experiencing at the moment is the sort caused by desire. Tonight I know exactly what I am doing. I want you, Amity, more than I have ever wanted any woman in my life."

A thrilling awareness flashed through her. She clutched his shoulders and met his eyes, letting him know that she was ready for the adventure that awaited her.

"I want you, as well," she said. "More than anything or anyone."

He pulled her head down to his and kissed her again, a heavy, drugging kiss that ignited her senses. She felt his hands glide up her thighs under the hem of the camisole. When he touched her intimately between her legs it was her turn to take a sharp, astonished breath, but she did not relax her grip on his shoulders. Everything inside her seemed to be melting.

He stroked her in places where no man had ever touched her, eliciting sensations that she had sensed existed but had never really known. She was an experienced traveler but this was one journey she had never undertaken, perhaps because she had never encountered the right travel companion, she thought. But tonight everything felt right. This was the man, the place and the time. Those factors might never come together again. She must seize the moment or forever regret her failure of nerve.

An unfamiliar tension was building inside her. She knew Benedict's hand was wet from the damp heat he had drawn forth with his touch. Part of her was embarrassed, but he certainly did not seem to mind and she was too excited to pull away.

He turned her onto her back and leaned over her, probing her gently. His mouth closed over one breast and she found herself arching against him in a silent plea for more.

He released her to open the front of his trousers. A shock of uncertainty went through her when she saw the hard, rigid length of him revealed in the silver light.

"I'm not sure—" she began.

He loomed over her again, blocking out the moonlight, and silenced her with a kiss.

"Touch me," he said against her mouth. "You don't know how I have longed to feel your hand on me."

Cautiously she encircled him with her fingers. He groaned. She started to move her hand slowly, experimentally. His breathing grew harsh in her ears, as if he was having to exert enormous control. His brow was as damp with sweat as it had been when he was in the grip of the fever.

He raised his head. In the deep shadows his face was stark and intense. His eyes gleamed with a dark desire. Knowing that he wanted her so badly was all it took to overcome the last vestiges of her uncertainty.

He stroked her until she was breathless. Until the tension inside her was wound so tight she thought she could not bear it any longer. She sank her nails into his shoulders.

Her release blindsided her. Without warning the tight, heavy, throbbing sensation inside her burst forth in a series of pulsing waves. A rush of euphoric surprise took her by storm and suddenly she was flying.

Benedict braced himself above her and used one hand to guide himself to her core. He thrust into her in one long, relentless stroke.

The invasion brought her crashing back to earth. She gave a small, choked shriek and instinctively tried to pull away. Her nails became claws on the front of Benedict's shirt.

Benedict gripped her hips tightly, anchoring her.

"Relax," he urged. He rested his damp forehead on hers. "Just relax."

For a moment she dared not move. Neither did he. She could feel the fierce knots of the muscles of his back beneath her hands. He was struggling for control of his passions while he waited for her to get over the initial shock. The knowledge that he was forced to work so hard to restrain himself reassured her.

Slowly her body adjusted to him. Taking a quick breath, she dared to wriggle a little in an attempt to find a more comfortable position. Benedict groaned and started to move, cautiously at first and then with increasing confidence. She found the sensation strange and uncomfortable but no longer intolerable.

"Are you all right?" he said into her ear.

"I think so," she said. "It is certainly no worse than riding a camel."

He uttered an exclamation that sounded like a cross between a growl and a laugh. And then he began to move more rapidly, increasing the speed and power of each thrust until she was once again breathless, once again clinging to him for dear life.

He drove into her one last time. Everything about him went taut, his sleek back bowed. And then he stunned her by wrenching free of her tightly stretched body. He spent himself into the handkerchief, his climax raging through him in powerful waves that seemed to go on forever.

When it was over Benedict collapsed beside her. His eyes were closed. In spite of the discomfort and the uncertainty of the future, the sheer wonder of the moment thrilled her.

She had just made one of life's most mysterious journeys and discovered what lay at the end of the adventure. She knew now what it was like to take a lover.

Seventeen

"Are you certain you are all right?" Benedict asked again.

It was the third or fourth time he had inquired after her health and each time he sounded a little more brusque; impatient, even. They were in his carriage, heading back to Exton Street. Benedict had hustled her away from the ball immediately after the encounter in the stables. It was just as well, Amity thought. Her hair had come free of the pins and she was still picking bits of straw off her gown.

"Do stop fretting, sir, I am quite well, thank you," Amity said. She suspected that with each reassurance she sounded more annoyed.

Good heavens, they were practically quarreling.

The ending to what should have been one of the most important, most exciting and certainly most romantic nights of her life was proving to be a colossal disappointment. So much for taking a lover, she thought. If this was all there was to the business, it was difficult to fathom why so many people went out of their way to engage in illicit liaisons.

She understood the necessity of the hasty retreat—neither of them needed any more scandal. But it was the cool, efficient manner in which Benedict had managed things that bothered her. He had arranged the departure from the Gilmore mansion with the skill and precision of a battlefield commander—no, not a military commander—an engineer. She was rapidly coming to the conclusion that he already regretted the passionate interlude.

Now, to make matters worse, Benedict kept asking her if she was all right. It was good for a gentleman to be concerned about his lover after a heated session of lovemaking. But there did not seem to be anything the least romantic about his inquiries. He sounded worried. Perhaps he expected her to faint from the shock of the experience.

An acute silence settled inside the cab. She kept her attention focused on the misty street scene. Gas lamps and carriage lights appeared and disappeared in the fog.

Benedict stirred on the opposite seat. "Amity—"

"If you inquire into my health one more time," she said, speaking through set teeth, "I promise you I won't be responsible for my actions."

In the low glow of the lamp his eyes narrowed and the hard planes and angles of his face tightened into a grim mask. "What the devil do you mean by that? It's only natural that I am concerned about you. I did not realize that you had never experienced passion."

"For heaven's sake, sir, I am not a naïve eighteen-year-old miss who had no idea what she was about tonight. How many times have I told you that I am a woman of the world?"

"Too many times, evidently, because I believed you."

"I assure you I am not going to suffer a fit of the vapors just because of what happened in the stables."

"Just because of what happened?" he repeated, his tone turning ominous.

"Well, it's not as if what passed between us was anything remarkably extraordinary or revolutionary, now was it? Couples do that sort of thing quite frequently, do they not?"

"I believe you remarked that it was no worse than riding a camel."

"Oh, right." It dawned on her that perhaps she had hurt his feelings. She gave him a reassuring smile. "Not to worry, sir. One soon grows accustomed to a camel's stride. With time and experience, the jostling and swaying become second nature."

Benedict looked as if he was about to respond to that comment, but fortunately the carriage came to a halt. He hesitated briefly and then, clearly frustrated and decidedly grim, he opened the door. He got out of the carriage and turned to assist Amity.

She collected her skirts and took his hand. His fingers clamped around hers. Without a word they went up the front steps. She took the key out of the tiny evening bag attached to the chatelaine that held the tessen. Benedict took the key from her and opened the front door. The hall lamps were still ablaze but the lights had been turned off in the rest of the house. Penny and Mrs. Houston had both gone to bed.

Amity knew a sense of relief and stepped inside. She really did not want to engage in an extended conversation with Penny at that particular moment. There would be questions about the state of her hair and the straw clinging to her gown.

Benedict loomed on the threshold. "I will call on you tomorrow."

"Yes, of course," she said briskly. "We must consider the new direction of our investigation."

He seemed to fortify himself. "Amity, I realize that tonight was not all that you expected or hoped it would be."

She flushed. "I would rather not discuss it."

"The location was hardly romantic and the timing was not good."

She took a tight breath. "If you are about to tell me that you regret the incident—"

"Not entirely," he said. "To say that I regret what happened would be a lie."

Not entirely. For some silly reason she was now on the verge of tears. She fought them, rallying her defenses.

"Neither do I," she said. She was aware that her voice sounded oddly tight. "Not entirely. And you must not blame yourself. It is my own fault that I had imagined a somewhat different experience, but in the end it was all very educational."

"Educational."

She managed a bright smile. "That is the lure of embarking on a new journey, is it not? To experience new sensations and explore the unknown? Now, if you don't mind, I would very much like to go to bed. I find myself quite exhausted."

He did not move, so she was obliged to close the door gently but firmly in his face. For a moment she stood there, listening intently. Eventually she heard Benedict go down the steps. The door of the carriage opened and closed. The vehicle rolled away into the night.

She waited a moment longer. The tears that she had managed to restrain squeezed out of her eyes. She used the back of her glove to wipe the moisture away.

She turned down the hall lamps and went up the stairs. Penny's door opened. For a moment Amity just looked at her, too choked up to speak.

"My dear sister," Penny whispered. "What has he done to you?"

"It is not what he did to me," Amity said. "It is that I think he wishes he had not done it in the first place. And it is, at least in part, my fault because I wanted him to do it."

Penny put her arms around her. Amity let the tears fall.

Eighteen

He could not have mangled the business more thoroughly if he had set out to do precisely that, Benedict thought.

He had not intended to make love to Amity tonight, but he had been thinking about taking her to bed ever since he had met her. The problem was that he had not made a plan. Instead, he had acted on impulse. When the opportunity arose, he had been unable to resist. Desire was a powerful drug. And now he was paying the price.

No worse than riding a camel.

What did you expect? he wondered. You made love to her in a stable.

The only thing he could say about the matter now was that it had certainly seemed like a profoundly brilliant notion at the time.

The carriage jolted to a halt in front of his town house. The windows were darkened. Mr. and Mrs. Hodges had drawn the drapes for the night and retired to their bed.

Benedict opened the door, got down and sent the coachman on his way. The vehicle rumbled off into the fog.

He took his key out of his pocket, went up the steps and opened the door. The house seemed even quieter than usual. Darker, too, he thought. All of the lights were turned down low, including those in the hall.

He shrugged out of his coat, pausing to take a deep breath when he caught Amity's scent. He immediately grew hard again. The aching need stirred deep inside him, stronger than ever even though he had slaked his desire once tonight. Perhaps it was because he now knew just how satisfying it was to sink into Amity's wet, tight body.

The coat would certainly never be the same and neither would he.

What he needed now was a strong, medicinal dose of brandy. He slung the coat over one shoulder and went along the hall toward the door of his study. He reached up automatically to loosen his tie and then stopped, smiling a little, when he discovered that the strips of silk were still hanging around his neck. He had neglected to retie them because he had been fixed on the goal of getting Amity away from the Gilmore house before anyone noticed that she was in a state of enchanting dishabille.

He was so consumed with the sweet, hot memories that he did not notice anything amiss until he heard an odd, strangely muffled sound coming from a dark corner of the room.

He turned swiftly, his hand seeking the gun inside his coat. Mrs. Hodges was sitting rigidly in a ladder-back kitchen chair. Hodges was equally upright in a matching chair. Neither the chairs nor the Hodges belonged in the study at that hour of the night.

"What the devil are you doing there in the corner?"

Hodges made another strange noise. There was just enough light from the low-burning lamp on the desk to reveal the gag in his mouth. His hands and ankles were bound with rope. Mrs. Hodges was secured in the same fashion. Hodges stared, wide-eyed, at Benedict and made more desperate sounds deep in his throat.

The room had been ransacked. Books had been pulled from the shelves and dropped on the floor. The drawers of the desk stood open. The pictures on the walls had been moved aside, no doubt in search of a concealed wall safe.

"Good lord, man." Benedict removed the gun from the pocket of his coat, tossed the coat aside and turned up the lamp. "What the hell happened?"

The curtains shifted in the corner near the French doors. Benedict turned quickly, gun in hand.

A man moved out from behind the heavy velvet drapery. The light gleamed on the revolver in his hand. The lower half of his face was covered by a black scarf tied at the back of his head.

"We've been waiting for you, Stanbridge," he said.

The accent was unmistakably American. It stirred a shipboard memory. It took only a second for Benedict to put it together with the physical aspects of the intruder—slender, sandy-haired, young and male.

"Declan Garraway," Benedict said. He shook his head in disgust. "The expert on psychology. So you're the spy. I should have known. I suppose the two careers do complement each other."

"I was afraid you would recognize me." Declan yanked the scarf away, revealing his deceptively earnest, honest face. "It's the accent, isn't it? For your information, I'm not a damn spy. I'm a private investigator. Sort of."

"A fine distinction, I'm sure. Who are you working for?"

"That's none of your damn business. Where is Foxcroft's notebook?"

Benedict looked around the study, affecting mild surprise. "You mean you didn't find it?"

"Get it or so help me, I'll—"

"What? Shoot me and my butler and maybe my housekeeper before I shoot you? I doubt it. I'm no expert with a gun, but I have practiced a bit and at this distance it would be hard to miss. Even if you got lucky on your first shots, how far do you think you'll get after committing several murders in a quiet, respectable neighborhood like this? Trust me, someone will have noticed you when you arrived."

"No one saw me come here," Declan said quickly.

"What about the hansom that dropped you off nearby? Do you really think the driver won't remember that he had an American in his cab tonight? One who got out close to the scene of the killings?"

"How did you know I came in a hansom?" Declan sounded appalled.

"How else would you have been able to find this street? I doubt that you know London well."

"Forget the hansom. I'm not here to kill anyone. Your butler interrupted me as I was starting to search the place. I had to tie him up. He was going to summon the police. And then the housekeeper showed up. I had to do something. Give me the notebook and I'll leave."

"You're an idiot, Garraway. Did you really think I'd leave it lying around in my study?"

Benedict took the small leather-bound notebook out of the pocket of his coat. He flipped it open and shut very quickly, just long enough to reveal the pages covered with cryptic notes and sketches.

"Is that it? That little notebook?" Doubt creased Declan's forehead. He took a step closer. "I thought it would be much bigger."

"Foxcroft kept his notes in a small, convenient notebook that could be carried in his pocket."

Benedict tossed the notebook into the low-burning fire.

"*No.*" Declan dashed across the room, heading for the fireplace.

Benedict seized a poker and swung it in a low arc that took Declan's legs out from under him. He tumbled to the floor. The gun landed on the carpet. Benedict scooped it up.

"Damn you, damn you, damn you." Anguished, Declan sat up slowly and dropped his head into his hands. "You've ruined everything."

"What, exactly, have I ruined?" Benedict used the poker to draw the little notebook out of the embers. The small volume was somewhat singed around the edges but otherwise unharmed.

"My father sent me to get that blasted notebook." Declan watched Benedict set the notebook on the desk. "It was my last chance to prove to him that I had what it takes to join the family business."

"Must be a rather unusual business." Benedict went to Mrs. Hodges and untied the gag. "Are you injured, Mrs. Hodges?"

"No, sir," she said.

Benedict removed Hodges's gag. "What about you?"

"Only my pride, sir."

Benedict went to work first on Mrs. Hodges's bindings. Declan sat on the floor and gazed morosely at the notebook.

"Don't look so woebegone, Garraway." Benedict finished untying the ropes that bound Mrs. Hodges's ankles. "That isn't Foxcroft's notebook. It's one of my own personal notebooks. There is nothing of earthshaking importance in it."

Declan groaned. "I should have known. You tricked me."

"I'm afraid so. What exactly is your family business?"

"Oil," Declan muttered. "My father and his brother own the Garraway Oil Company. They're getting ready to drill some wells in California near Los Angeles. They're convinced there's a vast quantity of oil in the ground, waiting to be pumped out. You can see the stuff seeping up from the floor of the ocean just offshore in some locations on the coast."

Mrs. Hodges got to her feet, massaging her wrists.

"I'll see to Mr. Hodges, sir," she said.

"Thank you," Benedict said. He turned back to Declan. "What does Garraway Oil want with a device designed to utilize the power of the sun?" But the answer came hard on the heels of the question. "Oh, right. They don't want to steal the design for Foxcroft's system in order to manufacture and sell it. Your father and uncle want to keep the engine and the battery off the market. Is that correct?"

"They say that if everyone can go to the local hardware store and purchase a solar system that can capture the free energy of the sun, the market for oil will collapse before there is an opportunity to prove how useful it is. My father and my uncle say the future is in oil. They want to make certain it stays that way."

"Because they've invested heavily in that future."

Declan shrugged.

Benedict looked at Hodges. "You're certain you are unhurt?"

"Quite fit, thank you, sir," Hodges said. "But it's going to take some time to put your study to rights."

"That young scalawag made a dreadful mess," Mrs. Hodges said. She glared at Declan. "You should be ashamed of yourself, sir."

Declan had the grace to hang his head.

Benedict angled himself on the corner of his desk and contemplated Declan. "Obviously you are not aware of the latest developments."

"What are you talking about?" Declan asked.

"Someone stole the Foxcroft notebook. The good news for you is that, given the fact that you came here tonight to search for it, I must assume you are not the thief."

"Son of a bitch." Declan looked baffled. "It's gone? But who took it?"

"An interesting question. I don't know the answer. And as you don't appear to have the answer, either, I don't think there's any reason to continue the conversation. Hodges, please summon the nearest constable."

"With pleasure, sir," Hodges said. He started toward the door.

Declan stiffened in fresh alarm. "You're not going to call the police."

"Why not?" Benedict asked pleasantly.

"Because we're both after the same thing," Declan said, exasperated. "Look, if you're telling me the truth when you say the notebook has been stolen—"

"It's the truth."

"Then perhaps we can help each other. My father and my uncle will make it worth your while, I swear it. They are very rich."

"I don't doubt that," Benedict said. "But, you see, here's the thing—I'm rich, too. I don't need their money."

"Is that so?" Declan's expression turned shrewd. "Then why did you travel all the way to St. Clare and then go on to meet with Foxcroft in Los Angeles? I know you went there, by the way. When I discovered that you had purchased a ticket on a train bound for California, I guessed where you were headed. But by the time I arrived you had already left with Foxcroft's notebook." Declan paused. "He's dead, you know. The cancer took him less than forty-eight hours after he gave you his notebook."

"I'm sorry to hear that," Benedict said. "He was a brilliant engineer."

"I don't suppose you'd care to tell me exactly what happened on St. Clare? Everyone on board the *Northern Star* said that you had been attacked by a thief, but I never believed that story. I think you were there for the same reason I sailed to the island—to examine Alden Cork's solar cannon. But it was gone and Cork was dead by the time I found him."

"When did you arrive at Cork's laboratory?"

Declan looked grim. "Not long after you did, evidently. Cork's body was still on the floor. But the local police had arrived and were starting to ask questions. It was obvious they had settled on the notion that Cork had been killed by a foreigner, someone off one of the ships that was in the harbor that day. I thought it best not to be seen so I immediately returned to the *Star.*"

"And took a shot at me along the way, perhaps?" Benedict asked.

"No, I swear it. I'm not the one who shot you. I've been one step behind you at every turn. It wasn't until I followed you to Foxcroft's laboratory in Los Angeles that I realized the importance of his solar engine system, though. The cannon won't function without it, will it?"

"No. How did you come to be familiar with Cork's and Foxcroft's inventions?"

"An agent of the United States came to see my father and my uncle. The agent wanted to know if a cannon fueled by the energy of the sun and powerful enough to serve as a battleship weapon was technically feasible. He said there were rumors that such a device had been constructed by a British inventor named Alden Cork who had established a laboratory somewhere in the Caribbean. My father and uncle were familiar with Cork's work, of course, but they weren't particularly worried about it."

"The world of inventors working on solar energy devices is a small one," Benedict said.

"As I said, my father and my uncle didn't think Cork's design could function as a battleship gun, but they were sufficiently concerned to send me to St. Clare to take a look at it. When I learned that you had been shot, my first assumption was that you were the person who had murdered Cork and that you had been wounded in the process. Later, when you took the train to Los Angeles after we docked in New York, I realized that in all probability you were on your way to see Elijah Foxcroft. So I followed you. Again I was too late."

"What made you so certain that I went to see Foxcroft?"

Declan's smile held no trace of amusement. "As you said, the world of inventors working on solar energy devices is small. At one time Elijah Foxcroft was an employee of Garraway Oil. He was fired because he wanted to focus his research on solar energy rather than oil. We were aware that he had set up his own laboratory in Los Angeles to pursue his dream of a solar engine." Declan paused. "Do you have any idea of who murdered Cork or who stole Foxcroft's notebook?"

"We assume the killer and the thief are one and the same and that he is in the employ of the Russians."

Declan nodded. "I am aware that the Russians and the British have been playing a dangerous game of strategy for some time now. Both sides want to control the future of Central Asia and the East."

"Personally, I'm of the opinion that neither empire can control that part of the world, but as long as the Russians are attempting to do so, the Crown is convinced it has to stop them."

Declan shook his head. "So the game goes on."

Benedict folded his arms. "A close look at a map of North and South America makes it clear that the U.S. government is playing a few strategic games of its own."

Declan shoved his fingers through his hair. "I can't argue with that. But I think it is safe to say that neither your government nor mine would want the Russians to have a superior battleship weapon. Damn it, we've got to work together on this."

"Given the disgraceful manner in which you have treated my housekeeper and my butler, I see no reason to assist you in any way. I am going to have Hodges summon the constable now. I imagine it will take the nearest one about two minutes to get here."

"You're going to regret this, Stanbridge."

"I'm sure I'll learn to live with that regret." Benedict looked at Hodges. "You may summon the police now."

Hodges inclined his head. "At once, sir."

"Damn it," Declan muttered.

He swung around, yanked open one of the French doors and rushed out into the garden.

Hodges looked at Benedict. "Do you still wish me to summon the police, sir?"

"Don't bother. I'm sure Garraway will be several streets away by the time a constable arrives. In any event, it may be more useful to leave him on his own for a while. I will inform my uncle about him in the morning. Cornelius can deal with the Americans. I have enough trouble of my own at the moment."

"Yes, sir."

Benedict surveyed the chaotic state of the study. "Do you see the decanter? If Garraway spilled my good French brandy, I'm going to very much regret letting him leave in one piece."

"I believe the brandy is still standing, sir," Mrs. Hodges said. She stepped over a pile of tumbled books and moved some newspapers to reveal the decanter.

"Pour three glasses, Mrs. Hodges. Make those large glasses. We all deserve some. It has been a rather trying evening."

"Yes, sir," Mrs. Hodges said.

She splashed brandy into three glasses and handed them around.

Hodges studied Benedict with a considering air. "Can we assume that your evening was no more satisfactory than ours, sir?"

"You have no idea," Benedict said.

Nineteen

"Your mother is here to see you," the attendant said. He peered through the bars on the door while he inserted a key into the lock. "Expect she wants to see how you're getting along."

The patient's spirits soared. Mother had come to see him. Perhaps she'd had a change of heart and decided to believe his side of the story. With luck he could convince her to free him from this prison they called a hospital.

Until recently he had always been able to convince her that he was not guilty of all the small incidents for which he had been blamed over the years. There had always been sound explanations. It was a fact that small pets frequently suffered fatal accidents and the servants could be so very careless when it came to lighting fires. And Mother did so want to believe him.

But in the wake of the discovery of the bodies of the three brides, persuading Mother that he'd had nothing to do with the killings had become increasingly difficult. The episode with Amity Doncaster had proved disastrous. Mother had finally concluded that he was, indeed, the killer.

He had to find a way to make her believe that he'd had nothing to do with the attack on Doncaster. It was so obvious that the wounds he had suffered had been inflicted by an enraged whore who had assaulted him with a knife when he refused to pay for her services.

Mother had come to see him. Surely that was a clear indication that she wanted to be convinced that he had recovered from his latest case of shattered nerves.

Thankfully he had also recovered from the knife wounds the bitch had inflicted.

"How nice of Mother to come all this way to visit me," he said.

He put down the photographs of the hospital gardens that he had been arranging and rose from the table. He moved stiffly. His wounds had healed but he still ached in places. Each twinge was a reminder of unfinished business. He smiled at the attendant. "I trust you told her that I was at home and happy to receive callers, Mr. Douglas?"

The attendant chuckled. "Yes, indeed, sir." He swung the heavy door wide.

The roaring relief crashing through the patient threatened to overwhelm him but he knew he could not afford to appear euphoric. Displays of strong emotions of any sort were discouraged by Dr. Renwick and the hospital staff. The goal of therapy was a calm, well-ordered mind.

The patient winced as he pulled on his coat. Every time he felt the aches and twinges he knew a flash of rage. But he managed to maintain an air of composure in front of the attendant.

During the course of his earlier stay at Cresswell Manor, he had discovered that the trick to gaining privileges such as permission to photograph the flowers in the Manor's gardens was to affect a serene, polite, attentive demeanor. There were so many times when he yearned to vent his fury, but for the most part he was able to fight the urges.

True, there had been that incident with one of the maids shortly after his arrival, but the promise of a bribe had kept her silent. In any event, it was not as if he had hurt her, at least not nearly as much as she deserved. He had merely struck her hard enough to send her to the floor. Really, what had she expected him to do after the way she had treated him? She was just a servant who had gotten above herself. She had dared to try to give him orders. The silly woman had actually had the gall to tell him not to touch her. She had even threatened to report him to Jones, the ruthless man in charge of the hospital staff.

He should have done more than strike the stupid maid, the patient told himself. He should have taken a knife to her as she deserved. He was quite certain she was no virgin. But he knew he could not start cutting up the women on the staff, so he kept his needs in check. In any event, the maid was not worthy of his attentions. Just a bloody servant.

Bloody. Yes, indeed, a little bloodletting was exactly what the maid deserved—and what he needed to regain his sense of control.

But he did not have to concern himself with the maid any longer because Mother was here.

"She's waiting in the gardens," the attendant said. "I'll escort you. Dr. Renwick says you don't need the leg shackles because you've been responding well to therapy."

"Thank you," the patient said. He was careful to keep his tone humble. "I have been feeling much better since I started the treatments again."

The good doctor's therapy was very modern. It consisted of daily doses of his special nerve tonic based on quinine and nightly injections of opiates in various formulations. All patients followed a vegetarian diet devoid of any spices that might excite the nervous system. There was an emphasis on a strict routine that consisted of therapeutic baths, exercise and evenings spent listening to Dr. Renwick play the piano. Renwick was convinced that music had the ability to soothe agitated nerves.

For the most part, the regimen, with the exception of the doctor's piano playing, was tolerable, if decidedly boring. Fortunately, Renwick believed that the arts, such as photography, were also good for the nerves. The patient had been allowed to take photographs of the hospital gardens and develop his own pictures in a darkroom provided by Renwick.

Nevertheless, the pressure to act like a sane man who had been wrongfully locked away in an institution was taking its toll. He could not stop thinking about the bride who had escaped. Thoughts of Amity Doncaster obsessed him, night and day. He had to convince Mother that he was innocent—that it was safe to take him back to London with her.

The attendant unlocked the doors at the end of the corridor and escorted the patient down the staircase and into the grand hall of the old mansion. Together they walked past the hospital offices, the doctor's personal laboratory where he concocted his medications and the kitchens.

They went outside into the sunlit gardens. Towering hedges and cascading ivy concealed the high walls and the iron gates that surrounded the hospital. A woman was seated on a stone bench in the charming gazebo at the center of the gardens. She had her back to him but he could see that she wore a wide-brimmed bonnet and a stylish gown. Mother always prided herself on being in the first stare of fashion.

He could convince her to take him back to London, the patient thought. Confidence swelled inside him. Mother did not believe him as readily as she had when he was younger, but he knew that she still desperately wanted—needed—to believe in him.

Smiling, the patient went forward eagerly.

"Mother," he said. "It was good of you to come to see me. I have missed you so much."

Twenty

One look at Penny's face was all it took to tell Benedict that he was in serious trouble.

"My sister is dressing," Penny said. "She will come downstairs in a moment. I wish to have a few words with you before she arrives."

They were in the drawing room. The carriage was waiting in the street. Earlier Benedict had sent around a message informing Amity that there had been developments he wished to discuss with her. In his note he had also mentioned that he hoped she would be free to go out, as he wanted to take the opportunity to introduce her to his brother and sister-in-law. He had received a crisp note in response. *I will await you at ten.*

He had arrived promptly at ten. But it was Penny who had appeared first.

"If this is about my relationship with your sister," he said, "I can assure you—"

"Last night you began an affair with my sister."

Benedict steeled himself. "If you are concerned about my intentions—"

"You have already made your intentions plain, Mr. Stanbridge. You wish to conduct a liaison with Amity and she appears to be amenable to such an arrangement."

That stopped him. "She is?"

"I will not stand in her way. She is an adult. Furthermore, she is a modern-thinking woman. She has every right to make her own decisions. But as widely traveled and as worldly as she believes herself to be, Amity is still quite naïve in certain respects. I expect you to protect her."

"You refer to the killer who has fixed his attentions on her. I swear I am doing everything in my power to stop him."

"I do not refer to that situation," Penny said coolly. "It is understood that you and Inspector Logan will find the killer and stop him. That is not the sort of protection I meant."

He went blank. "I don't understand."

"You will see to it that Amity does not become pregnant. Do I make myself clear, Mr. Stanbridge?"

A rush of embarrassed heat slammed through him. He knew he was probably turning red. He could not remember the last time he had blushed.

"Very clear, Mrs. Marsden," he managed.

Footsteps sounded on the stairs.

Penny lowered her voice. "I assume a gentleman of your experience is aware of condoms and how to use them?"

Amity was in the hall now.

He collected himself and his nerves. "Yes, Mrs. Marsden," he said through his teeth. "Rest assured I am aware of such devices."

"I am relieved to hear that. I expect you to employ them."

Amity appeared in the doorway, a bonnet dangling from one gloved hand. She was dressed in a demure, high-necked walking dress outfitted with what Benedict knew the ladies termed street-sweeper ruffles at the hem. The ruffles were designed to protect the expensive fabric of the gowns from dirt and grime.

Amity glanced curiously at Penny and then looked at Benedict.

"Whom are you going to employ?" she asked.

"Never mind," Benedict said. "I will explain later. Are you ready to go out?"

Amity did not appear satisfied with his response but she did not argue. "Yes." She put on her bonnet and tied the strings. "The day is quite pleasant. I won't need a coat."

Benedict inclined his head at Penny. "Good afternoon, Mrs. Marsden."

"One more thing before you leave, Mr. Stanbridge," Penny said in the same cool voice she had used to deliver the lecture on protection. "Are your brother and his wife aware that your engagement to my sister is a pretense?"

"No," Benedict said. "And I intend to keep it that way."

Amity looked startled. "But surely there is no need to conceal the truth from your family," she said. "Your brother and his wife will understand the reason for our charade."

"Quite possibly," he allowed. "But families are inclined to talk about such matters. And there is always someone listening." He smiled at Mrs. Houston, who waited out in the front hall. "I trust Mrs. Houston. She is a part of our little band of investigators."

Mrs. Houston looked pleased. "Thank you, sir."

"But there are always a number of people coming and going from my brother's house—servants, clients, friends. I don't want to risk having someone outside the family overhear a bit of gossip as interesting as a false engagement would prove to be."

"Your point is well taken," Penny said. She was clearly troubled by the thought. "For now I think you are right. The engagement must appear to be real."

Benedict met her eyes. "Absolutely real."

Twenty-one

"Declan Garraway is after the notebook?" Amity asked. "I must say I am somewhat surprised but not entirely shocked. I knew there was something slightly off about him."

"Did you? That's news to me. Every time I saw the two of you together you appeared to be charmed by Garraway."

"I liked him very much. He is a most interesting gentleman. But I did think from time to time that he was a bit too curious about you." Amity blushed. "His curiosity made me wonder if he might be a tiny bit jealous of you."

"I see."

"I never dreamed that he might be after the notebook. To think he actually broke into your house like a common burglar." She frowned. "You say that his family owns a petroleum company?"

She was oddly grateful for the disturbing news about Declan Garraway. Discovering that he was pursuing the notebook came as a relief—not because it explained a few things about his attentions to her on the *Northern Star* but because it provided a convenient topic of conversation.

She had not slept well last night and a certain portion of her anatomy felt a bit bruised. And the thought of seeing Benedict again had made her unaccountably anxious all morning. She had no idea how a woman was supposed to conduct herself the day after the first passionate tryst with a new lover.

She had deliberated between two approaches—pretending that nothing out of the ordinary had occurred or hurling herself into Benedict's arms. One look at his stern countenance when she had walked into the drawing room had settled the matter. She would carry on as though she was quite accustomed to such unusual events.

"It would be more accurate to say that young Garraway is working in the family business," Benedict said. "The Garraway Oil Company."

"Interesting. Garraway Oil must be extremely concerned about the potential competition that a solar energy system represents."

"One can see the company's point of view," Benedict said. "The Garraways are not alone in believing that petroleum will be the most important source of energy in the future. It's true that currently it is mostly used as a source of kerosene for lamps, but a significant number of inventors and engineers are developing machines and devices designed to operate on petroleum-based fuels. The oil companies have a reason to fear the development of a rival technology that utilizes a source of energy that is free to all."

"I suppose that does answer some of the questions I had about Declan Garraway," she said. "But I must say that I did enjoy our conversations on the topic of psychology. He had some very interesting theories about why otherwise normal people do seemingly irrational things."

"Human nature is complicated. No doctor can explain it, at least not with our current state of knowledge."

"I agree." She drummed her fingers on the seat cushion. "Nevertheless, it occurs to me that it might be useful to discuss the actions of the Bridegroom with Mr. Garraway. He might be able to cast some light on the killer's reasoning."

"Damnation, Amity, Garraway is after the notebook. Haven't you been listening? He broke into my house last night. That makes him a member of the criminal class."

"I'm sure the attempted burglary was a one-time event."

"One time is sufficient to throw some doubt on his character, as far as I'm concerned."

"He was probably quite desperate," Amity said. "From the sound of things, his father and his uncle are putting a great deal of pressure on him. I'm sure you realize such a situation can be extremely stressful."

"I don't believe this. Now you are feeling sorry for Declan Garraway?"

"I can't bring myself to believe that he's a bad person—not down deep inside."

"And you're certain of this because you had extensive conversations with him on board the *Northern Star*?" Benedict demanded.

"Well, yes."

The carriage rolled to a halt in front of a handsome town house.

Benedict glanced out the window, clearly irritated by the interruption. "We have arrived."

"I look forward to meeting your relatives," Amity said politely.

"You don't mean that."

"You're right. The truth is I am not at all looking forward to lying to your brother and sister-in-law, who, I am certain, are very nice people."

"Yes," Benedict said. He opened the carriage door. "They are nice people. We won't stay long."

Marissa Stanbridge was a very pleasant, very charming lady, Amity discovered. She was also a very pregnant lady. They sat together in the garden behind the town house. Benedict and Richard were closeted together in Richard's study. From where she sat Amity caught occasional glimpses of the two men through the French doors, which stood open.

"We will be leaving London as soon as possible after the baby is born," Marissa said. She touched her belly in a protective manner. "We want to raise our child at our estate in the country, where the air is clean and fresh. The fog here in the city cannot be good for young lungs."

"I agree," Amity said.

"The only reason I'm not having the baby at the estate is because Dr. Thackwell maintains his practice here."

Amity put her cup down in the saucer. "You are satisfied that Dr. Thackwell is a modern-thinking doctor, I assume?"

"Yes, indeed. Richard and I investigated him quite thoroughly. He holds with all the most advanced theories on the importance of cleanliness and sanitation. In addition, he keeps chloroform at hand in the event that the pain becomes unmanageable."

Amity smiled. "My father was a doctor. From the sound of it, I think he would have approved of Thackwell."

"I have read your pieces in the *Flying Intelligencer*," Marissa said. "You make globetrotting sound very exciting."

"It has its moments."

Marissa raised her brows. "Such as when you saved Benedict's life on St. Clare?"

"He mentioned that business to you?"

"Of course." Marissa took a sip of her tea. When she lowered the cup she looked at Amity with veiled curiosity. "We are all very grateful to you. It is appalling that you returned home from all your adventures abroad only to encounter that dreadful killer they call the Bridegroom. Benedict is extremely concerned about your safety, to say the least."

Amity stilled. "I am aware of his concern."

"It's only natural under the circumstances."

"Yes." Amity sensed that she was on dangerous ground. "But I'm certain that the police will soon locate the killer."

"Benedict indicated that they think the Bridegroom is a member of the upper classes—that he may actually move in Society."

"Benedict and the police are working from my impressions of the killer. I am convinced that he is well bred and wealthy and there are reasons to think that he learned about me when the rumors of my . . . association with Benedict began to circulate after the Channing ball."

"Those factors will go far to shield the monster from a police investigation." Marissa paused. "Which is, of course, one reason why Benedict is assisting in the inquiries."

"I know. As I said, I'm sure the police will find the killer soon."

"And then what will happen, Miss Doncaster?" Marissa asked gently.

Amity nearly choked on a swallow of tea. It took a moment to pull herself together.

"Sorry," she said. "Not sure I understand the question. What do you suppose will happen?"

"What I think," Marissa said coolly, "is that once the killer is caught there will no longer be any need for you and Benedict to remain engaged. When the danger is past, you will be free to publish your book and set sail on another journey to some exotic foreign port of call."

Amity froze. "Are you implying that you think my engagement to Benedict is a fraud?"

"Yes, Miss Doncaster, that is my great fear."

"I see. I'm not sure what to say, Mrs. Stanbridge."

"You must call me Marissa."

Amity glanced toward the open doors of the study, hoping that Benedict would miraculously emerge and take charge of the situation. But he and his brother both had their heads down over some papers spread out on Richard's desk.

Amity sighed. She was on her own.

"Marissa," she repeated.

"And as for what you can say to me, please assure me that you will not end the engagement once you are safe," Marissa continued briskly.

"I'm sorry," Amity said cautiously. "I'm afraid I don't understand."

"You can tell me that your feelings for Benedict are sincere, that the engagement is for real. You can assure me that you will not break Benedict's heart by buying a ticket on the next ship bound for the Far East as soon as your book is published and the police have arrested the Bridegroom."

Amity caught her breath, stunned. "You think that I am in a position to break Benedict's heart?"

She was aghast at the misunderstanding but she had no notion of how to go about correcting it.

"Benedict has waited a long time for the right woman to come into his life. He certainly has not lived a monkish existence."

Amity cleared her throat. "Yes, I am aware of his past association with Lady Penhurst."

"It meant nothing to Benedict." Marissa waved her hand in casual dismissal. "Which is not to say that Lady Penhurst did not have her own plans. She was out to snag a wealthy husband at the time and everyone, including Benedict, knew that. She thought she could seduce him into marriage, but Ben is not that easily fooled. He learned his lesson after the disaster of his first engagement. There was never any possibility that he would give Leona the Rose Necklace."

Amity remembered some of the whispers she had heard at the Gilmore ball. *I see that she is not wearing the family necklace.*

"Mrs. Stanbridge—Marissa—I don't mean to disagree with you but I don't think you understand the nature of my relationship with Benedict. Our engagement is a very modern arrangement. It is based on friendship and mutual interests and . . . and a number of other things."

Marissa did not appear impressed. "Has Ben told you about Eleanor, the woman he was engaged to marry when he was much younger?"

"No. I've been told that there was a prior engagement, but he has never mentioned the woman's name. The subject is no doubt far too painful." Amity took a deep breath. "If you don't mind, I'd like to change the topic."

Marissa ignored that. "It was a disastrous relationship from the start. There is no doubt but that Eleanor was forced into the engagement because her family's finances were in desperate shape. She was barely eighteen. She tried to do her duty. But I'm afraid that poor Benedict believed that she truly loved him. He loved her, you see, the way only a young man can love."

Amity reflected briefly on her own youthful passion for Humphrey Nash. She shuddered. "I see."

Marissa patted her hand. "We were all that young once. Luckily, some of us make the right choices at that point in our lives. But I'm inclined to think that success in that regard is mostly a matter of chance. How can a person of that age possibly know what to look for in an alliance that is destined to last a lifetime?"

"Good question," Amity said.

She cast another, hopeful glance in the direction of the study, but Benedict and Richard were still immersed in the papers on the desk. She knew the conversation with Marissa was veering into dangerous territory. Part of her was curious to know the truth about Benedict's past, but another part of her did not wish to hear how much he had loved his first fiancée—his real fiancée.

"In the end, as you are probably aware, Benedict was left at the altar," Marissa said. "Eleanor ran off with her penniless lover the night before the wedding."

"How very melodramatic of her."

"Indeed. But as I said, she was only eighteen and at that age everything is melodramatic, is it not?"

"Quite true."

"It was all very awkward at the time, but Richard assures me that when the dust settled Ben soon realized he'd had a narrow escape. And for her part, Eleanor was honest enough not to take the Rose Necklace when she ran off. Some women in her situation would have kept the necklace and used it to finance a new life with her lover."

Amity smiled. "So Eleanor wasn't such a bad sort, after all."

"No. Just very young. Trust me, Lady Penhurst would have kept the necklace."

Amity thought about the vindictive expression she had detected in Leona's eyes. "I think you're right. Does anyone know what happened to Eleanor and her lover?"

"Yes, as a matter of fact. They got married. Probably lived in a garret for a time. Isn't that what young runaway lovers do? But in the end Eleanor's family accepted the marriage. It's not as if they had a choice. And eventually Eleanor's husband obtained a respectable position as a clerk in a firm of solicitors. The husband made a few investments that turned a very nice profit and now the family lives a comfortable life. Last I heard they have a house in the country and another here in London."

"So there was a happy ending for Eleanor and her lover."

"Oh, yes," Marissa said. "They have three children, I believe."

Amity pondered that and then smiled. "How fortunate for all concerned that Eleanor's husband got the post as a clerk and that he had the insight to make those very good investments."

A secretive, amused smile edged Marissa's mouth. "Very fortunate, indeed."

"Benedict recommended Eleanor's husband for that post at the firm of solicitors, didn't he? He probably also suggested those investments that turned out well for the couple."

Marissa laughed. "You do, indeed, know Ben very well—far better than most people know him. Yes, he gave the couple considerable assistance at a time when they desperately needed it. When I heard the tale, I was surprised at his generosity. But as Richard pointed out, Ben quickly realized he'd barely avoided what would no doubt have been an unhappy marriage. It's Richard's opinion that helping Eleanor and her husband financially was Ben's way of expressing his gratitude and relief."

At long last Benedict and Richard walked out of the study into the sunlit garden. They headed toward the bench where Amity sat with Marissa.

Amity watched Benedict for a moment and then she smiled again.

"No," she said. "He helped Eleanor and her husband because he felt sorry for the couple. He realized that Eleanor had been pushed into the engagement in the first place and that it was not her fault she had wound up in such a disastrous situation. And because she had left the Rose Necklace behind."

"As I said, you seem to know Ben well," Marissa said softly.

Benedict and Richard arrived at the bench. Benedict had his small notebook in his hand. There was an air of barely suppressed anticipation about both men.

"What is it?" Amity asked.

"Did you discover something of interest?" Marissa asked.

"Perhaps," Benedict said. "Richard made inquiries at his club. He has learned some information about the recent travels of several of the men on the Channing guest list."

"There were a handful of men on the list who were out of London for extended periods of time during the past year," Richard said. "Only to be expected, of course. Most were said to have traveled to their estates to see to business matters. A couple claimed to be traveling abroad. Those stories can no doubt be verified by Logan."

"Between us, Richard and I drew up a time line," Benedict said quickly. "It is cross-referenced with the time line that Inspector Logan provided. It tells us which of the men were away from London in the interim between the first murder and the more recent killings."

"The list is quite short," Richard said.

"I will give it to Inspector Logan so that he can begin making inquiries from his end," Benedict said.

"Meanwhile, I will continue my inquiries at my club," Richard said.

"Uncle Cornelius will also continue to assist us," Benedict added. "It is the least he can do since he is in part responsible for this situation in the first place."

"That's not fair," Amity said.

"It's perfectly fair, as far as I'm concerned." Benedict's voice hardened. "Besides, Cornelius is well positioned to gain precisely that sort of information. His reach extends into every club in London."

"The killer would have needed medical attention and time to heal," Marissa said. "If he is alive, someone must know how badly he was injured."

Benedict looked grim. "Richard and Uncle Cornelius have made inquiries along that line. Thus far no one is aware of a gentleman who was attacked or injured in a so-called accident."

Amity thought for a moment. "Perhaps we are searching for someone who took a cure for a certain unspecified illness a few months ago and has now returned to the same spa for another round of therapy."

Benedict, Richard and Marissa looked at her.

"That is a brilliant notion," Marissa said softly.

"Excellent strategy," Richard added. "What better excuse could the killer use to conceal his wounds than to let it be known that he was taking a cure at an unnamed spa?"

Benedict smiled a slow, cold smile and looked at Richard. "You do see now why I am so happy to find myself engaged to Miss Doncaster."

Richard chuckled and slapped Benedict on the shoulder. "She does appear to be the perfect one for you, brother."

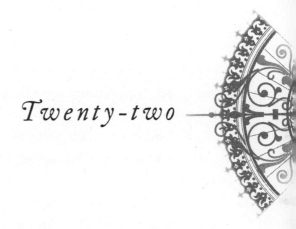

Twenty-two

"May I ask what you and Marissa were discussing out in the garden?" Benedict asked.

They were in the carriage and on their way back to Exton Street. She told herself that at least this time they had pressing matters to discuss. The investigation was moving forward at long last. But instead of focusing on the next step in the inquiry, Benedict wanted to know what she and Marissa had talked about.

"I congratulated her on the forthcoming birth of their first child," Amity said. "She is naturally quite excited."

"I saw the expression on your faces when I came out of the study with my brother," Benedict said. "Marissa told you about Eleanor, didn't she?"

Amity looked down at her folded hands. "I'm sorry, Benedict. I know it is none of my business."

"Of course it's your business. We're engaged."

She raised her chin. "In the eyes of the world."

"In my eyes, as well," he said very deliberately.

"Because of last night." She waved that aside. "Yes, I understand, but I assure you there is no need to feel honor-bound to actually marry me just because of what happened in the Gilmore stables. Indeed, I will not allow you to marry me for such old-fashioned reasons. I told you, I am not some innocent young woman who cannot take care of herself."

"I believe I have heard this lecture before. It grows tiresome."

She tightened her hands together in her lap. "Does it, indeed, sir? Forgive me for boring you."

"Never mind. This is not the time for an argument. We shall save it for later. What did Marissa tell you about my engagement to Eleanor?"

Amity took a deep breath and exhaled slowly. "She merely mentioned that Eleanor was quite young and that she had been pushed into the engagement by her parents, who were rather desperate to repair their finances. Eleanor abandoned you at the altar and ran off with her lover."

Benedict smiled somewhat ruefully. "That's about all there was to it."

"Not quite. Eleanor was a very honest young lady. She left the Stanbridge family necklace behind. And in return you helped the young couple get established financially. It is really a rather endearing tale—except for the bit about your heart having been broken, of course."

Amusement gleamed in Benedict's eyes. "Did Marissa tell you that my heart had been broken?"

"No. But I know you well enough to be certain that you would never have asked Eleanor to marry you if you were not in love with her."

Benedict exhaled deeply. "It was a long time ago and I was so much younger."

"You are hardly in your dotage now," Amity said.

"Thank you." Benedict smiled slowly. "That is good to know. You're right. At the time I certainly believed myself to be in love. Eleanor was quite pretty, very gentle and sweet. But the young man she loved was far more dashing and reckless and he read poetry."

Amity blinked. "Poetry?"

"I don't read much poetry," Benedict said. "Not if I can avoid it. I prefer the latest copy of the *Journal of Engineering* and the *Inventors Quarterly*. I can assure you that whatever I felt for Eleanor went up in smoke when I realized that she did not reciprocate my feelings."

"I see," Amity said.

She suddenly felt a good deal more cheerful.

Twenty-three

Dr. Jacob Norcott took the last shirt out of the wardrobe drawer and dropped it into the small traveling trunk. His precious medical satchel was already packed and latched.

He was about to close and lock the trunk when he heard the carriage out in the street. He went to the window and looked down. He was relieved to see that the cab he had sent for a short time ago had arrived. Soon he would be at the railway station and safely on his way to his brother's house in Scotland.

He turned away from the window and hurried back toward the bed, intending to close up the trunk. It was small enough that he could manage it on the stairs. He did not like to think about all of the plump fees that he would miss by taking this impromptu holiday, but there was no help for it. In any event, the money that he had received for saving the patient's life and arranging for him to be transported quietly to Cresswell Manor again would keep him in reasonable comfort for at least a year. He would not be a financial burden on his brother.

He was halfway to the bed when his gaze fell on the letter on the nightstand. It had arrived an hour ago and was dated the previous day. Each time he read it, his pulse fluttered and a terrible sensation of dread threatened to shatter his nerves.

Sir:

This is to inform you that the patient whom you referred to Cresswell Manor some three weeks ago and who entered this hospital under an assumed name departed this establishment in the company of his mother today. I tried to discourage the lady from taking him back to London, but my advice went unheeded.

I was informed that upon his return to London, the patient would be under your close supervision. I have nothing but the highest respect for your medical knowledge, as I'm sure you are aware. However, I feel it incumbent upon me to tell you that in spite of the progress the patient made while in my care, I do not feel that he is at all ready to resume his normal routine. Indeed, I am convinced that under certain circumstances, he might prove quite dangerous.

I trust that I have not given offense by offering this warning and that you will take this note in the spirit in which it is intended.

Sincerely,
J. Renwick
Cresswell Manor

"No offense taken, Renwick. I just wish you had sent me a telegram yesterday instead of using the post to warn me that the devil has escaped. I could have used the extra time, damn you."

Norcott put on his hat, pulled on his gloves and checked his pocket watch. Plenty of time to make it to the station. He took one last look around the bedroom to make certain that he had not left anything of value behind. His medical instruments and supply of drugs were his most important possessions. They were all safely stowed in the satchel. With the tools of his profession he could make a living somewhere other than London should it prove necessary.

Satisfied that he had packed everything he could reasonably carry, he closed and locked the trunk and hauled it off the bed. He hoisted the satchel with his free hand and went out the door.

He could feel his pulse pounding now. He wasn't accustomed to so much exertion, he thought. He labored to carry the heavy trunk and satchel down the stairs. But he knew it was not just the physical effort that was affecting him. His nerves were jangling wildly. He had to get out of the house as quickly as possible.

If only Renwick had sent a telegram yesterday instead of a letter.

If only I had gone to the authorities instead of agreeing to make arrangements for the bastard to be incarcerated at an asylum.

He consoled himself with the thought that he'd made the only choice he could under the circumstances. The patient's mother would have protected her precious son from the police. The scandal would have been unbearable for her. Rumors of insanity in the bloodline would have guaranteed that her son never made a respectable marriage. And Norcott knew that his own career as a doctor to the elite of Society would have been ruined.

The chances that the bastard would have been taken up on murder charges were almost nonexistent. Better to have him locked up at

Cresswell Manor, Norcott thought. Or so he had told himself at the time.

If only he had let the devil die of his wounds.

He reached the foot of the stairs, went past the closed door of his surgery and paused a moment to catch his breath. He set the satchel down and tried to fumble the key out of his coat pocket so that he could lock the door behind him. His state of near panic made things even more complicated.

He had just got the key in his hand when he heard the door of the surgery open behind him.

"I've been waiting for you, Dr. Norcott," the patient said. "I know that as a modern-thinking man of medicine you'll be thrilled to learn of my astonishing progress."

"No," Norcott whispered. *"No."*

He dropped the trunk and started to turn around. Simultaneously, he opened his mouth to scream for help, but it was too late. The cold blade of one of his own scalpels sliced across his throat.

He barely had time to realize that the patient was wearing one of the leather aprons from the surgery. It was now spattered with fresh blood.

My blood, Norcott thought.

And then he knew no more.

Twenty-four

Mr. Stanbridge suggested that I let you all view the limited evidence we have collected from the murder scenes," Logan said. "I agreed because in my experience, there is sometimes a great deal to be said for gaining a fresh perspective—in this case a number of fresh perspectives." He looked at Declan Garraway. "Yours as well, sir. Thank you for coming today."

"I will be happy to assist in any way I can," Declan said. He tugged uneasily at his tie and glanced at Benedict. "But I am by no means an authority in such matters. I had the privilege of studying under Dr. Edward Benson, who is a noted authority in the field of psychology, and I have a great personal interest in the criminal mind, but that is the sum total of my credentials. The science of explaining and predicting human behavior is still very much in its infancy."

"It is your academic background and wide reading in the field that make your opinion so valuable," Amity said. "In any event, the more observations, the better, as the inspector just observed."

They were gathered in Penny's study. Inspector Logan had arrived earlier with a small metal box that now stood open on the desk. Penny, Amity, Benedict, Logan and Declan were gathered around the desk.

Amity had been forced to be quite firm when it came to the issue of inviting Declan. Benedict had not been at all keen on the notion until she had reminded him that Declan possessed some training in the modern theories of psychology. Benedict had reluctantly relented, but he was not going out of his way to conceal his disapproval of Declan.

For his part, Declan was clearly uneasy about Benedict. The two were wary of each other, but Amity could tell that both were intrigued by the possibility of learning something new from the evidence.

"I must warn you that a number of men from the Yard have viewed these objects and come to no useful conclusions," Logan said.

Penny studied the contents of the trunk. "This is all that has been preserved from the scenes of the murders?"

"I'm afraid so," Logan said.

Amity considered the items. "Four plain gold rings and three lockets with chains." She looked at Logan. "You said you believed there was a fourth murder."

"Yes," Logan said. "But according to the records, the family kept the locket of the first victim. They wanted it as a memento of their daughter."

Declan frowned. "Not much to go on here."

"Hard to believe this is all that was considered worth salvaging from the scenes of such serious crimes," Benedict said.

Logan's mouth tightened at the corners. "I agree. Keep in mind that I was assigned to this case only recently after my predecessor failed to identify a suspect. I'm certain that there was more evidence but it was discarded as irrelevant." He paused. "There were other factors that limited the scope of the investigation, as well."

Penny nodded. "The families of the victims would have brought a great deal of pressure to bear on the police to keep things quiet."

"There is always a great fear of scandal in cases of this sort," Logan said. "The families did not want rumors and titillating accounts of their daughters' deaths appearing in the press. Not that they were able to prevent that from happening, of course."

Benedict looked at him. "I assume the lockets were tested for fingerprints?"

"Yes," Logan said. "But none were found."

"Presumably the killer wore gloves or wiped the jewelry clean," Benedict said.

"Most likely."

Amity looked at Logan. "There does not appear to be anything special about the rings."

"No," Logan said. "I was unable to trace them to the shop that sold them."

"May I open the lockets?" she asked.

"Certainly," Logan said. "The only items inside are photos of the women dressed in wedding gowns and veils."

"The lockets are not cheap," Penny observed. "The silver is good quality but the designs are old-fashioned."

"I showed them to a couple of jewelers who recognized the hallmarks," Logan said. "I was told that the lockets are all nearly a decade out of fashion and that they must have been made several years ago. I suspect the killer found them in various pawn shops."

Amity reached into the box and took out one of the lockets. She opened it with great care and set it on the desk.

They all looked at the photograph. The picture was that of a bride viewed from the waist up. Her veil was thrown back off her face to reveal the features of an attractive young woman with dark hair. There was a bouquet of white lilies in her gloved hands. She stared straight at the camera as though confronting a cobra. Even though the photograph was small, there was no mistaking the fear and dread in the victim's eyes.

Amity shivered. "Dear heaven," she whispered.

No one else spoke.

She took out the other two lockets, opened them and set them beside the first. There were definite, obvious similarities about the pictures.

"It appears that these portraits were all taken in the same studio," she said.

"I agree." Benedict took a closer look, frowning in concentration. "The lighting is the same in each picture."

"The flowers are all white lilies but they are slightly different in each photograph," Penny observed.

"That makes sense," Amity said. "It would be very difficult to make three bridal bouquets appear exactly the same."

For a time they all stood in silence, contemplating the photos.

"White," Amity said suddenly.

They all looked at her.

"She's right," Penny said. "The dresses and veils in the photographs are all white. The Queen set the style for white gowns when she was married decades ago, but only the very wealthy follow the fashion."

Declan looked at her. "Why is that?"

Penny smiled. "White is a very impractical color for a gown. Impossible to clean, you know. Most brides are married in their best dresses. If they do buy a new gown for the ceremony, they usually purchase one in a color and a style that can be worn after the wedding. Only the very wealthy wear white. In these photographs the gowns are all white and the veils are quite elaborate." She looked at Logan. "But, then, we know that these three young ladies moved in wealthy circles."

"That is correct," Logan said.

"Nevertheless, there's something about these three dresses." Penny picked up one of the lockets and took a closer look, frowning in concentration. "I think these women are all wearing the same wedding gown and veil."

"What?" Logan spoke sharply. "I had not noticed."

"It is a detail that a woman is more likely to observe," Penny said. "But I'm quite sure this is the same gown and veil in each of the photographs." She opened a desk drawer and took out a magnifying glass. She examined each of the lockets in turn. "Yes, I'm certain of it. Same gown. Same veil. Take a look, Amity. What do you think?"

Amity took the magnifying glass and studied each of the small photographs. "You're right. They are all attired in the same bridal gown. It is harder to be certain about the veil, but I think the headband is the same, too."

"There is something else about the dress," Penny said. She retrieved the magnifying glass and took another look at all three pictures. "It is, I believe, about two years out of date."

Benedict looked interested. "How can you tell?"

"This particular sleeve and low neckline were very much in fashion for formal gowns about two years ago," Penny said with cool authority.

"Interesting," Logan said. He made a note. "I suppose it makes sense that he used the same gown for all three victims. A man can hardly go to a fashionable dressmaker and start ordering a number of wedding gowns, not without causing comment."

"So he bought one gown two years ago and reuses it for each victim?" Amity mused.

Declan cleared his throat. They all looked at him. He turned red under the scrutiny.

"What is it?" Benedict said. "Speak up, man."

"It just occurred to me that perhaps the gown has some special significance," Declan said.

"It's a wedding gown," Logan said. "In and of itself, that fact implies a great deal of significance."

"No, I mean, perhaps that particular gown has some personal meaning for him," Declan said.

"Yes, of course," Amity said softly. "What if the gown was made for his own bride?"

Logan flipped through his notes and paused at a page of names. "Five of the men on this list that Mr. Stanbridge and his brother drew up are married. The other three are not."

"I have a feeling that we are looking for one of those who is not married," Declan said quietly. "At least not any longer."

A short, stark silence fell on the room. Amity was aware of a chill on the nape of her neck.

Benedict looked at Logan. "Are there any widowers on our list? Or men who remarried after losing their first wives?"

"I don't know," Logan said. "But it shouldn't be difficult to find out." He turned back to Declan. "What makes you think that the first bride to wear that gown is dead?"

"Because there is a horrible kind of twisted logic to the thing," Declan said. "I remember Dr. Benson lecturing on the subject of murderers who killed again and again. He believes that there is always a pattern—a ritual—involved. If he's right, I would not be astonished to discover that the first murdered bride was the wife of the killer."

Benedict looked at Logan. "You said the body of the first victim was found about a year ago. She was engaged to be married but not yet a bride."

"That's right," Logan said. "None of the young women was ever married."

Declan exhaled slowly and shook his head. "I was just speculating. I've never done anything like this before."

"If he murdered his first wife," Benedict said slowly, "then that narrows the suspects on our list to a man who was married approximately two years ago and who was widowed."

"It's worth pursuing that angle," Logan agreed.

"And don't forget, we also know that the killer indulges in cigarettes that are scented with spices," Amity added. "That should help narrow the list a bit."

"So he smokes coffin nails, does he?" Declan said.

"I beg your pardon?" Amity said.

"That's what we call cigarettes in America," Declan explained. "Coffin nails. Not that it stops anyone from smoking them, mind you."

Logan glanced at him. "I heard cigarettes were good for the nerves."

"Not according to Dr. Benson," Declan said.

Penny stirred. "I may be able to help you narrow the list a bit more."

Logan watched her with close attention. "How will you do that?"

Penny glanced at Amity. "By consulting an expert."

Amity smiled. "Madame La Fontaine, your dressmaker."

"She is an authority on all things relating to fashion," Penny said. "Amity and I will pay a visit to her this very afternoon and see what we can discover."

"Excellent." Logan slipped his notebook and pencil back into the pocket of his coat. "I appreciate all of the help you four have provided today. I feel as if I know considerably more about this killer than I did before I arrived here."

Benedict gave Declan a speculative look. "I must admit that I am quite intrigued by your observations. Maybe you should consider a career as a consultant to the police."

"My father would be furious," Declan said. He made a face. "The future is in oil, you know."

"Yes, you did mention that," Benedict said.

Twenty-five

Madame La Fontaine used Penny's magnifying glass to study the photographs in the lockets arrayed on the counter. Amity and Penny waited, tense and silent. The dressmaker muttered to herself as she moved from one picture to the next. When she reached the last one, she nodded emphatically and put down the lens.

"*Oui*, Mrs. Marsden, you and your sister are correct," she announced in her fake French accent. "There is no doubt but that it is the same gown in all three pictures and it is most certainly a design from the fall season two years ago. The truth is all there in the details of the sleeve, the neckline and the beading on the headpiece of the veil."

"Thank you," Penny said. "We thought as much but we wanted to be certain."

Madame La Fontaine eyed her with a shrewd expression. "It is a very expensive gown. And in white satin, no less. So impractical. But perhaps the three young ladies in the pictures are sisters who decided to share the dress to save money?"

"No," Amity said. She scooped up the lockets and tucked them into the small velvet bag she had brought with her. "They were not sisters."

"Friends of yours, perhaps?" Madame La Fontaine asked.

Amity tugged on the strings to cinch up the bag. "No. Why do you ask?"

"I am aware that you are engaged to be married and will soon be in the market for a wedding gown yourself," Madame La Fontaine said smoothly. "I merely wondered if perhaps one of these brides had offered to sell you that white satin gown and veil at a reduced price."

"Oh." Amity managed to regain her composure. "No, absolutely not. Trust me when I say that this particular gown is the very last dress I would want to wear for any reason whatsoever—especially not my own wedding."

"Ah, you show exquisite taste in fashion, Miss Doncaster." Madame La Fontaine's voice warmed with approval. "That dress is sadly out-of-date. No self-respecting bride would want to be caught dead in it."

There was a short silence. Amity cleared her throat.

Penny fixed Madame La Fontaine with a polite smile infused with charm and respect. "You are the most knowledgeable dressmaker I know, madam. That is why I would not patronize any other modiste. Naturally my sister will come to you for her wedding gown when the time arrives."

Madame La Fontaine beamed. "I will be delighted to design your gown and your veil, as well, Miss Doncaster."

"Yes, well, thank you," Amity said. She knew she was blushing furiously.

"Very gracious of you, madam," Penny said smoothly. "But to return to the subject of this particular wedding gown, is there anything else you can tell us about it?"

Madame La Fontaine's brows shot upward. "I can't imagine why you are interested in it. I told you, it is not at all in the current fashion."

Penny gave her a bland smile. "We found the lockets quite by accident. They appear to be rather valuable. We are trying to track down the three women in the pictures so that we can return their jewelry to them. As we do not recognize the young ladies, we thought we might start by identifying the dressmaker who created the gown they all shared."

"I see." Madame La Fontaine relaxed somewhat. Evidently any suspicions that her clients might be seeking a replacement for her services had been allayed. "Very kind of you to go to the effort. I can tell you with absolute certainty that both the dress and the veil were made by Mrs. Judkins. Calls herself Madame Dubois, but between you and me she's no more French than that streetlamp out in front of my shop."

Amity looked at Penny. "Isn't it amazing how many people attempt to pass themselves off as something other than what they are?"

"Astonishing," Penny said.

Some twenty minutes later Amity stood with Penny at the sales counter of Madame Dubois, also known as Mrs. Judkins. The dressmaker examined the three images in the lockets with an air of confusion mingled with dismay.

"Yes, I made that dress," she said. "But this is all very odd."

Her accent was somewhat more refined than Madame La Fontaine's but equally false.

"What is strange about the gown?" Amity prompted.

Madame Dubois looked up, brow wrinkled in bewilderment. "I did not make it for any of these young ladies. I suppose it's possible that they all borrowed or purchased the dress secondhand, but I can't imagine why anyone would do such a thing."

"You mean because it's out of style?" Penny asked.

"No," Madame Dubois said. She removed her reading glasses and dropped the French accent, instantly transforming into Mrs. Judkins. "It easily could have been remade in the current style. I meant I can't imagine why any young lady would want to be married in a gown that had such a tragedy attached to it. Very bad luck."

Amity knew that she and Penny were both holding their breath now.

"What is the story behind this gown?" Amity asked. "It is very important that you tell us."

"Ah." Mrs. Judkins inclined her head in a knowing way. "I see you were thinking of purchasing the dress for your own wedding."

"Well—" Amity began.

"I strongly advise against it, Miss Doncaster. No good can come of wearing that gown. The bride for whom it was made died a tragic death within weeks of her wedding. She was still on her honeymoon, as a matter of fact."

"That would have been two years ago, correct?" Penny said.

"Yes." Mrs. Judkins made a *tsk-tsk-tsk* sound with her teeth and tongue and shook her head. "So very sad."

"Who was the bride?" Amity asked, hardly daring to believe they were closing in on the answers to the questions she and the others had been asking.

"Adelaide Briar," Mrs. Judkins said. "I have the details in my files but I don't need to look them up. I remember the whole business quite clearly, not only because the bride was very lovely and the gown was so expensive but also because it was such a hurried affair. My seamstresses had to work night and day to complete the dress in time. Just between the three of us, I'm quite sure the bride was pregnant or, at the very least, concerned about the possibility, if you take my meaning."

"She had been compromised," Penny said.

"I suspect that was the situation," Mrs. Judkins said. "It's certainly not the first time I've been asked to produce a gown in a great rush. But that hurried wedding cost the young lady her life."

Amity instinctively touched the tessen blade on her chatelaine. "What happened to her?"

"I'm not certain, exactly. The papers said something about a terrible accident. The couple went to the continent for their honeymoon. They stayed at an old castle that had been turned into a very exclusive hotel. In the middle of the night she somehow fell from an upstairs window. The fall broke her neck, but in addition she must have been cut up quite badly by the broken glass. According to the accounts, there was a great deal of blood. No, Miss Doncaster, you do not want to be married in that gown."

Amity swallowed hard. "I believe you."

Penny watched Mrs. Judkins very steadily. "Do you remember the name of the groom?"

"How could I forget?" Mrs. Judkins said.

Twenty-six

H is name was Virgil Warwick," Amity said.

"Damnation." Benedict flattened his palms on Penny's desk and glared at the names on the sheet of paper in front of him. "He's not even on the guest list. No wonder we weren't getting anywhere with our inquiries."

An icy rage threatened to override his self-control. They had been chasing the wrong quarry. So much time wasted.

"We had to start somewhere," Amity said gently. "It was logical to begin with the Channing ball connection. After all, the gossip about me started the day after that event. That could not have been a coincidence."

It was as if she had read his mind, Benedict thought. And not for the first time. He straightened away from the desk.

"I know," he said. "But when I think of all the time Cornelius and Richard spent interrogating men in their clubs about suspects who have proven to be of no interest—"

"As an engineer, I'm sure you're accustomed to the necessity of having to perform any number of experiments that fail before one gets it right," Amity said.

Logan looked amused. "That's certainly how it works in my profession. We needed a starting point, one that got us into the Polite World. The guest list from the ball provided that. And by the way, do not discount the value of those interviews your brother and your uncle conducted. They helped us discard a number of suspects."

"You're correct, of course," Benedict said.

He went to stand at the window. The sensation that time was running out clawed at him. Part of him was certain that the monster was out there, somewhere, and he was stalking Amity.

"I would also point out that the fact Virgil Warwick's name is not on the list does not mean he did not hear the rumors about Amity from someone at the ball," Logan said. "That possibility still holds."

"I think that is very likely," Penny said. "But we no longer need to search for the connection between the guest who attended the ball and the killer. We have Virgil Warwick's name."

"Thanks to you, Penny—Mrs. Marsden," Logan said, hastily correcting himself. "And you, Miss Doncaster."

"It was Penny who recognized the significance of the gown," Amity said proudly. "It was a brilliant notion."

"Thank you," Penny said. She blushed. "I'm glad it worked out well."

"I don't care to contemplate what else in the way of evidence was lost or discarded before I was assigned the case," Logan said grimly.

"We still don't know for certain that Virgil Warwick is the killer," Amity said.

"No," Logan agreed. "But I must tell you, Miss Doncaster, that I have noticed a pattern over the years. Whenever a wife is found dead under mysterious circumstances, it is often the husband who is guilty." He paused before adding dryly, "And vice versa, although women tend to be more subtle about the crime. Poison is usually the weapon of choice."

Benedict turned back to face the others. He thought he saw Penny and Amity exchange glances, but they both looked away so quickly he could not be certain.

"I assume the next step is to interview Virgil Warwick?" Amity asked.

Penny put down the guest list and looked at Logan. "Will you do that, Inspector?"

"In a perfect world, yes," Logan said. "But we all know that it is unlikely that Warwick will see me, even if he happens to be innocent of any crime."

"He's not innocent," Benedict said. "I can feel it."

"Unfortunately, I cannot arrest a gentleman of his rank without something more in the way of proof," Logan said.

"He'll talk to me," Benedict said.

"Are you acquainted with him?" Logan asked, his tone sharpening.

"Not personally," Benedict said. "I don't spend much time in social circles. But I promise you, I can and will get past his front door."

Logan raised his brows but he did not say anything.

"What good will it do to speak with Warwick if you don't take me with you?" Amity asked.

"No," Benedict said automatically. "I'm not putting you within arm's reach of that bastard."

"I appreciate your concern," Amity said. "But as we all know, I am the only one who might be able to identify him. I need to hear his voice, see his hands and smell the scent of his cigarettes."

"No," Benedict said again.

Logan and Penny remained quiet. Benedict knew that he was fighting a losing battle.

"Keep in mind," Amity said, "that he does not know that I might be able to recognize him. He wore a mask. I'm sure he considers his secret safe."

Benedict closed one hand into a fist and then forced himself to relax his fingers.

"Damn it to hell," he said very, very softly.

She was right. There was no other option.

Less than an hour later, Benedict stood with Amity on the front steps of Virgil Warwick's town house. The drapes were closed on all of the windows. No one responded to a knock on the door.

"The bastard is gone," Benedict said.

The door of the neighboring house opened. The housekeeper, a middle-aged, sour-looking woman in a grimy apron peered out at them.

"Mr. Warwick ain't home," she announced. "Heard he left for Scotland nearly a month ago. Got a hunting lodge there, someone said."

"Is that so?" Amity said politely. "How did you discover that?"

"The housekeeper mentioned it. She was let go, you know. She was told that she would be notified when it was time to open up the house again. Expect she'll find a new post before he comes back, though, just like the last housekeeper did when he disappeared for months on end."

Benedict took Amity's arm. They went down the steps and walked toward the housekeeper.

"When do you expect him to return?" Benedict asked, taking some coins out of his pocket.

The housekeeper eyed the money with acute interest.

"Got no notion," she said. "Last time he went off to Scotland, he was gone some six months. Real fond of Scotland, he is. Can't imagine why."

"When did he leave on that first trip?" Benedict asked.

"About a year ago."

Amity smiled. "Did you happen to notice if he took a lot of luggage with him this time?"

"Never saw him leave, not this time or the last time, for that matter." The housekeeper snorted. "On both occasions he just went out one night and never bothered to come home."

"Thank you," Benedict said. He dropped the coins into the housekeeper's outstretched hand. "You've been very helpful."

The woman closed the door and shot the bolt.

Benedict looked at Amity. He could see the excitement in her eyes. He had a hunch there was a very similar gleam in his own expression. Neither of them spoke, however, until they were back in the cab.

"Mr. Warwick was gone for some six months the last time he disappeared to Scotland," Amity said.

"And now he has disappeared again," Benedict said. "The timing certainly fits Logan's theory that the killer was out of town between the first killing and the more recent murders."

"Do you suppose he actually is in Scotland?"

"Perhaps he went there the first time," Benedict said. "But it strikes me that a man who was badly injured would not be in any condition to undertake a long journey by train or private carriage. It seems likely he would select a closer lair in which to recuperate."

An excited Mrs. Houston opened the front door before Amity could take out her key. But one look at their faces and the housekeeper's initial anticipation transformed into a look of dismay.

"He wasn't the right man, then?" she asked.

"I think that Warwick may, indeed, be the killer," Benedict said. He followed Amity through the door. "But he's disappeared again."

"Oh, dear," Mrs. Houston said. She closed the door.

Logan and Penny were waiting in the doorway of the study.

"What do you mean, he's disappeared?" Logan asked.

Before Benedict could respond, he was interrupted by a frantic banging on the front door.

"What on earth?" Mrs. Houston opened the door again.

A young out-of-breath policeman was on the front step.

Mrs. Houston beamed. "It's you, Constable Wiggins. Nice to see you in the daylight. Did you get some sleep this morning?"

"Yes, Mrs. Houston, thank you." Wiggins looked at Logan. "I've got good news, sir. Constable Harkins found the driver."

"What driver?" Amity asked. Then her eyes widened. "Good heavens, do you mean the driver of the killer's carriage?"

"Yes, ma'am," the constable said. He grinned. "We're getting somewhere now, aren't we?"

"Maybe," Logan said. "Where is the driver?"

"According to Harkins, he spends his free time in the Green Dog. It's a tavern near the docks."

"Summon a cab, Constable," Logan ordered.

"Yes, sir."

The constable took out a whistle and hurried off toward the far end of the street.

Benedict looked at Logan. "I'm coming with you."

"Glad to have you along," Logan said.

Twenty-seven

His name was Nick Tobin. He reminded Benedict of a terrier—small, wiry and probably very fleet of foot. But he wasn't running now. He was more than pleased to talk to Benedict and Logan—for a price. He pocketed the money that Benedict placed on the table, took a long pull on his ale and told his story. It was not a long tale.

"Aye, a gennelman 'ired me to drive his carriage for him," Nick said. He wiped his mouth on the sleeve of his well-worn coat. "Said he was meeting a lady who didn't want to be seen in public with him. That's the way it is with some of them high-class whores. But I expect you gennelmen know that."

Benedict tamped down his anger. "The lady mistook the carriage for a cab."

"Well that's 'ow it was supposed to work," Nick said patiently. "I was to make it look like she was getting into a cab. How was I to know she was a lunatic?"

"What made you think she was mad?" Benedict asked.

"Cut me customer up somethin' terrible, she did." Nick shook his shaggy head. "Never saw the like. Blood all over those fine cushions. A real shame. Then she jumped out and ran off hollerin' like a mad-woman."

"What happened to your fare?" Logan asked.

"When the bint ran off the customer flew into a right panic, I can tell ye that much. He screamed at me to get him away from that street. Naturally I did what he said to do. Not like I wanted to hang about, either."

"Where did you take him?"

"As soon as we was away from the madwoman I opened the trap-door in the roof and asked him where he wanted to go next. Imagine my surprise when I saw all that blood."

"Did he instruct you to take him to his address?"

Nick appeared surprised by the question. "No, sir. He never said where he lived, sir. He ordered me to take him to an address in Crocker Lane and that's what I did. When we got there I 'ad to help him up the front steps. He pounded on the door. Bleeding all over the steps, he was. Someone opened the door. Me customer went in-side. That was the end of it."

"Not quite," Benedict said. "What about the carriage?"

"A man came out of the house and gave me some money. He said it was to pay me for my time. He said he would deal with the horse and that strange carriage. I was to take myself off and forget what had happened. And that's exactly what I did. Next thing I know, I 'eard that two gennelmen wanted to talk to me and would make it worth my while." Nick squinted at Logan. "Course, I didn't know that one of the so-called gennelman was from the Yard."

Logan gave him a cold smile. "We appreciate your cooperation."

"Always pleased to do a favor for the Yard," Nick said.

"It won't be forgotten," Logan promised.

Nick nodded, satisfied.

Benedict studied him. "You do realize that the carriage you drove that day belonged to the killer they call the Bridegroom?"

Nick stared at him, deeply offended. "No, sir, that's not possible. That was a gennelman's carriage, I tell ye. Real fine vehicle it was, even if it was odd inside. Not the kind of vehicle a crazed killer like the Bridegroom would go about in now, is it?"

"I want the address of the house in Crocker Lane," Logan said.

Nick turned wily. "Well, now, that'll cost you a bit more, sir."

Logan looked as if he was about to argue the point. Benedict shook his head ever so slightly and took out more money.

"The answer had better be correct," Benedict said.

"It's not like I'd forget a fare like that," Nick said cheerfully. He rattled off a number.

Logan narrowed his eyes. "Where were you going to take them?"

Nick's bushy brows scrunched together. "Take who, sir?"

"The gentleman and the lady who did not want to be seen getting into the carriage," Logan said evenly. "Where were you supposed to take them?"

"Can't help ye there, sir. Never did find out exactly where we was headed on account of the little whore going crazy like she did. I was supposed to get my instructions after we picked her up."

Logan and Benedict got to their feet.

"One more thing," Benedict said.

Nick looked up. "What's that, sir?"

"What was it about the carriage that struck you as odd?"

"The way it was all sealed up inside. Reminded me of one of those wagons they use to transport prisoners. The windows were covered with wooden shutters. There were even bars in the trapdoor in the roof. The door could be locked from the outside so no one could break in, I reckon."

"Or escape from the vehicle, perhaps?" Logan suggested.

"Aye, if ye locked it from the outside, the person inside would be trapped, right enough," Nick said. "Hadn't thought about that bit. My client allowed as to how he was afraid of being attacked by robbers when he traveled around London."

"He had a point," Benedict said. "The streets are dangerous."

"Aye, sir, that's the truth, it is."

Twenty-eight

Twilight and fog were descending by the time they arrived at the house in Crocker Lane. Benedict stepped down from the hansom cab. Logan followed him. They went up the front steps. The light of a nearby gas lamp made it just barely possible to read the small plaque on the front door. *Dr. J. M. Norcott, By Appointment Only.*

"Norcott is a doctor," Benedict said. "That certainly explains why Warwick ordered the driver to bring him here."

"Warwick knew the address of this house well enough to be able to summon it from memory in a moment of panic when he must have been in some fear of bleeding to death," Logan observed.

"In other words, Warwick may well have a long-standing acquaintanceship with Dr. Norcott."

"I think so, yes," Logan said.

Benedict studied the dark windows. "Doesn't look like anyone is home."

"Perhaps Norcott has been called out to treat a patient," Logan said.

He raised the knocker and clanged it with some force. They could hear the muffled echo from deep inside the front hall but no one responded.

"I suggest we try the kitchen door," Benedict said.

"I could point out that we don't have a key, let alone a warrant," Logan said, his tone perfectly neutral.

"I could point out that there are other ways to gain entry into a house. I might also mention that there is a considerable amount of fog tonight."

Logan looked thoughtful. "Excellent points, all of them. Let's try the kitchen door."

Benedict raised a hand to wave the hansom on its way. When the cab was out of sight, he followed Logan around to the rear of the house.

They went into the small garden. At the kitchen door Benedict struck a light and held it steady while Logan made short work of the lock.

The smell of death wafted out of the house the moment they opened the door. No longer concerned with the neighbors, Benedict turned up a lamp.

The body was in the front hall. A shiny length of sharpened steel gleamed in the middle of the dry blood pool.

"That must be Norcott," Benedict said.

Logan crouched beside the body and examined it with a professional eye. "I think this was done sometime yesterday. The killer used one of the doctor's own scalpels."

"It would seem that Virgil Warwick has returned from Scotland," Benedict said. "He came back to murder the one man who could testify to the nature of his wounds."

Logan got to his feet. "But why kill him now?"

Benedict glanced at the trunk on the floor near the door. Careful to avoid the dried blood, he stepped around the body and hunkered down beside it.

"Locked," he said.

Without a word Logan reached into the dead man's coat. He withdrew a key and handed it to Benedict.

Benedict opened the trunk. The hall lamps gleamed on an array of carelessly packed clothing and shaving gear.

"He was on his way out of town," Benedict said. "Running, I think. This suitcase looks like it was packed in a hurry."

"I agree." Logan fished a ticket out of the victim's front pocket. "He was scheduled to catch a train to Scotland."

Benedict circled the body again and opened a door. When he turned up the lamps inside the room, he found himself looking into a neatly organized office. There was another door in a side wall of the office. He opened that one, too, and saw an examination table and an assortment of medical instruments.

Logan went straight to the desk and opened a leather-bound volume.

"This is Norcott's appointment book," he said. "Looks like he expected to be busy all week with patients."

Benedict headed for the door. "I'll have a look around upstairs while you go through his desk."

"Right." Logan sat down in the chair and went to work in an efficient, methodical manner.

Benedict took the stairs two at a time. There was only one room that looked as if it had been recently occupied. The furniture in the others was covered with heavy dust cloths. Norcott lived alone.

He saw the letter on the bedside table as soon as he turned up a lamp. He read it quickly and then went swiftly back down the stairs. When he walked into the study, Logan was in the process of closing a drawer.

"You found something?" Logan asked.

"The killer wasn't in Scotland." Benedict held out the letter. "He was a patient at a hospital called Cresswell Manor. Two days ago he was taken away by his mother."

"Let me see that." Logan snapped the letter out of Benedict's hand and read it quickly. "Cresswell Manor is an asylum. It is common for respectable and upper-class families to send their mentally ill relatives to such institutions under false names in order to protect the privacy of the patient."

"To say nothing of the family's privacy," Benedict said. "The patient's relatives will do whatever they can to bury such a secret."

"And they will pay any price to guarantee silence." Logan held up a ledger. "According to these financial records, Dr. Norcott received a very nice commission for referring the patient known as V. Smith to Cresswell Manor."

"If the referral commission was that large, one can only imagine the size of the fees that were paid directly to the proprietor of the Manor."

"Bloody hell," Logan said softly. "I very much doubt that Virgil Warwick willingly checked himself into an asylum. Someone else in the family was no doubt responsible for paying the fees."

"We need to track down Virgil Warwick's parents," Benedict said.

"That shouldn't be too difficult now that we've got a name." Logan looked around. "I think we have done all we can here. I'll call a constable and arrange to have the body removed."

Benedict went back into the hall. He glanced once more at the body and the trunk.

"Interesting," he said.

"What?" Logan asked.

"I wonder what happened to the doctor's satchel. I can't see a man of medicine leaving it behind, even if he was trying to flee from a killer. Medical instruments and medicines are a doctor's tools, his stock-in-trade, the means by which he makes his living. They are valuable."

"We've established that Norcott was in a hurry, probably fleeing for his life."

"Yes, but if he hoped to practice medicine after leaving London, he would have taken the instruments of his profession with him," Benedict said. "I think the killer stole the doctor's medical supplies."

Logan eyed the bloodstained scalpel. "Which would include sharp blades like that one."

"And chloroform," Benedict said. "Warwick is preparing to take his next victim."

Twenty-nine

It was not hard to create a list of Virgil Warwick's close relatives," Penny said. "I checked with Mrs. Houston to confirm
my own recollections. She went to see a friend of hers who once
worked for the family. Warwick's father died a few years ago. Virgil
has no brothers or sisters. There are, I believe, some distant cousins,
but they moved to Canada. As far as we could determine, he has only
one close relation here in town. His mother."

"Warwick is the sole heir to a sizable inheritance," Amity said.
"Which explains the trappings of luxury that I noted when I was
kidnapped."

The four of them were in the study. She and Penny had been closeted there, scouring the guest list one more time in a search for answers, when Benedict and Logan had returned with the news of Dr.
Warwick's murder. One look at their grim, determined faces had
been enough to tell her that the discovery had deepened their con-

cerns. But the steel in their eyes made it clear that they were closing in on the answers.

Benedict pulled a letter out of his pocket. "According to this, Warwick was referred to Cresswell Manor—which appears to be a private asylum—for unspecified treatment a little more than three weeks ago. Warwick's records indicate that it was the second time Warwick had been admitted to the Manor."

"Let me hazard a guess," Amity said. "The first time was approximately a year ago."

"Yes," Logan said. "Immediately after the body of the first dead bride was discovered. It appears he was sent back after the attack on you, and now he has been released again."

Penny frowned. "Why would his mother take him out of the asylum again?"

"In her heart she probably knows or at least suspects that he is capable of terrible things, but she continues to hope that he can be cured by modern medical knowledge," Amity said.

"She certainly didn't allow much time for him to receive therapy on this last occasion," Penny said.

"Perhaps she has been convinced that he is not guilty of murder, after all," Amity said. "I'm sure he told her that I attacked him, not vice versa."

"And she wishes to believe that is what happened," Penny said. "She is his mother, after all."

"Regardless of her reasoning, Virgil Warwick's mother is the one who is responsible for his release and she may be the one person who knows where he is," Logan said. "I must speak with her."

Penny shook her head. "Even if she believes her son to be innocent, the last person she will speak with is a policeman."

"I will find a way," Logan vowed.

"It will be easier and no doubt faster if I do the interview," Benedict said.

Amity looked at him. "I am going to accompany you."

Benedict gave that a brief consideration. "Yes, I think that would probably be best."

Logan raised his brows. "How do the two of you plan to get past the front door? If you use your real names, she will become suspicious immediately and have her butler inform you that she is not at home."

"What made you think that I plan to use my real name?" Benedict asked.

"Speaking of names." Penny held up a sheet of paper. "It just so happens that Mrs. Charlotte Warwick is on the Channing ball guest list."

"So there was a connection," Logan said.

"That certainly explains how her deranged son came to hear the gossip about my supposed shipboard affair with Mr. Stanbridge," Amity said.

"It appears he may have gotten the news from his mother," Logan said.

Amity sighed. "I'm sure she had no notion of what he would do with the information."

❦

An hour later Amity stood on the front steps of the Warwick mansion and watched with interest as Benedict dealt with the supercilious butler.

"You may inform Mrs. Warwick that Dr. Norcott and his assistant are here to discuss a matter of utmost importance."

The butler eyed Benedict's expensive coat and trousers and then gave Amity's elegant walking gown a similar perusal. He did not appear convinced.

"Your card, Dr. Norcott?" he said.

"Sorry. All out of cards. Trust me, Mrs. Warwick will see us."

"I will find out if she is at home to callers today," the butler said. He closed the door in their faces.

"Do you think this is going to work?" Amity asked.

"I think that, under the circumstances, Mrs. Warwick will be afraid not to see Dr. Norcott. She must know that he is one of the few people who are aware that her son is likely a killer."

"But if she does refuse to see us?"

"Then we go in anyway," Benedict said.

"We could find ourselves under arrest," Amity pointed out in neutral tones.

"Mrs. Warwick is unlikely to summon the police to remove a doctor and his assistant who just happen to know her darkest secret. She would be terrified that the scandal would be all over town by morning."

"Indeed," Amity said. "Your powers of reasoning never cease to amaze me, sir."

"I'm glad to hear that because at the moment I am not at all in a reasonable mood. I want answers."

"So do I."

The door opened.

"Mrs. Warwick will see you," the butler announced. He looked as if he strongly disapproved of the decision.

Amity gave him a cool smile and stepped briskly into the spacious, elegantly appointed front hall. Benedict followed her.

The butler escorted them into the library. A woman in a dove-gray gown stood at the window, looking out into the garden. Her once-dark hair was rapidly turning the same shade as her dress. She carried herself with a rigid elegance, as if the only thing that kept her upright was a steel corset.

"Dr. Norcott and his assistant, madam," the butler said.

"Thank you, Briggs."

Charlotte Warwick did not turn around. She waited until the butler closed the door.

"Have you come here to tell me that my son's case is hopeless, Dr. Norcott?" she asked. "If so, you made an unnecessary journey. I have resigned myself to the knowledge that Virgil must spend the rest of his life at Cresswell Manor."

"In that case, why did you insist that he be released into your custody?" Amity asked.

The shock that went through Charlotte was visible. She gasped and stiffened.

Recovering, she turned quickly, her lips parted in astonishment and, perhaps, panic.

"What do you mean?" Charlotte began. She stopped. Anger refocused her expression. "Who are you?" She glared at Benedict. "You are not Dr. Norcott."

"Benedict Stanbridge, madam," Benedict said. "My fiancée, Miss Doncaster. You may have heard of her. She is the woman who was recently kidnapped by your son."

"I have no idea what you are talking about. How dare you lie to get into this house?"

Charlotte reached for the velvet bell pull.

"I'd advise you not to summon your butler, madam," Benedict

said. "Not unless you want to be responsible for leaving Virgil free to commit more murders."

"I don't know what you mean," Charlotte said. She sounded as if she was having trouble breathing. "Get out of here."

"We will leave as soon as you tell us where your son is hiding," Benedict said. "If he is truly insane, he will not hang. He will be sent back to the asylum. We all know that you have the money it takes to ensure such an outcome."

Charlotte collected herself. She went to stand behind her desk, gripping the back of the chair with clenched hands.

"It is none of your business, but let me be perfectly clear," she said evenly. "My son is currently taking a cure for a disorder of the nervous system. His health is a private matter. I do not intend to discuss it, certainly not with you."

"Your son has murdered at least four women that we know of and very probably his wife, as well," Benedict said. "Three weeks ago he kidnapped my fiancée with the intention of murdering her, too."

"No," Charlotte insisted. "No, that's not true. His nerves are far too delicate. He would never do something so violent."

"What do you mean by delicate?" Amity asked.

"He cannot stand any great strain or pressure. It takes very little to agitate him. I have always handled the details of life for him, his finances, his social engagements, his household staff."

"Your son enjoys the hobby of photography, doesn't he?" Benedict said, unrelenting.

Charlotte hesitated. "My son possesses an artistic temperament. That explains his delicate nerves and his moods. He found his métier in photography. How did you know that? Not that it matters. It is a common enough hobby."

"The day he tried to seize me I fought back," Amity said. "He was badly injured."

"He told me that he was attacked by a common whore," Charlotte whispered. "It was an argument about money. He may have over-reacted."

Benedict tensed and started to move forward. Never taking her eyes off Charlotte, Amity put her hand on his arm. He stopped but she could feel the fierce energy roiling inside him.

Charlotte never noticed the byplay. She concentrated on the story she was telling. Amity knew that she was desperately trying to convince herself.

"He agreed to the . . . encounter," Charlotte said, her voice very tight. "But there was a dispute over the fee. The whore went into a rage and attacked him."

"I think you and I both know that is not what happened," Amity said quietly. "Virgil kidnapped me. I barely managed to escape. Yes, I did defend myself with a blade. He was bleeding badly when I left him behind in the carriage. He sought the help of the only doctor he knew, the one he could be certain would keep his secret. Dr. Norcott treated his injuries and then summoned you."

Charlotte sank into the chair, appalled. "You know that much?"

"We found Norcott's body earlier today," Benedict said. "His throat had been sliced open with one of his own scalpels. Just like the throats of the victims of the Bridegroom. We suspect that Virgil's wife died in a similar manner, although the exact nature of her injuries was masked by the fact that he threw her out a window."

Charlotte shook her head. "No, it was an accident."

"Norcott is dead." Benedict said. "Now Virgil has evidently gone into hiding—with Norcott's medical kit, I might add."

Charlotte composed herself. "It can't have been Virgil. Don't you understand? He is currently in a special clinic."

"He is no longer at Cresswell Manor," Amity said. "Two days ago he was released into the custody of his mother."

Charlotte seemed to sink in on herself. She closed her eyes. "Dear heaven."

"You know what he is," Benedict said. "That is why you committed him to Cresswell Manor not once, but twice. Why did you take him out of that place this last time?"

A heavy silence descended. Amity wondered if Charlotte would ever respond. But eventually she stirred and looked at them with haunted eyes. A strange grayness enveloped her, as if life was slowly seeping away.

"It was the witch," she said. "It must have been her. Why she took him away from Cresswell Manor, I cannot say. You must ask her."

Amity exchanged glances with Benedict.

"Who is the witch?" Amity asked carefully.

For a moment it seemed that Charlotte would disappear into the grayness that surrounded her. But eventually she pulled herself together.

"Shortly after my husband died I discovered that for years he had been paying blackmail to a woman who operated an orphanage for girls," Charlotte said. "She contacted me and made it clear that if I did not continue to pay she would see to it that certain matters were made public in the press."

"What orphanage?" Benedict asked.

"Hawthorne Hall," Charlotte said. "It is located in a village outside of London, about an hour away by train. At least that is the address I was given when I took over the blackmail payments. The Hall no longer serves as an orphanage, but the former director continues to live there."

"What are the matters that you paid her to keep quiet?" Benedict asked.

"My husband fathered a child by another woman."

Amity took a few steps closer to the desk. "Forgive me, Mrs. Warwick, but we all know that it is not rare for men of wealth and rank to father children outside marriage. Such situations are understandably embarrassing but hardly shocking. Most women in your position would turn a blind eye to the matter. Why would you pay blackmail to conceal the fact that your husband produced an out-of-wedlock child?"

Charlotte turned her gaze to the view of the garden, but Amity was quite certain she was looking into the past.

"The witch claimed that she had noticed evidence of mental instability in my husband's daughter. She suggested that perhaps my son was also unhinged."

"I see," Amity said. "She threatened to take her theories about Virgil's mental health to the press."

"I may be deranged as well," Charlotte said quietly. "Because I have spent a great deal of time imagining ways of murdering Mrs. Dunning."

"I assume that she is the former director of the orphanage," Amity said.

"Yes," Charlotte said. "She is the one who is blackmailing me."

"What stopped you?" Benedict asked.

Charlotte turned back to him. "At the start Dunning made it clear that if anything happened to her, she had made arrangements for letters suggesting insanity in the Warwick bloodline to be sent to the press. But a year ago it got worse. She let me know that those letters would contain evidence that my son had murdered his wife and a young lady, as well. She intended to announce to the world that Virgil was the Bridegroom."

Benedict looked thoughtful. "Is your son aware that Dunning has been blackmailing you?"

"No, of course not," Charlotte said. "I never wanted him to know that he has a half sister, you see."

A stark silence gripped the room. Amity looked at Benedict.

"We must go to Hawthorne Hall," she said.

"Yes."

Charlotte stared at them. "My son—"

"If you have any notion of where he may be hiding, you must tell us," Benedict said.

"I swear to you, I don't know. I believed him to be at Cresswell Manor." Charlotte looked genuinely bewildered. "Mrs. Dunning claims to be well aware of my son's nervous affliction. I was paying the blackmail. Why would she set him free?"

Thirty

M rs. Warwick asked an excellent question," Benedict said. He surveyed the high wrought-iron gates of Hawthorne Hall with a sense of grim certainty. There were answers to be found here, he thought. "Why would the director of the orphanage take Warwick out of Cresswell Manor?"

He and Amity had set out for the Hall soon after ending the interview with Charlotte Warwick. He had allowed only a brief stop at Exton Street so that Amity could collect her cloak and a few necessities for the train trip. There had been no time for a visit to Logan. Penny had promised to convey the information they had gained to the inspector as soon as possible.

The village where the Hall was located was, indeed, an hour from London by train, just as Charlotte Warwick had said. The cab trip from the station to the old orphanage, however, took another forty minutes over bad roads.

Hawthorne Hall proved to be an aged mansion that was slowly crumbling into the ground. It loomed, dark and isolated, at the end of a long lane.

Benedict glanced back over his shoulder. He had paid the cab to wait. The horse and driver were only a short distance away, but they were slowly being swallowed up by the fog that had set in with on-coming night.

"We won't know why Dunning removed Warwick from Cresswell Manor until we ask her," Amity said.

He contemplated the gates. "You make a very logical point."

The gates were unlocked—probably because there was little to protect, Benedict concluded. In a few spots the grounds were over-grown with weeds, but for the most part there was nothing left of the gardens except bare earth.

The last of the orphans had been removed years ago, according to the cab driver. He had explained that Mrs. Dunning was the only current occupant of the house. There was no permanent staff. A woman from the village went in twice a week to clean. She had told everyone that Mrs. Dunning lived on the ground floor. The upper floors had all been closed, the furniture draped in dust cloths. Mrs. Dunning went into the village to shop occasionally and some-times took the train to London, where she stayed for a week at a time. But aside from those meager facts, she was a mystery to the locals.

Benedict pushed open one wing of the iron gates. It moved pon-derously and with a great deal of groaning.

He took Amity's arm. Together they walked toward the front steps of the old hall. The paving stones were cracked and chipped. The windows of the upper floors were dark, but weak lamplight leaked out from around the edges of the curtains on the ground floor.

At the top of the steps Benedict clanged the knocker. The sound echoed inside the house, but there was no immediate response.

"Someone is home," Amity observed. "The lamps have been turned up."

Benedict banged the knocker louder than before, but again no one came to the door.

"She is in there and we are not leaving until we have spoken with her," he said. "Perhaps she cannot hear our knock. Let's try the back door."

"What good will that do?" Amity asked. "If she doesn't want to see us, she won't answer it, either."

"You never know," Benedict said.

He kept his tone deliberately casual but he saw understanding in her eyes. She knew exactly what he intended to do.

"Oh," she said. She lowered her voice still further. "I see. You do realize that entering a house without permission is quite illegal."

"That is why we are going around to the rear of the house where the driver of the cab cannot see us."

Amity smiled. "You always have a plan, don't you?"

"I try to formulate one whenever I can."

"I expect it's the engineer in you."

She did not sound put off by that fact, he concluded. She merely accepted it as a part of who he was.

She followed him down the steps and around the side of the big house. A high wall enclosed the gardens at the rear, but the gate was unlocked. Inside the walls they found another mostly barren stretch of ground.

Benedict rapped sharply on the kitchen door. This time when he got no response he tried the knob. It was unlocked. A chill of knowing went through him.

"Just like this morning," he said, more to himself than to Amity.

She gave him a quick, searching glance. "You mean when you found Dr. Norcott's body?"

"Yes." Benedict took the pistol out of his pocket.

Amity breathed out slowly, as if fortifying herself. Then she reached beneath her cloak and unhooked the tessen from the chatelaine. She held the fan-shaped blade in the closed position in her gloved hand.

Benedict considered ordering her to remain outside, but then concluded that she was no safer there than she was with him. Together they could protect each other if it transpired that Warwick was waiting for them inside the house.

He used the toe of his boot to prod the door open. A dimly lit hallway loomed in front of them. When no madman with a scalpel leaped out of the shadows, he moved into the gloom. Amity followed.

The house reverberated with emptiness. A single ray of lamplight slanted out of a room halfway along the hall.

"Watch the rooms on the left side of the hall," he said. "I will keep an eye on the right."

"Yes," she said.

They made their way toward the wedge of light, passing the kitchen, a morning room, a pantry and a closet. All the doors were open except the one on the closet. Benedict tried the knob. It turned easily enough. The shelves inside were stacked with linens and cleaning supplies.

They continued down the long hall. The unmistakable smell of death drifted out of the lamp-lit room.

"Dear heaven," Amity whispered.

Benedict stopped in the doorway and swept the space with a single glance. The body of a middle-aged woman dressed in a dark gown lay on the floor near a desk. As was the case with Warwick, there was a great deal of blood. Most of it had soaked into the carpet and appeared to be dry.

"So much for Charlotte Warwick's assumption that her son did not know about Mrs. Dunning," Benedict said. "The bastard does like the scalpel. He cut her throat."

"He killed her the same way he murdered his other victims."

"Stay here. I want to make sure there are no surprises in the front hall."

He checked the last room on the floor, a sparsely furnished library. The few leather-bound volumes on the shelves were covered in dust. He went quickly back to where Amity waited, her fan at the ready.

"What is going on?" she asked. "Why is Warwick murdering these people?"

"It's probably unwise to speculate on the motives of a madman, but I have a feeling that he is killing those who know his secret."

"But why now? And why these two? Dr. Norcott very likely saved Warwick's life the day that I cut him with the tessen. And evidently Mrs. Dunning was the one who got him out of Cresswell Manor."

"Perhaps he doesn't think he needs them anymore," Benedict said. "He believes they had become liabilities because they knew the truth about him."

Comprehension widened Amity's eyes. "And because he knows we are hunting him. He realized that sooner or later we would likely track down both Norcott and Dunning."

"We must return to London immediately and inform Inspector Logan of what we discovered."

"What about the body? We cannot simply leave it here."

"Yes," Benedict said. "We can and we will."

Amity reattached her tessen to the chain at her waist and studied the desk with a speculative expression.

"Mrs. Dunning is a rather interesting piece of this puzzle," she said. "It might be useful to take a quick look through the drawers of her desk."

"Odd you should mention that," Benedict said. "I was just thinking the same thing."

He took two steps before he felt the slightly raised object under the carpet. At the same time he heard a faint, muffled click. A small spark flashed underneath the desk.

"Run," he snapped. "Back door. It's the closest. Move, woman."

Amity whirled, grasped handfuls of her skirts and cloak and fled down the hall. He followed.

Amity stumbled, swore, regained her balance and kept going. But she was not moving fast enough. He realized it was the weight of her gown and the cloak that was slowing her down. The heavy folds threatened to trip her. He seized her arm and half dragged, half carried her down the hall and out through the back door.

They burst outside into the dead gardens seconds before the explosion erupted in Dunning's study.

Within moments the house was consumed in flames. Dark smoke billowed into the air.

Benedict took Amity's arm and steered her back through the iron gates. Once they were safely outside the grounds he drew Amity to a stop. They both turned to watch the house burn.

"He set a trap," Benedict said. "Well, now, isn't that interesting?"

Thirty-one

Amity listened to the frantically galloping hooves of a terrified horse bolting down the long lane.

"So much for our cab," she said.

She could not take her eyes off the burning mansion. Her pulse was pounding harder than it had the day she and her guide had rounded a corner on a Colorado mountain trail and found themselves confronting a bear. The extraordinary spectacle of the blazing ruins and the knowledge that she and Benedict had very nearly died in the explosion riveted her senses.

"He intended us to die in that house," Benedict said.

"The driver will no doubt assume that we were killed in the explosion," she said.

"Yes," Benedict said. "I believe he will."

She got the impression that he was doing some intricate calculations in his head. She took her attention off the inferno long enough to glance at him.

"You have another plan in mind, don't you?" she said.

"Perhaps."

She turned back to the view of the fire. The flames roared, consuming the interior of the mansion. Even though she and Benedict were some distance away she could feel the waves of heat. The stone walls would stand, she thought. But by morning Hawthorne Hall would be a burned-out hulk.

"Do you think this fire will ignite the woods?" she asked.

"Doubtful," Benedict said. "There is little to burn in the immediate vicinity of the house and it has been a damp summer. In any event, there is another storm coming. The rain will suppress the blaze." He studied the dark clouds. "We need to find shelter soon."

"Surely the driver will summon help."

"He will no doubt carry the tale back to the village, but there is no way the local fire brigade can defeat a house fire of this size. A few curiosity seekers may show up this evening, but even that is unlikely."

"Like the driver, everyone in the village will assume that we are dead."

"Yes," Benedict said. "And that may prove quite useful."

"I detect the engineer at work again."

"We may have something of a grace period tonight, a time to think about what we have learned. I have been overlooking an important piece of the puzzle, Amity. I can feel it."

"Isn't it possible that the killer was watching the house and saw us flee into the woods?"

"Certainly, but I'm inclined to doubt that he is anywhere nearby. The village is small. This isn't London. Around here everyone would remember a stranger who arrived at the railway station, inquired about directions to Hawthorne Hall and then failed to take the train back to London until after the explosion."

"I see what you mean," she said. "In order to remain as anonymous as possible, he would have wanted to be seen leaving the village long before the explosion occurred. But you are assuming he came and went by train. What if he hired a carriage?"

"Again, that is a possibility," Benedict conceded. "But it is a very long trip from London by carriage. No, I suspect that he took the train, just as we did, and that he returned to the city hours ago. At the moment he is no doubt anticipating news of the explosion at Hawthorne Hall and the deaths of three people in tomorrow's papers."

A chill swept through Amity. "Dear heaven, the press reports. Yes, of course. My sister will surely see the accounts and believe that we are dead. We must get word to her."

"We will do so first thing in the morning," Benedict promised. "There is no hiking back to the village tonight, not with that storm about to break over our heads."

"But Penny will be worried when we do not return on the midnight train."

"There is no help for it, Amity," Benedict said gently. "She is accustomed to losing track of you from time to time due to the vagaries of your travels. She will not panic."

"I hope not." Amity paused. "She is aware that I am with you. That will no doubt reassure her."

"Come, we must find some shelter."

He started around the side of the burning house. Amity collected the folds of her cloak and fell into step beside him.

"As you pointed out, the nearest farm is some distance from here," she said.

"We won't be able to get that far before the rain comes. We will have to content ourselves with that cottage we saw at the far end of the lane."

"That should do nicely," Amity said. "I've certainly stayed in far more uncomfortable accommodations."

She tried not to think about the obvious but it was impossible to ignore. She would be spending the night alone with Benedict.

"It won't be the first time," Benedict said. "You spent three nights on the *Northern Star* in the same cabin with me if you will recall."

She smiled. "There are occasions, Mr. Stanbridge, when I wonder if you can actually read my mind."

"From time to time I have wondered if you can read mine. But as neither of us claims to be psychic, I think we must look to another explanation for these occasional flashes of mutual intuition."

"And what would that explanation be, sir?"

To her surprise, he hesitated, as if searching for the right words.

"I think that we know each other perhaps better than we realize," he said finally. "I expect that lurching from crisis to crisis together as we have been obliged to do lately has that effect on two people. We know what to expect from each other in a pinch."

"That is very insightful of you," Amity said.

"You are surprised?" He smiled faintly. "I may not possess Declan Garraway's knowledge of psychology, and as I have noted, I'm not a fan of poetry, but I can usually add two plus two and arrive at four."

"Something to be said for a sound foundation in mathematics."

"I like to think so."

"What made you realize that Hawthorne Hall was about to go up in flames?" Amity asked.

"I knew there was a problem as soon as I stepped on the trigger mechanism hidden under the carpet and saw the spark. I admit that I leaped to the conclusion that the spark might ignite a fuse, but it seemed prudent to act on the assumption."

"In hindsight, it was a positively brilliant assumption, Mr. Stanbridge."

❧❧❧

The cottage at the end of the lane was empty, but it was in better shape than Amity had expected. There were no signs that rodents or other forms of wildlife had taken up residence on the premises. The well pump functioned and there was a shed that contained a supply of firewood.

The storm arrived with a crack of lightning and a rumble of thunder just as Benedict came through the door with the last of several logs. Amity closed the door behind him, shutting out the blast of rain.

"I think that the owner of this place probably rents it out at least occasionally," she observed. "Everything is in reasonably good condition, including the bed."

She winced as soon as the word *bed* left her lips. That particular item of furniture stood in the corner, but it seemed to dominate the small space.

Mercifully, Benedict politely chose to ignore both the comment and the bed.

"We will go hungry tonight," he said. "But at least we will have water to drink and we'll be warm. I'll get a fire started."

Amity smiled, feeling decidedly smug. "We won't go hungry."

He was on one knee in front of the fireplace, preparing to strike a light to ignite the kindling that he had brought in from the shed. He paused, looking at her with great interest.

"You found something to eat?" he asked.

"I brought something to eat." She went to where her cloak hung on a peg near the door and opened the folds to display the many pockets sewn inside. With a flourish, she took out two small water-proof pouches. "I long ago learned that one should never set out on a journey without at least some biscuits and tea. One never knows what awaits at the other end."

Benedict's eyes gleamed appreciatively when she opened one of the pouches and removed a small packet wrapped in paper.

"I do admire a lady who is always prepared," he said.

She found a kettle and used it to boil water from the well. When she opened a cupboard, she discovered a pot, some mugs and a few chipped plates. She smiled.

"It is as if we were expected," she said.

Benedict watched her with a bemused expression.

"I am acquainted with a number of people—male as well as female—who would long since have begun complaining about the poor quality of the accommodations," he said.

"When one travels as much as I have, one learns that the definition of poor-quality accommodations is subject to considerable flexibility depending on the circumstances," Amity said.

Benedict glanced at the cloak. "Between the items you carry on your chatelaine and the number of pockets in your cloak it is no surprise that you occasionally clank when you walk."

She cleared her throat. "You think that I clank?"

He nodded appreciatively. "I think that you are the kind of woman who is able to cope with unforeseen circumstances."

She smiled and reminded herself that he did not read poetry.

When she had the small repast ready, they sat down at the table in front of the fire to dine on biscuits and tea.

They ate in a companionable silence and contemplated the cheerful blaze on the hearth. Outside, the bluster of the storm turned to a gentle, steady rain.

When they finished, Benedict helped rinse the mugs and plates.

And then they were left with the issue of the single bed in the corner of the room. Amity determined to take a brisk, no-nonsense lead. She was, after all, the kind of woman who could cope with unforeseen circumstances.

"It will be just like camping out in the West," she said. "Except that we will not have to sleep on cold, hard ground and there will be no need to fret about wolves and bears."

"Just a human predator who kills with a scalpel," Benedict said.

Amity looked at him. In the firelight his face was hard and grim.

"Have you changed your theory about the present whereabouts of the killer?" she asked. "Do you think he is out there somewhere in the storm, watching us?"

Benedict looked into the fire for a moment and then shook his head. "No. I think he is being careful now. He got rid of the two people who knew his secret and who might conceivably go to the police. He will have returned to his lair for the time being. In any event this cottage is reasonably secure. The windows are too small for a man to crawl through and he cannot break down the door without an axe. That is not his style."

"He might use an explosive device such as the one he left behind at Hawthorne Hall."

"No." Benedict sounded more certain now. "That sort of trap requires time, planning, access and—above all—the right materials. It is highly unlikely he traveled all this way prepared to set two explosive devices. In any event, he could not possibly know that we would escape the first explosion and seek shelter here."

She watched Benedict for a moment.

"What is it that worries you so much tonight?" she asked. "Beyond the obvious fact that we are hunting a killer, of course."

He took his attention off the fire and met her eyes. "Damned if I know. But there is something about this affair that I am not seeing."

"It will come to you in time," she assured him.

"I fear that time is the one thing that we do not have in great measure."

"We have tonight," she said.

Benedict smiled. It was a wry smile but a real one.

"Yes," he said. "We have tonight."

He gazed at her as if he was in some sort of trance. She understood that he was waiting for a response from her, but she was not sure what to say. When she just looked at him, mute, he stirred and pulled himself out of the stillness.

"I got the bed the last time we spent a night together," he said.

"The bunk in your stateroom, do you mean?"

"Yes. It is only fair that you get the bed tonight. I'll sleep in front of the fire."

A sinking feeling came over her.

Well, it had been a rather long and difficult day, she reminded herself. What else could one expect except a sinking feeling?

Thirty-two

Soft, rustling sounds and the scrape of wood on wood brought her out of a fitful sleep. She opened her eyes and watched Benedict add another log to the low-burning fire. He had removed his boots, coat and tie before wrapping himself in the quilt and stretching out on the floor. She could not help but notice that at some point after she had settled down on the lumpy mattress, he had also taken off his shirt. The garment hung over the back of a chair.

She held herself very still, pretending to be asleep, and contemplated Benedict with a sense of wonder and deep, feminine pleasure. The flames illuminated the lean, sleekly muscled lines of his body. His shoulders were broad and strong. He handled the firewood with easy competence and an economy of motion that was at once graceful and masculine. She remembered the feel of his hands on her skin. A rush of longing swept through her. She yearned for him to touch her again.

At that moment he turned toward her. Firelight revealed the scar just below his rib cage. The wound had healed but he was marked for life.

"You're awake, aren't you?" he asked.

"Yes," she said.

"Sorry. Didn't mean to disturb you. Just putting another log on the fire."

She sat up slowly. Earlier she had removed her cumbersome petticoats and unfastened several of the hooks at the throat of her traveling gown. But even though she was not wearing a corset, the stiffened bodice of the dress did not allow for any degree of genuine comfort or relaxation.

"It doesn't matter," she said. "I wasn't getting much sleep. I keep seeing Mrs. Dunning's body and hearing that click that we heard just before the fuse on the explosive ignited."

"What a coincidence. I'm having the same visions, except mine include the sight of you struggling to run in that cumbersome gown and cloak you wore today."

She made a face. "I can only be grateful that as a member of the Rational Dress Society, I don't wear a corset and I limit my underclothing to no more than seven pounds."

"Good lord. Seven pounds of undergarments?"

She shrugged. "A lady dressed in the first stare of fashion can find herself wearing over thirty pounds of clothing. Fabric is heavy when it is gathered into a great many drapes and pleats. To say nothing of boots and cloaks."

He smiled. "You don't dress like that when you travel abroad."

"No. Only when I am home in London."

She could see the stark hunger in his eyes. Like some psychic power it elicited a response deep within her. There was a palpable tension in the atmosphere between them. Her pulse beat a little faster. She knew he would not make the first move, not unless she let him know that she would welcome it.

She got to her feet. The skirts of her dress, no longer reinforced with the petticoats, collapsed around her legs.

"You saved us today, Benedict," she said. "If you had not understood what that click meant when you stepped on the carpet . . ."

"I've spent years designing and experimenting with various types of mechanical devices. I know the click of a switch when I hear it."

"Yes." She took a few steps toward him and then stopped, uncertain how to proceed. "Definitely something to be said for your knowledge of engineering and . . . other matters, as well."

He frowned. "You refer to mathematics?"

His genuine bewilderment gave her some confidence. She took a steadying breath and went to stand directly in front of him. She was aware of the warmth of the fire and another kind of heat, as well.

"Not mathematics," she said. She drew her fingertip along the hard edge of his jaw. "I was referring to your expertise in the art of kissing."

He raised his hands slowly and cupped her face between his rough palms. "If I am any good at kissing you it is because it comes naturally to me, as naturally as breathing. There is nothing I want to do more at this moment."

She caught her breath. "There is nothing I want more at this moment than to be kissed by you."

"Are you certain?" His voice was ragged now.

She flattened her palms on the fire-warmed skin of his chest and thought about the nights when she had touched him to see if he was feverish. She had been so worried those first few days on the ship. There were certainly other things to concern her now, but she did not want to think about them until morning. She remembered the question that had been in his eyes earlier when she had gone to the room's only bed and he had spread the quilt on the floor. She had not known how to answer him then. But now she did.

"We have tonight," she said.

She stood on tiptoe and brushed her mouth against his.

And that was all the answer he needed.

He pulled her to him and took her mouth with a fierce tenderness that thrilled her senses. She gripped his shoulders and hung on for dear life.

He deepened the kiss until she was breathless; until she could not think about anything else except the deep, aching urgency that was building inside her.

He unhooked the rest of the fastenings on the bodice of her gown. The dress fell away, pooling at her feet. She was left in her stockings, drawers and chemise.

"At least tonight we have a bed," he said against her throat. "Not a pile of straw."

"Yes." She sank her nails into the muscles of his broad shoulders. "Yes."

He lifted her, cradling her in his arms, and carried her the short distance to the bed. He set her down on top of the blanket and straightened long enough to strip off his trousers and drawers.

The rigid length of his erection fascinated her even as it made her wary. She remembered how uncomfortable it had been to take him inside her that first time in the stable. She reassured herself that it would be easier this time.

"We will go slowly tonight," he promised.

He put one knee on the bed, testing to make sure it would take his weight. Her nerves were in such a jangled state that she actually giggled.

"The bed seems sturdy enough," she said. "I don't think you will send us crashing to the floor."

He smiled in the shadows. "I hope you are right."

Cautiously he lowered himself along the length of her, cloaking her in the heat of his body. He braced himself on his elbows to keep from crushing her into the mattress and bent his head to kiss her.

Everything inside her quickened. She gave herself up to the embrace. The sense of urgency coiled and tightened into a demanding ache. Impulsively she lifted her hips against the rigid thrust of Benedict's erection.

He wrenched his mouth away from hers and kissed her throat.

"I love the smell of you," he whispered.

She gripped his shoulders. He caught hold of the hem of her chemise and pushed the garment up to her waist. He slipped one hand inside the open center seam of her drawers and found the part of her that was melting.

"So warm," he said. "And so ready." He kissed her breast through the fabric of the chemise. "For me."

"Yes," she managed, her throat constricting with the sheer, overwhelming force of the whirlwind threatening to sweep her away. "For you."

He kissed her mouth again—not in a sensual manner this time but rather as if sealing a solemn vow. She was still struggling to comprehend the meaning of the kiss when he eased two fingers inside her.

She flinched, but not from pain. Instinctively she tightened herself around his gently probing fingers. She was so sensitive now that every touch sent little shocks through her.

Benedict stilled and raised his head. "Did I hurt you?"

"No." She pulled him back to her. "No, please. Whatever you do, don't stop."

"I have to stop."

"Why?"

"Because your sister warned me that if I got you pregnant she would have my head on a platter."

"*What?* Penny said that? I don't believe it."

"Those may not have been her exact words, but as I recall it was something along those lines. The point was to make certain that I used a condom." He paused. "But given your lack of experience, you may not understand what I am talking about."

"I may lack experience, but I do not lack medical knowledge," she said primly. "My father explained the use of condoms to me."

"Of course he did." Benedict sounded torn between amusement and chagrin. "I don't suppose you carry a spare in one of the pockets of your cloak?"

She flushed. "Now you are teasing me."

"Yes, I am." He shifted his weight. "Hold on. I'll be right back."

He got up off the bed and went to where his overcoat hung on the wall. She levered herself up on one elbow to see what he was doing. In the firelight she watched him take a small leather case out of one pocket.

"Do you mean to say that you brought one with you?" she asked, dumbfounded. "On a journey to investigate a murder?"

He froze, evidently uncertain of the correct answer.

"Ah," he said. He stopped and then came to a decision. "I have been carrying it everywhere since I bought it."

"That would have been when, precisely?"

"Shortly after your sister gave me the lecture."

"Good heavens." She realized that she was not sure what to say. After a moment's reflection, she smiled slowly. "It would appear that I am not the only one who travels prepared for any eventuality."

He laughed—a husky rumble that was clearly fueled by relief—and came back to the bed. He opened the leather case and took out the condom. Amity watched, fascinated, as he sheathed himself in the little sack.

He leaned down to kiss her.

"This time you will enjoy the experience, I promise," he said against her mouth.

"I believe you."

He did not enter her immediately. Instead, he stroked her until she was once again throbbing and desperate. He found the exquisitely sensitive place just inside her and the nubbin at the top of her sex. He focused his attentions on those regions until she could not think of anything else.

When her release pulsed through her, she gasped, cried out and gripped Benedict's shoulders tightly.

He pushed into her slowly, deliberately, riding the hot currents of her climax. There was no pain this time but the too-full, too-tight sensation set off another series of rippling little pulses. She was utterly breathless now.

She heard his hoarse groan. His back was a solid wall of muscle beneath her hands.

He reached down between their bodies. She realized that he was using one hand to secure the condom while he thrust into her. At the last possible instant he pulled out of her. She held him close while he spent himself into the condom.

He shuddered and collapsed beside her.

Thirty-three

A long time later Benedict stirred and sat up on the side of
the cot. He removed the condom and dropped it into the
chamber pot under the bed. The things were so expensive
many men rinsed them out and reused them. Fortunately, he could
afford the luxury of a fresh device each time one was required.

He looked at Amity. In the fading light of the fire, she looked soft
and warm and delicious. He realized he was getting hard again. He
reminded himself that he had just discarded the only condom he had
brought with him.

"You did not use the device as it was intended," she said. "Even
though you wore it you still pulled away at the last moment, just as
you did the first time in the barn."

"Neither the skin nor the rubber version are entirely reliable," he
said. He leaned down and kissed her. "It's best to take extra precautions."

She stretched like a cat. "Always planning for disaster."

"I have been told that I am rather boring," he said before he could give himself time to think about the wisdom of bringing up the subject.

She blinked, startled. Then she laughed. "That's absolutely ridiculous. Since I met you my life has been anything but dull. Indeed, it seems to me that we have gone from one adventure to another with very little time to relax in between."

"Yes, but that is because things have been quite extraordinary lately. Under ordinary conditions, life might prove quite monotonous with a man of my temperament."

She smiled a slow, provocative smile. "I sincerely doubt that. However, should boredom ever threaten, we can always resort to the sort of experiment that we just carried out a short time ago."

The tension inside him eased.

"I believe you likened the first experience to the sensation of riding a camel," he said.

"It was much better this time," she said. "Rather like riding a wild stallion into a storm. Somewhat dangerous, perhaps, but that is no doubt part of the lure. It was all quite exhilarating."

For a moment he allowed himself to simply enjoy the sight of her in the firelight. She almost glowed, he decided. No, he was quite certain that she actually did glow. There was a luminous quality about her that riveted his senses.

"Rest assured that I stand ready to relieve any tedium in your life with such methods at any time, Miss Doncaster," he said.

"Very kind of you to offer, sir."

He got to his feet, pulled on his drawers and crossed the room to throw another log on the fire.

When the flames leaped high again he turned back toward the bed. Amity watched him, waiting for him. A rush of satisfaction crashed through him. *She was waiting for him.*

And just like that, the missing piece of the puzzle fell into place.

He stopped in the center of the room.

"It's all connected," he said.

Amity sat up slowly on the edge of the bed. "What are you talking about?"

"Everything. We've been dealing with Virgil Warwick's attack on you as if it were a separate issue from the theft of Foxcroft's notebook. But there is a link between them. There must be."

"Why do you say that?"

"The explosion at Hawthorne Hall." He crossed the room to where his coat hung on the peg. He took his small notebook out of the pocket and flipped it open. "Don't you see? It clarifies a number of things."

"Such as?"

"Such as the fact that Virgil Warwick most likely did not murder Mrs. Dunning."

Thirty-four

"Explain," Amity said.

Benedict's cool, controlled energy was contagious. A moment ago she had been drowsy and more than ready to slip into sleep. But now she was wide awake and very curious.

She got up from the bed and tugged the blanket around her shoulders. She could feel the chill of the floorboards through her stockings but she ignored the sensation.

"Whoever set that trap for us today is skilled in the rather arcane art of explosive devices," Benedict said. He sat down at the table and opened the small notebook. "Do you remember what Charlotte Warwick said about her son's personal inclinations?"

"She described him as having an artistic temperament and said that he had seemed to find his métier in photography."

"Precisely. She gave us no indication that he was ever interested in engineering or scientific matters. It is highly unlikely that he would know how to construct a complicated mechanism for an explosive device, let alone put it together at the scene of the murder without blowing himself up in the process."

"But Mrs. Dunning's throat was cut with a sharp blade. She died just like Dr. Norcott and those poor brides."

"Everyone who has been following the news of the crimes in the press—that would be most of London—knows how the killer committed the murders. It would be no great trick to duplicate the technique."

Amity shuddered. "Assuming one didn't mind the blood."

"Assuming that," Benedict said. He returned to his notes.

Amity watched him.

"Do you think someone other than Virgil Warwick murdered Dr. Norcott as well?" she asked after a moment or two.

"No. I can't be certain, but that murder has some twisted logic behind it."

"Yes, I know. You said that it made sense that Warwick got rid of the one man who knew how dangerous he was. He was afraid that Norcott might go to the police."

"Right. But the killer also took Norcott's medical satchel. That feels like something Virgil would do. However, even if he did know about his half sister and the fact that Mrs. Dunning was blackmailing his mother, it is very difficult to believe that he learned how to wire that explosive device and set it to go off when someone stepped on the carpet. That requires training and experience."

"But who else would want to murder Mrs. Dunning?" Amity asked.

Benedict put down the pencil and sat back in his chair. The flames were reflected in his eyes. "The same person who tried to murder me on St. Clare and then arranged to make you the target of a crazed killer. When those plans failed, that individual went to Hawthorne Hall and murdered Mrs. Dunning because she knew too much about the Warwicks' personal history."

Amity tightened her grip on the quilt. "You're saying Virgil Warwick is involved with the plot to steal Foxcroft's notebook? But he seems far too unstable to be a successful spy."

"I agree," Benedict said patiently. "And I don't think that he is the spy. But I believe that he is somehow connected to the person who took the Foxcroft notebook."

"The person who tried to murder you on St. Clare."

"Yes. That person knew Virgil Warwick well enough to try to use him the way one would a weapon. She aimed him at you but things did not go as planned."

"She?"

"I think we are looking for a woman, after all."

"Dear heaven." Amity tried to stitch the pieces together in her head. "If you're right when you say that she deliberately set Warwick on me, that means she knows what kind of monster he is and how to play to his obsession. Who except Mrs. Dunning and Virgil's mother would know that?"

"The sister who was raised in an orphanage," Benedict said very softly.

Amity absorbed that logic. "Yes, of course, the sister."

"We will take another look at the guest list from the Channing ball when we return to London," Benedict said. "But there is only one woman on it who is the right age to have been fathered by Warwick and who also possesses a motive for sending a killer after you."

Amity took deep breath. "Lady Penhurst?"

"I think so."

"But why would she want me dead?"

Benedict looked at her. "You are the first woman in whom I have displayed any serious interest since I ended my association with Leona two years ago."

"Oh, dear," Amity said. "Of course. A woman scorned."

Thirty-five

W elcome home, Miss Doncaster." Mrs. Houston held the door wide. "Nice to see you again, Mr. Stanbridge. I must tell you that Mrs. Marsden was quite alarmed when you did not return on the train last night. Inspector Logan made inquiries of the police in the village and was told there had been reports of a fire at Hawthorne Hall and that no one had seen either of you afterward."

"You got my telegram this morning?" Benedict said.

"Yes, indeed, and it arrived none too soon. Mrs. Marsden and Inspector Logan were preparing to set out for the village."

Rapid footsteps sounded in the hall. Penny appeared. Relief blazed in her face. Logan was directly behind her.

"Amity," Penny said. She rushed forward. "Oh, thank heavens."

Amity hugged her. "It's all right, Penny. We're fine. I'm so sorry you were concerned. There was no way to send word until shortly after dawn when we found a farmer who drove us into the village."

Penny stepped back. "I understand. It's just that I've been so worried. The morning papers carried the news of the fire at the Hall. I knew you were all right because we got your telegram very early, but you were not at all explicit about what had occurred."

Logan looked at Benedict. "What the devil did happen?"

"It's a long story," Benedict said.

Mrs. Houston smiled. "I'll just go and put the kettle on."

Sometime later Benedict concluded his tale. Amity could feel the tension in the atmosphere. Logan looked grim.

"From the sound of things, it is going to be next to impossible to prove anything against Lady Penhurst," he said.

"We must leave her to Uncle Cornelius," Benedict said. "He will deal with her. Meanwhile, none of this changes the situation with regard to Virgil Warwick. He must be found and stopped before he kills again."

"I agree." Logan got to his feet and went to stand at the window. "He is out there, somewhere. He cannot remain in hiding forever. We will find him."

Amity cleared her throat. "If I might make a suggestion?"

They all looked at her. But it was Benedict who understood before everyone else.

"No," he said.

"What is it?" Logan asked.

"Lady Penhurst may have tried to use her brother as if he were a weapon, but I doubt that she can control him now that he has been launched in my direction," Amity said. "I am his target. He is an obsessed man. Why not set a trap?"

Penny's eyes widened in alarm. "With you as bait?"

"Yes, exactly," Amity said. "I could leave the house by myself as if I was going shopping. The police could follow me at some distance—"

"No," Benedict said again.

"No," Penny said.

"Absolutely not," Logan said.

Amity sighed. "I don't understand why you are all so set against the idea."

Benedict fixed her with a stern look. "Give it some thought. I'm sure the answer will come to you."

"For heaven's sake," Amity said. "It seemed a perfectly good plan to me."

"Fortunately, for my own peace of mind, I have a better one," Benedict said.

Thirty-six

Y ou may be right about Lady Penhurst," Cornelius said. He propped his legs on a hassock and toyed with his unlit pipe. "But she has vanished. I sent young Draper, my secretary, around to her address this morning after you told me what had transpired at Hawthorne Hall. Lord Penhurst has no idea where his wife is at the moment. The household staff seems to believe that she is on a trip to Scotland."

Amity looked at Benedict, who was sprawled in a chair near the window. He raised his brows.

"There appears to be a lot of people traveling to Scotland this summer," he said.

"Yes, indeed." Amity drummed her fingers on the arm of the chair. "First you were told that Virgil Warwick was on his way to a hunting lodge there and now we learn that his sister may be headed to the same destination."

"And we mustn't forget that Dr. Norcott possessed a train ticket to

Scotland," Benedict said. "Although in his case it was the truth. Evidently he actually did plan to seek safety there."

"Yes," Amity said.

She had been quite pleased when Benedict had suggested that she accompany him to the home of his uncle. It was an indication that not only did he trust her—she knew that much already—but he had come to consider her an equal partner in the case.

For his part, Cornelius Stanbridge appeared much improved. He still wore a small bandage, but he insisted that he had recovered from the blow to his head.

Benedict got to his feet. Amity watched him walk to the window. She could sense the restless energy driving him.

"I very much doubt that either Warwick or Leona is in Scotland," he said.

Cornelius grunted. "I have asked young Draper to look into Lady Penhurst's past."

Benedict's jaw flexed. "Leona is Virgil Warwick's sister and she is in the pay of the Russians. It is the only answer that explains the twists and turns in this case."

"I believe you are correct." Cornelius tapped the stem of his pipe against the arm of his chair. "As the wife of Lord Penhurst, she is certainly in an excellent position to play the part of an espionage agent. Penhurst may be going senile but he is still extremely well connected. He knows everyone and, at least until quite recently, he enjoyed the trust of a number of high-ranking men in government. There is no telling how many secrets he has been privy to over the years."

"And no telling how many he has unwittingly divulged to Lady Penhurst," Amity said.

"Indeed." Cornelius squinted a little. "I think you both should take a look at the note that I received shortly before you arrived here today. I was about to ask you to call on me when I discovered you on my doorstep."

Benedict turned around, eyes darkening with understanding. "You heard from the thief?"

"Yes," Cornelius said. "And the timing of the note suggests that the thief is aware that you and Miss Doncaster survived the explosion at Hawthorne Hall. It arrived after you returned to London unharmed. However, it appears the spy is now extremely anxious to complete the transaction." Cornelius gestured with the pipe stem. "Go on, take a look and see for yourselves. I'd like your opinions. The price for the return of the notebook is rather interesting."

Amity jumped to her feet and hurried toward the desk. Benedict took two long strides from the window and joined her.

He read the message aloud, his voice increasingly dark with each word.

The transaction will occur tomorrow evening at the Ottershaw ball. Miss Doncaster will bring the Rose Necklace as payment for the notebook. She will wear a black domino with the enclosed mask. She will be contacted at the ball and given final instructions for the exchange.

"Son of a bitch," Benedict said. "There can be no doubt now. Leona sent this."

"I'm inclined to agree," Cornelius said. "I cannot imagine anyone else insisting on a specific necklace as payment for the notebook."

Amity looked at him, bewildered. "But this makes no sense. She must realize that demanding the Stanbridge family necklace is a very risky venture. It is bound to bring suspicion down on her head. Too many people know that she was offended when Benedict did not ask her to marry him."

"I think that Lady Penhurst has allowed her desire for revenge to overcome her common sense," Cornelius said.

"I wonder if the Russians have begun to realize that their agent has allowed her personal desire for vengeance to override common sense," Benedict said.

Amity smoothed the letter with one hand. "Charlotte Warwick told us that Mrs. Dunning claimed to have observed evidence of mental instability in Virgil's sister. Perhaps our engagement has completely unhinged her."

Benedict started to pace the study. "So it seems."

Amity looked at Cornelius. "Where is the mask?"

Cornelius pointed the pipe stem at a box on the desk. "In there."

Amity lifted the lid and set it aside. She studied the beautiful mask. It was elegantly made and lavishly trimmed with feathers and small glass jewels that caught the light. It was designed to conceal the upper portion of the face. And it was crimson red.

"Not very subtle, is she?" Amity said. "She wants me to go as a Scarlet Woman."

Benedict stopped his pacing and gave the mask a hard look. "You aren't going to that damned ball."

Amity noticed that Cornelius did not attempt to interfere. Instead, he waited to see how she would respond.

"Of course I am going to the ball," she said. "Leona will know if you try to bring another woman in my place. Not that I would allow you to take any other female."

"If she wants to make the trade she can damn well make it on our terms," Benedict said.

Cornelius coughed a little. "We need to unmask Lady Penhurst. Literally, it appears."

"Your uncle is right," Amity said. "We must catch her. This is our best chance to expose her as a spy."

Cornelius grunted. "Miss Doncaster is correct in terms of strategy. As I have mentioned, in this sort of ransom situation, the moment of the exchange is the time when the thief is most vulnerable."

"I realize that the necklace is probably quite valuable and that it has great meaning and significance to your family, Benedict," Amity began. "But if we are careful we can protect it."

"I don't give a damn about the necklace." Benedict's eyes tightened at the corners. "That mask is an insult to you."

"Only if I choose to take it that way," Amity said. "I prefer to see it as part of the costume that I will wear in a play. Really, sir, there is no need for agitation and anxiety. What can possibly go wrong in the middle of a crowded ballroom?"

"Let me count the ways," Benedict said.

"Benedict, surely you can see this is our best chance, not only to catch Lady Penhurst but to find out where her brother is hiding. If anyone can lead us to Virgil Warwick, it is most likely his sister."

Benedict looked grim.

"We need a plan," he said at last.

Amity smiled. "Well, then, come up with one."

Cornelius snorted. "She's right, Ben. You're the one who has a talent for planning for various and assorted disasters."

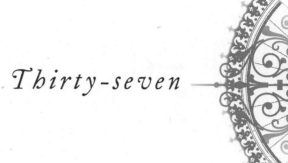

Thirty-seven

The vast ballroom of the Ottershaw mansion was dimly lit with colored lanterns that cast seductive shadows over the throng of elegantly costumed guests. Under other circumstances, Amity thought, the scene would have been wonderfully romantic. For the first time since meeting Benedict she was actually dancing with him—a waltz, no less, the most romantic music in the world.

Not that Benedict appeared to appreciate the romanticism of the moment. He danced the way he did most things—with a fine, efficient competence. But there was a clockwork precision to his steps that made it clear his attention was on other matters. She could almost hear the internal metronome inside his brain counting off the steps. He searched the crowd with eyes that glittered darkly behind a plain black mask. He, too, wore a black domino, the hood pushed back to allow him a better view of the room.

She had also folded her hood back, framing her face to make certain that the scarlet mask was visible. She was very aware of the weight of the Rose Necklace around her throat. It was hidden beneath the domino. Benedict had insisted that was the safest location for it. When he had clasped it around her neck, she had taken one look in the mirror and nearly been blinded by the dazzling rubies and diamonds.

Benedict steered her into a crisply paced turn while he checked another quarter of the heavily shadowed ballroom. She smiled. He was manipulating her as if she were a tool, she thought, a device that he just happened to need to produce the correct pattern of the dance.

"It's as dark as the inside of a cave in here and everyone is wearing a mask," he said.

"Well, it is a costume ball," Amity reminded him.

"Believe it or not, I am aware of that. Damn it, it's nearly midnight. We've been here over half an hour already. When is she going to make contact?"

"Probably when we least expect it. Relax, Benedict. You are making me nervous. Perhaps I should say more nervous than I already was before we arrived."

"Sorry." He cranked her through another perfectly executed turn. "It's just that I don't like any of this."

"No one does. But it's not as if we have any choice."

"Don't remind me."

The music rose to a dramatic crescendo and ceased abruptly. Benedict stopped as if someone had flipped an invisible switch. Amity was forced to halt so quickly that she accidentally stumbled into another dancer. She could not tell if her victim was male or female because the individual was wearing a long black domino with the hood pulled up around a full-face mask.

"Your pardon," she started to say.

The dancer thrust a note into her hand. Before Amity understood what had happened, the costumed figure vanished into a sea of black dominos. Amity clutched the note very tightly, trying to peer through the throng. It was hopeless.

"Benedict." She yanked on his arm to get his attention.

"What?" He did not look down at her. He was too busy studying the crowd.

"I think Lady Penhurst—or someone—just made contact. I was given a note."

"What the devil?" He stopped, turning quickly to survey the crowd behind her. "Describe the costume."

"It was just another black domino. She was wearing a mask that covered her entire face. There was nothing to see. Except—"

"Except what?"

"Now that I think about it, I'm quite certain that the person who thrust the note into my hand was wearing gloves. Kid gloves, I believe. And she was about the same height as Leona. But that's beside the point. We need to find a place where we can read the note."

Benedict steered her through the crowd and out a side door. Amity pushed her mask up onto her forehead and fumbled beneath the domino to touch her tessen. It dangled from the chatelaine, together with the dainty evening bag that contained a tiny sewing kit of the sort that ladies frequently carried to balls. The kits were designed to make it possible to do emergency repairs to ripped hems and petticoats.

When she looked around, she discovered they were in a hallway lit with gas lamps. At the end of the hall she could see footmen dashing about. Silver platters clanged. Someone swore. Someone else called out orders.

"More champagne and another tray of lobster canapés needed in the buffet room."

"Let me see that note," Benedict said.

She handed it to him and then leaned around his broad shoulders to read it aloud while he studied it:

*The ladies' withdrawing room. Five minutes. I will not wait
any longer.*

Amity straightened swiftly. "Good heavens, I must find the with-drawing room immediately. There is no time to waste."

"I don't want you going anywhere without me."

"Nonsense. It is the ladies' room, for heaven's sake. There will be chambermaids and any number of guests coming and going."

Benedict looked deeply suspicious. "Where is this withdrawing room?"

"I don't know. I'll ask one of the footmen. Come, we must hurry."

She grabbed Benedict's hand and drew him down the hall to a room swarming with sweating servants. The first one to see her looked shocked.

"Can I help you, madam?"

"The ladies' withdrawing room, please," she said.

"Not in here," the footman said. "Opposite side of the ballroom. There will be a maid at the door."

"Thank you."

She yanked the mask down over her eyes.

"We're losing time," she said.

She towed Benedict back along the hall and out into the darkened ballroom. She paused briefly to let her eyes adjust to the shadows.

"Damn it, I can't see over the heads of the crowd," she said.

"I'll get you there," Benedict said.

He moved through the crowd, an implacable force of nature,

drawing her along in his wake. When they reached the far side of the throng, he stopped in front of a discreetly shadowed hallway.

A maid appeared. She bobbed a quick curtsy.

"The ladies' withdrawing room, please," Amity said.

"I will escort you, madam." The maid turned to move down the hall. "This way, please."

Once again Amity pushed the mask up onto her head and pulled up her hood. She started to follow the maid. Benedict put a hand on her arm.

"I'm coming with you," he said.

The maid halted and turned quickly. Her eyes widened.

"Oh, no, sir, I'm sorry, sir, but it is the ladies' room. You cannot go in there."

"She's right," Amity said. "Wait here. I'm sure this won't take long." She looked at the maid. "Which door?"

"The one on the right at the end of the hall, madam." The maid moved forward again.

Amity left Benedict standing in the hall and hurried after the maid. The woman opened the door for her and stood aside.

Amity stepped into an elegantly appointed sitting room. The door closed behind her. She had just concluded that she was alone and was wondering if she had come to the right location for the meeting when the door on the far side of the room opened.

A figure draped in a hooded domino, her face covered with a full mask, stepped out. She had a pistol in one hand.

"Good evening, Leona," Amity said.

The figure in the domino froze.

"What?" Amity said casually. "You didn't realize that we knew you were the one who stole the notebook?"

"You don't know what you're talking about." Leona pushed back the hood of the domino and removed her mask. "Give me the necklace."

"Since this place is obviously not the ladies' room, I'm assuming you paid the maid to bring me here?"

"I told her I wanted to surprise you." Leona's hand tightened on the gun. "Where is the necklace?"

"I'm wearing it, of course."

"Not any longer. It's mine."

"Where is the Foxcroft notebook?"

"Do you think I'm an idiot? I didn't bring it with me. I will send word to tell you where to find it after I am safely out of the country."

"Of course you will." Amity smiled. "You're a liar and a thief and quite capable of using your brother's murderous tendencies for your own benefit. Did you take Virgil with you to Hawthorne Hall so that he could perform the messy work of cutting Mrs. Dunning's throat? Or did you handle it all yourself?"

Leona raised her brows. "You know about my connection to Virgil? I'm impressed. You have been busy. Yes, I am his long-lost sister. Dear Papa threw me into an orphanage after my mother—his mistress—died giving birth. Mrs. Dunning fired up her blackmail scheme shortly thereafter, but she was content with small payments. I suppose Papa found it easier to pay her than to get rid of her and risk the scandal that might occur if he became involved in a murder investigation."

"When did you discover the truth about your father?"

"When I turned sixteen. Dunning sent most of the girls away as soon as they were old enough to work as governesses. Except me. She offered me a post as a teacher at the orphanage. I declined. I knew I could do much better out in the world. But her offer made me curious. I went through her records and discovered her blackmail scheme.

Imagine how thrilled I was to discover that I had a half brother. I forced Mrs. Dunning to make me a partner in her extortion scheme. The first thing I had her do was raise the price, of course. She was not charging Papa nearly enough for her silence."

"When did you realize that your half brother was a murderer?"

"Not until his wedding. We had become quite close before that, however, although his mother was not aware of it. I was aware of his various hobbies. Let's just say that I was not the least bit surprised when his bride suffered a fatal and rather bloody accident on her honeymoon. By then, of course, I had begun my career as an espionage agent. It occurred to me that Virgil might come in handy one day. The problem is that—like a bullet or an arrow—once he had been fired he was rather difficult to control."

"Your first husband died rather conveniently, I'm told."

Leona laughed. "Dear Roger suffered from a very severe case of gastric distress."

"Brought on by steady doses of arsenic."

"Heir powder, I believe the French call it. It is also very popular with women who wish to become widows."

"When you discovered that your first husband had not left you nearly as much money as you had expected—"

"Not nearly as much as I had *earned*." Leona's cheeks blazed with sudden fury. "Do you know what it is like to be married to a man who is old enough to be your father? It is a living hell."

"So you got rid of him and set out to seduce Benedict. But that plan failed, didn't it? You seem to have much better luck with gentlemen who are in their dotage."

A wild rage flashed in Leona's eyes. "It is Benedict's fault that I was forced to marry that old fool Penhurst. He proved to be a cheap bastard. He actually changed his will shortly after we were married.

When he dies I will be left with nothing—only a fraction of his estate."

"Ah, so that is why he is still alive. I wonder if he realizes how fortunate he is."

"The Rose Necklace should have been mine," Leona said, her voice raw and tight. "It *will* be mine. You should have been dead by now. Virgil was supposed to make you one of his brides."

"Why take the risk of using your unstable brother to try to murder me?"

Leona smiled. "Because I knew that Benedict would feel responsible for your death. After all, if it wasn't for the gossip about the two of you, the Bridegroom would never have selected you as his victim. I wanted Benedict to pay a price for the hellish marriage he forced me into."

"Why do you need the necklace? Surely you have earned a nice income working for the Russians."

"Not nearly enough to allow me to live in the style I deserve. But the Rose Necklace will change all that."

"Where will you go?"

"Who knows?" Leona shrugged. "Perhaps I shall take some guidance from one of your essays in the *Flying Intelligencer*. What was it you wrote? *'In the American West, there is no past, only the future. One is free to reinvent oneself.'*"

"I don't think that's going to work for you, Leona."

"It will work. Give me the bloody necklace."

"Or you'll shoot me? Don't be silly. Benedict is out in the hall. He will hear the shot and come at once."

"But that will be much too late to save you."

"Very well."

Amity reached up slowly to unfasten the long, sweeping cloak. She pulled the folds of the domino aside at her throat, revealing the spectacular necklace.

Leona's eyes widened. "It is even more amazing than I imagined."

Amity reached up slowly to unclasp it.

The door opened behind her. Benedict walked into the room. Logan and Cornelius, dressed in black dominos like so many others at the ball, were directly behind him.

"I think we've heard enough, Inspector, don't you?" Benedict said.

"Yes," Logan said. "With your testimony and that of Miss Doncaster there will be no problem sending Lady Penhurst away to prison."

"No." Panic and fury lit Leona's eyes. She edged toward the door behind her. "If you arrest me you'll never get the Foxcroft notebook."

"Actually, the notebook isn't all that important," Cornelius said. "What I was really after tonight was the Russian agent. That would be you, my dear."

"It's over, Leona," Amity said. "Put the gun down."

"No, stay away from me," Leona whispered. She leveled the gun at Amity. "Stay away or I'll kill her, I swear it. She deserves to die. This is all her fault."

No one moved toward her.

Leona was at the door. She opened it with her free hand, revealing the dimly lit hall. At the last instant she whirled and fled, the folds of her domino whipping out behind her.

Her footsteps rang in the hall and then grew faint.

Amity looked at Benedict.

"You're sure this plan is going to work?" she asked.

"It was the best I could do on the spur of the moment," Benedict said. "We knew it was unlikely that she would deliver the notebook in exchange for the necklace. But now that she hasn't got the jewelry, the only thing of value that she has left is that notebook. She will try to retrieve it and attempt to sell it to the Russians."

"She will escape into the street and hail a hansom," Logan said. "There are three waiting. She will have her choice. My men are driving all three of the cabs. They have been directed to accept no fare unless the customer is a lady who is alone."

"Leona is a clever woman," Amity warned.

"Yes," Cornelius said, "but now she is a very desperate woman. I am convinced that she will get the notebook and lead us to her Russian contact. As Benedict said, whoever that person is, he or she is Leona's only hope now."

A crack of muffled thunder sounded in the distance. For an instant they all froze.

Cornelius frowned. "Odd. There was no sign of rain earlier."

"Gunshot," Logan said.

"The ballroom, I think," Benedict said.

A woman screamed somewhere in the distance.

Both men broke into a run, heading down the hall toward the ballroom. Cornelius followed.

Amity found herself fighting the long folds of the domino and the skirts of her gown. In addition, she had a great fear of losing the Rose Necklace so she kept one hand clamped on it beneath the costume. It made for awkward sprinting.

She caught up with the three men at the edge of the shadowy ballroom. The music had come to a crashing, discordant halt. The dancers were milling about in confusion. An earthquake of exclamations—shock, horror and confusion—rumbled through the crowd.

"Police," Logan called out in a voice that rang with great authority. "Stand aside."

No one argued with him. The crowd fell away to reveal the body on the floor. The domino had fallen open, displaying skirts and pet-ticoats.

Logan and Benedict crouched beside the figure. Cornelius loomed above them, looking down as Logan removed the victim's mask.

Astonishment reverberated throughout the room. Amity heard the whispers around her.

"It's Lady Penhurst."

"Shot herself in the middle of a ballroom. It's unbelievable."

Amity stopped at the edge of the scene. A number of people were already hurrying discreetly away, heading for the front door and their carriages. Benedict, Logan and Cornelius were not paying any atten-tion to the murmurs of the crowd or the retreating onlookers. They were conducting a quick search of the body.

She was about to move closer when she caught the stale odor of cigarettes scented with exotic spices.

She felt something sharp press against the back of her neck.

"I have your sister," Virgil Warwick said into her ear. "If you call out or try to run I will vanish into the crowd. No one will see me. I will escape but your sister will die. Get rid of your nasty little fan. Do it now or I will leave here without you and pretty Penny dies."

Amity reached beneath her domino and removed the tessen from her chatelaine. There was so much commotion in the room that no one heard the fan when it fell to the floor.

Thirty-eight

He's got Amity and Penny," Benedict said. He did not take his eyes off the tessen where it lay on Penny's desk. "The bastard was there in the crowd tonight. He kidnapped her while I was no more than a few yards away."

"It wasn't your fault," Logan said. "It's obvious he used Penny to force Amity to leave the ballroom quietly. That's the only thing that makes sense, the only reason for taking both of them. He probably terrified Amity by telling her that he would murder her sister if she didn't go with him."

"I thought he was a new constable," Mrs. Houston whispered. She rocked back and forth in the chair, dabbing at her eyes with her apron. "I can't believe I offered him tea and a fresh muffin."

"You were overpowered, Mrs. Houston," Cornelius said. "He used chloroform on you and very likely on Mrs. Marsden, as well."

They had arrived in Exton Street to find Constable Wiggins unconscious in the park and Mrs. Houston sprawled on the kitchen floor. The house was dark. Penny was gone.

Fury and fear were stirring up an icy witch's brew of emotion in Benedict. It was all he could do to tamp down some of the toxic sensations so that he could think. When he met Logan's eyes across the short distance of the study, he knew the other man was exerting the same exacting self-control. They were both well aware that their only hope now was to remain coolheaded enough to think through the logic of the situation.

The knocker sounded on the front door. Mrs. Houston leaped to her feet and hurried away to answer it. Benedict heard voices in the front hall. A moment later Declan Garraway appeared. He looked as if he had just been dragged out of bed and given only a few minutes to dress—which was, indeed, the case, Benedict thought.

It had been his idea to send for Garraway, but Logan and Cornelius had welcomed the plan, such as it was. They needed all the insights they could get.

"What is it?" Declan asked. He clutched his hat and stared at the small group in the study. "The constable said that Mrs. Marsden and Miss Doncaster have been kidnapped by that monster they call the Bridegroom."

"The bastard's name is Virgil Warwick and he's got them both," Benedict said. "We have to find them by morning. Our only hope is to locate the studio where he photographs his victims."

"I'll help you in any way I can, of course," Declan said. "But I don't know how I can be of service."

"We know considerably more about the son of a bitch than we did the last time you gave us your opinions." Logan swept out a hand to indicate the small notebooks on the desk. "Stanbridge and I have arranged everything for you to review with us. If there is any clue in our findings, we must discover it and soon."

Declan took a deep breath and moved closer to the desk. He looked down at the notes.

"Tell me what you have learned about him in the past few days," he said.

A short time later Declan put down the notes that he had made while Benedict and Logan filled him in on the new discoveries.

"I think," he said, "that Virgil Warwick would value control above all else. He is a perfectionist when it comes to his photography. It takes time to get a portrait right. He will need a secure studio, one in which he can be assured of privacy. He'll take his victims to a place in which he is certain he will not be discovered."

Cornelius shifted in the depths of the reading chair. "That makes sense. But he won't risk taking them to his own house or his mother's, either. He will know that we are aware of both of those locations."

Benedict looked at the notes spread out on the desk. A great certainty settled on him.

"There is only one way Virgil Warwick can be relatively certain that he won't be discovered," he said.

Thirty-nine

Charlotte Warwick sat rigidly upright in the chair behind her desk. She had been in bed when Benedict and Logan had arrived on the doorstep. She had sent word that she would see them in the morning. When Benedict had informed the butler that the visit concerned her son, she had donned a dressing gown and slippers and come downstairs to meet with them. The three of them were now closeted in the library.

"You said this was about Virgil." Charlotte gripped the polished wooden arms of the chair as though hoping it would keep her afloat in the storm that had overtaken her. She stared at Benedict and Logan. "I have told you everything I know. What do you want from me?"

"Your son abducted two women tonight," Logan said.

"Dear heaven, no." Charlotte's face twisted in anguish.

"He will murder them both before this night is over if we do not stop him," Benedict said.

Charlotte released her desperate grip on the chair and buried her face in her hands. "This cannot be happening."

Benedict planted both hands on the top of the desk and leaned toward her. "Look at me, Mrs. Warwick. You know what your son is. You have known all along and that is something you will have to live with for the rest of your life. All we want from you tonight is an address."

Charlotte raised her head, her eyes wet with tears. "Virgil's address? But you already know it."

"Not his house," Logan said, "his studio—the place where he takes his victims to photograph them before he murders them."

Charlotte looked dazed. "I don't know what to tell you. If he is not at his house there is no telling where he may have gone."

"We have reason to believe that he will have established his killing ground in a place that he believes is safe," Benedict said. He saw the tremor that went through Charlotte when he used the words *killing ground* but he ignored it. "We know that he takes his time with his victims. He is a perfectionist when it comes to his photography. That means he requires privacy."

"We have concluded that the most logical way that he could be assured that he won't be discovered or interrupted is if he has established his studio in a building that he owns or controls," Logan said.

Benedict saw comprehension begin to filter into Charlotte's expression.

"When Miss Doncaster and I came here to ask you about your son, you mentioned that you managed the details of his life, including his finances. Inspector Logan and I stopped at Virgil's house before we came here. There are no financial records at his house. You keep his accounts, don't you?"

"Yes," she whispered. "But I don't see how that information can help you find him."

"Does he own any property here in London?" Logan asked.

Mrs. Warwick blinked several times. "Yes, as a matter of fact. My husband left him several properties that were intended to provide income for him. The majority of the properties are rented to shopkeepers and the like who live in the rooms above their establishments."

"Perhaps there is one that is not rented?" Benedict prodded.

Charlotte hesitated. "One of the properties is an old house near the docks that has been standing empty for nearly two years. My business manager has mentioned on a number of occasions that it should be leased or sold."

"Why are there no tenants?" Benedict asked.

Charlotte squeezed her eyes shut. When she opened them again there was nothing but resignation and a mother's grief in her gaze.

"Virgil told me that he had plans for the property," she said. "He insisted that the old house be left unoccupied until he was ready to remodel it. He said he was working with an architect. I was pleased that he was finally showing some interest in financial matters. But when I asked him how the project was coming along, he said that he had changed his mind about the original design and fired the architect. Shortly thereafter he had his first nervous breakdown and I was forced to send him to Cresswell Manor."

"Have you ever been to the house that he said he intended to remodel?" Benedict asked.

"No." Mrs. Warwick shook her head. "There was no reason to pay a visit to the property. My manager kept an eye on it while Virgil was being treated at the Manor to make certain that no one broke in or attempted to take up residence."

"What did the property manager tell you about the house?" Logan asked.

"Very little," Mrs. Warwick said. "He just mentioned that the windows were boarded up and that the locks on the front and back doors appeared to be very modern. He was satisfied that the house was secure."

Forty

The photography studio looked very much like other studios Amity had seen—except for the large, ornate, wrought-iron cage in one corner. Penny was huddled on the floor of the cage. She was dressed in the plain housedress and soft shoes that she had been wearing earlier in the evening. She staggered to her feet when Amity walked into the room with Virgil Warwick.

"Amity, my dear sister." Penny's eyes were stark with horror and dismay. "I was so afraid of this. He said you would come with him willingly once you knew that he had taken me."

Amity looked around. There was a large, expensive-looking camera on a tripod in the center. The lens of the camera was aimed at an elegant, white satin chair. A small vase filled with white lilies sat on a nearby table. In one corner there was a folding screen of the sort designed to provide privacy for dressing. The panels of the screen were painted with an elaborate floral design.

"What else could I do?" Amity said briskly. "Don't worry, we shall both be leaving in a short while. Warwick is quite insane. By definition that means he cannot think logically. Benedict and Inspector Logan, however, are eminently capable of rational thought. They will find us soon."

"Shut your mouth, you lying whore," Virgil hissed. "Or I will kill your sister while you watch." He walked toward the cage and pointed the pistol at Penny.

Amity looked at him and said nothing.

Virgil gave her a cold smile.

For some reason the most jarring thing about Virgil Warwick was that he appeared so normal. There was nothing remarkable about his neatly combed light brown hair, his thin face or his lean build. It would have been quite easy to pass him by on the street without taking any notice of him whatsoever. But that was the thing about the true monsters of the world, Amity thought. They were so dangerous because they were able to hide in plain sight.

"Excellent," Virgil said. "You seem to have grasped the fact that you are not the one in control here tonight." He gestured toward the privacy screen. "Time to change into your wedding gown for your sitting."

Amity looked down at her bound wrists. "How am I supposed to take off one gown and put on another with my hands tied?"

Virgil frowned. She realized that he had not planned for this particular eventuality.

"How did you manage the changing of the gowns with the other brides?" she asked, keeping her voice at a conversational tone.

"I made them dress inside the cage," he said.

He looked annoyed. For a horrifying instant Amity realized he might murder Penny in order to solve the problem.

"There is room for both of us inside," she said quickly.

Virgil came to a decision. "Very well. The gown you will wear for your portrait is over there behind the screen. Get it."

She went around the screen and took the white satin-and-lace gown off the peg. A shiver went through her when she recognized the design of the bodice. It was the same gown that the victims had worn in the photographs.

"It's very beautiful," she said.

"Nothing but the best for a pure and virtuous bride," Virgil said. "Of course you are not exactly pure or virtuous, are you? No, you are tainted. Stanbridge may not realize it but I am doing him a favor. When he comes to his senses he will thank me. After all, once a whore, always a whore. Take the gown to the cage. Hurry."

The dress was very heavy. The dressmaker had used a vast amount of fabric in the skirts. There was so much beading on the stiffened bodice that Amity suspected it alone weighed several pounds.

Virgil motioned for Penny to step back out of the way. When she obeyed, he took a key out of the pocket of his coat and unlocked the cage. Amity carried the wedding gown inside.

Virgil slammed the door shut and locked it. He went to the workbench, picked up a knife and walked back to the cage.

"Put your hands through the bars," he ordered.

Amity did as instructed. Virgil sliced through the bindings on her wrists. Relief swept through her. She and Penny were hardly free, but at least, for the moment, they were both unbound.

Virgil crossed the room, picked up the folding screen and positioned it in front of the cage. Amity looked at Penny, brows raised.

"Evidently Mr. Warwick has some respect for a lady's modesty," Penny said coolly.

On the far side of the screen Virgil uttered a guttural laugh.

"You know what they say, bad luck to see the bride in her gown before the wedding," he said lightly.

But there was more to it than that, Amity realized.

"You don't like to see women nude, do you?" she asked.

Virgil grunted on the other side of the screen. "Women like you are unclean. Dirty. Tainted. Their wedding gowns conceal the truth about them until the groom has been deceived into marriage."

Penny helped Amity out of the domino and the simple gown that she had worn beneath it. They both went about the business as slowly as they dared. Trying to buy time, Amity thought. She touched the Rose Necklace that she still wore around her neck as if it were a talisman. Benedict and Logan would even now be searching for them.

"Is that why you murdered your own bride?" Penny asked, sounding for all the world as if she was making polite drawing room conversation. "Because you felt she had deceived you?"

There was a short, startled silence from the other side of the screen.

"How did you discover that?" Virgil demanded.

"This is your wife's gown, isn't it?" Amity asked. "How long did it take you to realize that she was not the virgin you assumed her to be?"

"I believed her to be a paragon of womanhood," Virgil said. "But she dared to come to me pregnant with another man's child. She tried to deceive me and for a time I believed her lies. But when she miscarried three weeks after the wedding I knew the truth."

Amity stepped into the heavy white satin skirts and pulled up the bodice. She noticed that the gown was cut rather full around the waistline. Madame Dubois had done a very good job of concealing that feature, however.

"To be fair, you lied to her, as well, didn't you?" Amity said.

"What are you talking about?" Virgil snapped.

"I imagine that you failed to mention the streak of insanity in your family bloodline," Penny said casually.

"The Warwick bloodline is untainted," Virgil roared. He slammed the privacy screen aside just as Penny started to do up the bodice of the gown. His face was splotched with fury. "How dare you imply that there is insanity in the family!"

"I had an interesting conversation with your sister tonight before you murdered her," Amity said. "Out of curiosity, may I ask why you killed her in the middle of a ballroom?"

"You think I killed her?" Virgil asked. He looked first surprised and then amused. "You silly woman. Put on the veil. It is time for your sitting."

Penny picked up the veil. Her eyes were filled with dread.

Amity turned toward her, partially blocking Virgil's view. She pressed the little evening bag that she had carried to the costume ball into Penny's hand. Penny's fingers closed around it. Her eyes flickered in understanding. Amity knew she had just remembered the little sewing kit inside.

"Good-bye, sister," Amity said, raising her voice to a sorrowful wail. "He will kill me as soon as he takes my photo and then he will murder you, as well. He is quite mad, you see."

Penny hastily opened the pretty evening bag and took out the small scissors.

"Enough!" Virgil screamed. "There will be no more talk of insanity."

"Be ready." With her back to Virgil, Amity mouthed the words the way she and Penny had done when they were children trying to convey a silent message across the dinner table without their parents being aware of it.

Penny concealed the scissors in the folds of her skirt.

Amity readied herself. Until that moment she had been careful to move slowly, making no moves that might alarm Virgil. She could only pray that he would not be anticipating a sudden burst of energy from her.

"Put your hands outside the bars," Virgil ordered.

Amity turned around and extended her wrists. He was obliged to set the pistol aside while he bound her a second time.

"Stand back, both of you," Virgil ordered. Hastily he retrieved the pistol.

Amity and Penny obeyed.

Virgil stabbed the key into the padlock. It took him two tries to unlock the door. There was a feverish excitement about him now.

When the lock finally gave way, Virgil tugged the heavy door open. In that one brief moment he was forced to juggle the door, the lock and the pistol.

Amity gave a shrill, piercing scream and flung herself at the door. The force of her full weight slamming into the iron bars caught Virgil off guard. He staggered back a couple of steps.

"Lying whore!" he screamed. "Lying, cheating harlot. I'll teach you your place."

He used his grip on the door to slam it closed but Penny, wielding the little pair of scissors like claws, stabbed his hand. The sharp points of the blades bit into flesh.

Virgil howled. Blood flowed.

Reflexively he released his grip on the iron bars and staggered back out of range. Amity took advantage of the opportunity to shove hard against the door a second time. It swung wide open. Penny dashed out first. Amity flew after her.

Virgil fell back again, his attention fixed on Amity. He raised the gun, aiming it at her. She grabbed the only weapon at hand—the long wedding veil with its elaborate crown—and tossed it at him. The yards of diaphanous lace cascaded over his face and chest. Furious and clearly panicked now, he swiped at the billowing veil with both hands.

The roar of the gun was deafening. Amity didn't know if Virgil had pulled the trigger by accident or intent. The only thing that mattered in that moment was that she and Penny were both on their feet. Neither of them had been hit.

Penny seized the nearest heavy object—the medical satchel—and hurled it at Virgil. It caught him on his upper shoulder. It didn't do much damage but he stumbled again. He had evidently unlatched the satchel earlier because the contents spilled out. Small glass vials filled with medicines, bandages, a stethoscope and a number of gleaming instruments scattered across the floor.

Virgil yelled and swung the pistol toward Penny. Amity grabbed his gun arm with both hands and hauled on it with all of her strength. The second shot slammed into the wooden floorboards.

He managed to shake free of her grip but Penny came at him from behind, a scalpel in her hand. She stabbed wildly at the back of his neck, missed and struck his shoulder.

He shrieked in pain and whirled around. He still had the gun. He tried to level it at Penny. Amity hoisted the heavy skirts of the wedding dress and kicked Virgil behind his right knee with all the strength she could muster.

He screamed again, lost his balance and went down on both knees. This time he lost his grip on the gun. It fell to the floor. Amity kicked it out of reach.

Penny grabbed the big camera off the tripod. Amity realized that she intended to smash it against Virgil's head.

A gun roared. Not Virgil's, Amity realized. The sound had been muffled.

The studio door slammed open. Benedict and Logan thundered into the room. Amity realized that Benedict had shot the lock off the door.

It seemed to her that for an instant everything and everyone in the scene except Benedict and Logan froze. The two men did not stop. They were intent only on the destruction of their prey. And their prey was Virgil Warwick.

Virgil erupted from the brief trance. He scrambled to his feet. Amity made no attempt to stop him. Neither did Penny. They both knew that he would never escape the wrath of the two men who were between him and the door.

Virgil must have seen the ice in Benedict's and Logan's eyes. He stopped short, frantic now.

"No!" he shrieked. "I've done nothing. It's the whores. They are trying to kill me."

"Stop," Logan said. "I am arresting you on charges of murder."

"No!" Virgil screamed. "I'm Virgil Warwick. You can't touch me."

He whirled around and reached out to grab Amity. She realized he intended to use her as a shield. She lurched out of his path. Her foot caught on the thick, treacherous folds of satin in the skirts of the gown. She lost her balance, but the fall took her out of range of Virgil's desperately flailing hands.

He changed direction and went after the gun he had dropped during the struggle.

Benedict aimed his pistol and pulled the trigger.

The roar of the gun bounced off the walls. Virgil stiffened as if he had been electrified. He looked down, staring in disbelief at the growing bloodstain on the front of his crisply pleated white shirt. Then he raised his eyes and stared at Benedict, bewildered.

"I'm Virgil Warwick," he said. "You can't do this to me."

He crumpled to the floor.

A great hush descended upon the room. Amity grabbed Penny's hand. Penny's fingers closed around hers. They both watched Logan crouch beside Virgil.

"Is he dead?" Benedict asked.

"Not quite," Logan said. He took his fingers away from Virgil's throat. "But he will be soon, which, under the circumstances, is a very good thing. We will not have to worry that he might be released again from an asylum."

Virgil's eyes fluttered. He stared up at Benedict with fading eyes.

"Where is Mother?" he rasped. "She will take care of everything."

"Not this time," Benedict said.

Forty-one

The first light of dawn was illuminating an overcast sky when the hansom cab stopped in front of Benedict's address. He paid the driver, descended the narrow steps to the pavement and turned to look back at Logan.

"Can I offer you a brandy, Inspector? I think we've both earned one. It's been a long night."

Logan hesitated and for a moment Benedict thought he might refuse. Then he got out of the cab.

"A brandy sounds like an excellent notion," Logan said. "Thank you."

They went up the steps. Benedict reached into his pocket for the key. His fingers brushed across the Rose Necklace. Another sharp pang of dismay splashed through him, weighing down his spirits. He relived the moment in Warwick's ghastly studio when Amity had looked as if she would fling herself headlong into his arms. Instead, she had composed herself and said something about his always excellent timing.

They had all agreed that it would be best if he escorted the ladies home before the press arrived. The story was bound to be a sensation, but the uproar would be even greater if the killer's last two intended victims were discovered at the scene.

Unable to tolerate another moment in the wedding gown the killer had forced her to wear, Amity had insisted on taking the time to change back into her own dress before leaving the studio.

She did not remove the Rose Necklace until they were back in Exton Street. Benedict had the feeling that she had forgotten it. There, on the front steps, Amity had paused to thank him again, ever so politely, and then she had reached up to unclasp the necklace.

In the hazy glow of the gas lamps he thought he saw some emotion in her eyes, but he could not read it. Shock, he concluded. What else? She had been through a terrible ordeal.

"You mustn't forget your necklace, Benedict," she said, handing it to him. "I know how important it is to you and your family. I don't want to take any more chances with it."

He had left Amity and Penny in Mrs. Houston's capable hands and returned to the grim, boarded-up house that Warwick had used as a photography studio. He had been very conscious of the weight of the necklace in his pocket while he waited for Logan to finish with the business of collecting evidence.

When Logan had eventually appeared, he had been surprised to see Benedict and the hansom in the street. But he had accepted the offer of a ride without hesitation.

"I must call on Mrs. Warwick before I go home," he said.

"I will go in with you if you like," Benedict said.

Logan nodded once, his face grim. "I would be glad of your company. I'm not sure what to say to a mother under these circumstances."

In the end, however, the meeting with a stoic Charlotte Warwick had been mercifully short. Benedict knew from the shadows in her eyes that she had been braced for the news they had brought her. They had left her alone in her library, tears glittering in her eyes. Benedict had gotten the odd impression that they might have been tears of relief as well as grief, but he could not be certain.

He opened the door of his house and moved into the dimly lit front hall. Hodges appeared in his nightcap and dressing gown.

"Tea or brandy, sir?" he asked.

"Brandy," Benedict said. "But I'll see to pouring it."

"Yes, sir."

Benedict led the way into the study, turned up the lamps and splashed healthy doses of brandy into two glasses. He handed one of the glasses to Logan and motioned him to sit down. He watched Logan lower himself into the chair with a familiar ease that indicated he was as comfortable in a gentleman's study with a brandy glass in his hand as he was drinking tea in a lady's drawing room.

"When did you take a notion to become a policeman, Logan?" Benedict asked.

The question clearly caught Logan by surprise but he recovered readily enough.

"Shortly after I found my father dead from a self-inflicted pistol shot to the head and discovered that he had died bankrupt after a series of disastrous financial investments." Logan swallowed some brandy and lowered the glass. "It was either take up gainful employment here in London or emigrate to Canada or Australia. I haven't ruled out the last two possibilities, by the way. In fact, I am giving both countries a great deal of consideration at the moment."

Benedict took the Rose Necklace out of his pocket. He studied the brilliant jewels in the lamplight for a moment and then set the thing on the desk. The heavy gold links clinked on the polished wood.

He crossed the room and lowered himself into the chair across from Logan.

"You are not the only one who is considering his prospects in Canada or Australia tonight," he said. He drank some brandy. "And for similar reasons, I suspect."

Logan glanced at the necklace. "She gave it back to you?"

"Yes."

"But you did not ask for it to be returned."

"No."

"Well? Did you tell her you wanted her to keep it?"

Benedict frowned. "There was no opportunity to discuss the matter. She simply dropped it into my hand before she closed the door. I thought the gesture rather telling."

"We are men, Stanbridge. We are not always very good at comprehending women."

"You are in no position to lecture on the subject," Benedict said.

"Is that right?"

"Bloody hell, man, even I can see that you and Penny—Mrs. Marsden—have warm feelings for each other."

Logan's jaw hardened. He drank some more brandy. "At the moment I am in no position to propose marriage to her. I have made a few small investments but none have proved to be especially lucrative. Perhaps in time." He raised one shoulder in a small shrug. "For the most part I am obliged to survive on an inspector's salary, at least for now."

"Well, at least she hasn't flung a damned family necklace back in your face."

Logan scowled. "I can't imagine Miss Doncaster actually flinging the necklace at you."

"I may have exaggerated slightly on that point, but there is no mistaking the fact that she gave the thing back to me."

"Huh." Logan cradled the brandy glass in his hands.

Benedict swallowed some brandy and lowered the glass. "Have you let Mrs. Marsden know that you are considering emigrating to Canada or Australia?"

"The subject of my future has not come up."

They drank their brandies in silence for a time.

"The ladies suffered a terrible shock to the nerves tonight," Benedict said after a while.

"We all did," Logan said. "I certainly doubt that my nerves will ever be the same. When I think of that scene in the bastard's studio, I feel like reaching for a vinaigrette."

"So do I. What we need to keep in mind is that by the time we arrived Penny and Amity were in command of the situation."

Logan smiled grimly. "I do believe they would have killed the monster."

Benedict recalled the fierce expressions on Amity's and Penny's faces. "No doubt about it. They are both quite resourceful."

Logan nodded. "Indeed, they are."

"And brave."

"Absolutely," Logan said.

"Extraordinary," Benedict said.

"Indeed."

They drank some more brandy in silence.

Benedict rested his head against the back of the chair. "It occurs to me that you ought to clarify the matter of your future with Mrs. Marsden."

"I don't think I have any choice." Logan finished his brandy and set down the glass. "I can't imagine continuing to live here in London knowing that she is living in the same city, wondering if I'll see her on the street or at the theater, unless I can be with her."

"You aren't the only one who needs clarification," Benedict said.

He drained his glass, got to his feet, picked up the decanter and poured two more glasses of brandy.

"We need to make a plan," he said. "Two plans."

Forty-two

I would just like to point out that, when all is said and done, the Channing ball guest list was the key," Logan announced. He smiled at Penny. "But we were not using it correctly. Lady Penhurst was, indeed, on that list and on the Gilmore list, as well."

Penny smiled and blushed.

"One of several aspects of this case that I don't comprehend is, why did Virgil Warwick kill his own sister?—and in the middle of a ballroom, no less," Amity said. "After all, it must have been Leona who convinced or bribed Mrs. Dunning to pose as Virgil's mother so that he could be freed from the asylum the second time."

It was ten o'clock in the morning. Penny had sent invitations to breakfast to Benedict, Logan and Declan. They had all arrived on time and immediately set to making heavy inroads on the mounds of eggs and potatoes and toast that Mrs. Houston had prepared.

"Perhaps Warwick concluded that he no longer needed Leona," Logan suggested. "As for the location he chose for that murder, what could be a more anonymous venue than a masked ball? It was ideal for his purposes. And it created the perfect distraction to make it possible for him to grab you, Miss Doncaster. It's all very neat when you consider it. He was able to dispatch his sister and kidnap his victim at the same place while wearing a disguise that no one would question."

Benedict looked at Penny. "Did Warwick tell you anything that might explain why he murdered Leona?"

"No," Penny said. She swallowed some coffee and cradled the cup very carefully in both hands. "When I woke up in that cage, he spoke only of Amity. He was obsessed with her. When he left to kidnap her, he put on a domino and a mask. He was excited." She shuddered. "In a most unwholesome fashion."

"He obviously knew that he would find her at the costume ball," Declan said. "That means that he knew of Leona's plans to obtain the necklace from Miss Doncaster at that affair."

Amity pursed her lips. "He even knew the details of her scheme. It was a large crowd yet he found me quite easily. It was as if he had been waiting for me to appear from that particular hallway."

"Leona briefed him on her plans," Benedict said.

"Yes, but that still doesn't explain why he killed her," Declan said.

"Leona had her own agenda," Benedict pointed out. "But she was also working for the Russians. It's the only reason she would have gone to great lengths to obtain the Foxcroft notebook. Trust me when I tell you that she had no personal interest in engineering and scientific matters."

Amity looked at him. "During our encounter in the ladies' room, she made it clear that all she cared about was the Rose Necklace. She also said that she had not brought the notebook with her, but aside from that she did not seem concerned with it. She was fixed on going to the American West to reinvent herself."

"Did she say anything else?" Declan asked.

Amity wrinkled her nose. "Well, she did admit that she was the one who aimed Virgil at me. She wanted you to suffer, Benedict. She seemed to think that if I was murdered in a spectacular fashion because of my connection to you that you would feel some responsibility."

Benedict had been about to slather some butter on a slice of toast. His hand tightened into a fist around the knife. "That would be putting it mildly."

Penny set down her coffee. "It makes sense that Leona went a little crazy with rage after your engagement was announced. But why did she want Virgil to murder Amity before that announcement? After all, as far as she knew, the two of you had merely indulged in a shipboard liaison."

"Penny is correct," Logan said. He frowned. "There was no mention of a formal engagement until you returned from America. Yet Leona started the rumors about an affair some three weeks before you returned to London."

Amity felt an awkward warmth rush into her cheeks, but no one seemed to notice her embarrassment.

"Isn't it obvious?" Benedict asked around a bite of toast. "It probably wasn't Leona who decided to murder Amity back at the start. More likely it was her Russian contact. He simply used Leona and her crazed brother to accomplish the mission. As soon as he realized that Amity had saved my life on St. Clare and that we had been quite close for the duration of the voyage to New York, he leaped to the obvious conclusion."

"Yes, of course." Amity set her cup down with a clang. "The Russian contact assumed that I was also a spy and that I was working with you, Benedict."

"I'm sure he knew that I was not a professional espionage agent," Benedict said. "After all, everyone knows that I spend a great deal of my time locked away in my laboratory. But the master spy in this affair could not be certain about you, Amity. He probably views you as his rival or even as his nemesis. What better cover for an agent of espionage than a career as a lady globetrotter?"

Amity smiled slowly, pleased. "An excellent point, sir. What better cover, indeed?"

He glared. "You needn't look so thrilled with the notion."

Declan stepped in before Amity could respond. "So it was very likely Leona's Russian connection who decided to get rid of Miss Doncaster at the start of this business."

"Yes," Benedict said. "But I'm afraid that after I announced that Amity and I were engaged, Leona took it personally. I imagine the Russian spy connection started to lose control of her and of the situation at that point."

Declan nodded. "Because Leona proved to be as unstable and as obsessive as her brother."

"Right," Benedict said. "The master spy is the one who shot Leona at the ball last night. He is also the one who murdered Mrs. Dunning and set the explosive device at Hawthorne Hall. He's been masterminding this affair from the beginning—or, rather, trying to mastermind it. But things keep going awry. Must be very frustrating for him."

They all stared at him for a moment.

He looked at Logan. "It occurs to me, Inspector, that your career would benefit nicely if you happened to be the detective who arrested a spymaster who tried to steal a certain notebook containing secrets that the Crown would prefer to keep out of the hands of the Russians."

Logan's brows rose. "Doing a favor for the Crown never hurts a man's career prospects. Can I assume you are aware of the identity of this spymaster?"

Benedict looked at Amity. "I think so, yes. We are looking for someone who arrived on St. Clare shortly before I did, murdered Alden Cork and stole the plans for the solar cannon. That same person was still in the vicinity when my ship docked. He watched me go to Cork's laboratory and realized that I was very likely working for the Crown."

"Why try to murder you?" Amity asked. "After all, the spy already had the plans for the solar cannon."

"We may never know. But for whatever reason, Cork did not give him the name and address of the inventor with whom he was collaborating," Benedict said. "Cork may have realized that he was dealing with a Russian agent at that point. Perhaps at the last minute he was struck with a burst of loyalty to his country."

"He refused to tell the agent about Foxcroft," Logan said. "The agent killed him and then you showed up at the scene."

"He had no way of knowing that I had discovered Foxcroft's letter to Cork, but he decided it would be best to get rid of me just to be certain I would not prove to be a problem," Benedict said. "He must have been furious when he realized that Amity had managed to get me safely on board the *Northern Star*. At that point all he could do was hope that I succumbed to my wound. He booked passage on board another ship bound for New York and, ultimately, London."

"You survived and headed west to California," Declan said. "All the spy could do at that point was sit back and wait to see what you discovered."

"He assumed that I had found something useful when I returned with a certain notebook, which I delivered almost immediately to my uncle. Cornelius let it be known in certain circles that he had Foxcroft's notebook and that it was the real secret to the solar cannon. As far as the spy knows, he possesses the correct version of Foxcroft's design."

"So now we are looking for the Russian spy." Penny said, "The puppet master who has been pulling the strings."

"I think it is safe to say that we know who he is," Benedict said.

Declan frowned. "Don't keep us in suspense. Who is Inspector Logan going to arrest?"

Benedict's smile lacked any hint of warmth. "The one person involved in this affair besides Amity who possesses the ideal cover for a spy, a façade that allows him to travel anywhere in the world without raising questions."

Forty-three

Humphrey Nash was waiting in his study. He rose and smiled politely when Amity was shown into the room but he made no secret of his impatience.

"My housekeeper said that you wanted to see me immediately and that the matter was quite urgent," he said. "Please sit down."

"Thank you for seeing me." Amity perched on a chair. She gripped the satchel on her lap and looked around the room. "What lovely photographs. You really do possess great skill with a camera."

"Thank you." He sat down at his desk.

Amity glanced at the leather-bound volumes of the *Inventors Quarterly* that were neatly lined up on a nearby shelf.

"I see you have an interest in scientific and engineering matters," she said. "I don't recall that you mentioned that six years ago."

"I have always had an interest in mechanical devices."

"I do remember that you were always obsessed with the very latest in photography equipment."

Humphrey clasped his hands on top of his desk. "I saw your name in the morning papers. I congratulate you on your second narrow escape from the clutches of the Bridegroom. According to the accounts in the *Flying Intelligencer*, the police arrived just in the nick of time."

"Thank heavens." Amity shuddered. "If not for them my sister and I would both be dead by now."

"I am relieved to know that you are safe, of course." Humphrey cleared his throat. "Dare I hope that you are here today because you have changed your mind about collaborating on a travel guide?"

"Not exactly," Amity said.

Humphrey dropped his smile. "What is it, then? As it happens, I am in the midst of packing for a trip to the Far East to do another series on the monuments and temples."

"Yes, I saw the trunks in the front hall." She smiled. "I assume that in addition to the odd monument or temple, you will also photograph various harbors and fortifications while you are abroad?"

Humphrey went quite still. But in the next instant he managed to appear utterly bewildered. "I beg your pardon?"

"Come now, there is no reason to be coy, sir. I am aware that you are in the pay of the Russians."

Humphrey stared at her. "My dear, Amity, I have no idea what you are talking about."

"I am also aware that you are in possession of a certain notebook. It's missing a few vital pages, by the way."

"Amity, are you by any chance prone to bouts of female hysteria?"

"No. I am, however, in need of a healthy dose of revenge. I believe you can be of some assistance to me in that regard, sir."

"You are making less and less sense," Humphrey said.

"Perhaps you have not heard the most recent gossip about me."

He frowned. "What do you mean?"

She clenched her fingers around the satchel. "There is no point keeping it a secret. The word will be all over town by nightfall. Mr. Stanbridge has ended our engagement."

Humphrey looked bewildered.

"I see," he said.

"After all I did for him." Amity whipped out a hankie and blotted her eyes. "I saved his life. If not for me he would have died in an alley on St. Clare. And how does he repay me? By compromising me on board the *Northern Star*. Within days after arriving in London my reputation was in tatters."

"I see," Humphrey said again. He sounded cautious now.

She choked back a sob. "I was so relieved when he announced our engagement. I believed that he had done the gentlemanly thing and saved me from ruin. But I have discovered that he was only using me for his own ends."

"Uh, what ends would those be?"

"He and his uncle, who is connected to certain parties in the government, were searching for a spy, if you can imagine. They did, indeed, find her—with my assistance, I might add. And what is my thanks?"

Humphrey ignored the last bit. "What is the name of this spy, Amity?"

"Lady Penhurst." Amity flicked the hankie, waving the details aside. "I'm sure you heard that she took her own life last night. In the middle of a ballroom, no less. But that is neither here nor there. What matters is that last night Mr. Stanbridge informed me that he no longer requires my assistance in the case. He terminated our engagement and demanded that I return the Stanbridge family necklace. By tomorrow my reputation will have been destroyed beyond repair."

Humphrey cleared his throat. "About this notebook you mentioned."

"Yes, of course. I brought the missing pages with me." She opened the satchel and removed two sheets of paper covered with drawings, symbols and equations. "Mr. Stanbridge doesn't know that I took them, not yet. But by tomorrow he will have discovered that they have vanished. I cannot wait to see the expression on his face when he realizes they are gone."

Humphrey eyed the pages. "What makes you think that I have any interest in those pages?"

"Lady Penhurst told me everything last night. She was delighted to chat about her Russian contact. But all she really wanted was the Rose Necklace. I was to bring it to the masked ball. Of course she did not realize that the notebook that one of you stole is missing the crucial pages detailing certain specifications for Foxcroft's solar engine and battery." Amity smiled. "I can see by the expression on your face that you were not aware of that fact until now yourself. But, then, you probably haven't had time to take a close look at the notebook."

Humphrey was starting to appear alarmed. "Are you certain that those pages are from the Foxcroft notebook?"

"Yes, of course." Amity waved the hankie again. "Mr. Stanbridge explained the plan to me when he asked me to assist in the capture of the spy. They hoped to catch her at the costume ball. But that effort failed because Lady Penhurst took her own life rather than hang as a traitor. Personally, I suspect you are the one who murdered her, but I don't care a jot about that. I never did like the woman."

"The only thing you want is revenge, is that what you are saying?"

"Well, I don't mind telling you that a small financial gesture of gratitude would also be appreciated. We both know how expensive it is to live the globetrotting life."

"Indeed." Humphrey did not take his eyes off the pages in her hand.

"I am rather low on funds and my sister refuses to part with any of the money she inherited from her late husband," Amity continued. "She does not approve of my globetrotting. I was hoping that my travel guide for ladies would prove successful, but given the disaster to my reputation it is unlikely to ever see the light of print."

"May I examine those pages, Amity?"

"What? Oh, certainly. Not very interesting, really. Just a lot of drawings and calculations. Oh, and a list of materials for something called a photovoltaic cell."

She rose and set the pages down on the desk. Humphrey examined them intently for a few minutes. His frown tightened with each passing tick of the clock.

"What makes you think that these pages are from the Foxcroft notebook?" he asked.

"Aside from the fact that Mr. Stanbridge told me, do you mean? Well, there is the rather obvious matter of the signatures."

"What signatures?"

"At the bottom of each page," Amity said. "Evidently Elijah Foxcroft was obsessed with the fear that his drawings would be stolen. So he signed and dated every page in the notebook just as an artist signs his work. See for yourself. Lower right-hand corner."

Humphrey stared at one of the pages. Disbelief warred with uncertainty on his face. Then anger took hold, tightening his handsome face into a dangerous mask.

"That son of a bitch," he rasped very softly.

"Whom do you refer to?" Amity asked politely. "Elijah Foxcroft?"

"Not Foxcroft. Stanbridge. The bastard tricked me."

"Very untrustworthy, our Mr. Stanbridge. As I have learned to my great cost."

"Bloody hell." Humphrey opened a desk drawer. "I don't give a damn about the damage to your reputation, Amity."

"How very open-minded and modern of you."

"Tell me, does Stanbridge or his uncle know that Leona and I were associated?"

"No. I intended to tell him but what with one thing and another last night, I did not get the opportunity until after the police had rescued me from the clutches of the Bridegroom. By then I was so upset because of my ordeal I completely forgot that Leona had told me she was connected to you. I was going to inform Mr. Stanbridge first thing this morning, but he arrived on my sister's doorstep early today to announce that he was ending our engagement. I was so upset I decided not to give him any more information." She wiped her eyes with the hankie. "He was just using me."

"My sympathies and my apologies, Amity. I'm afraid I am going to use you, as well."

She lowered the hankie and saw that he had a gun in his hand.

"I don't understand, sir," she whispered.

"I can see that. Really, how did you survive all those journeys to dangerous lands? One would have thought that you would have picked up a modicum of cleverness along the way."

She rose slowly. "You can't shoot me here. Your housekeeper is moving about upstairs. She will hear the shot."

"I have no intention of shooting you, not unless you leave me no other choice."

He was lying, Amity thought. She could see it in his eyes.

"What, exactly, are you going to do with me?" she asked.

"I am going to gag you and lock you up in the darkroom in my basement, where you will not be able to cause me any trouble until I am well away from London. On your feet. Open the door and turn to your left. Hurry."

Amity rose and crossed the room. She opened the door and went briskly out into the hall.

Humphrey followed, moving swiftly. His attention was focused on her. He did not notice Benedict until it was too late.

Benedict seized Humphrey's gun arm and twisted savagely. The pistol roared. The bullet thudded into the wood. All movement ceased overhead. A muffled scream sounded.

The housekeeper, Amity thought.

Benedict snapped the pistol out of Humphrey's hand.

"There's been a change of plans," Benedict said. "But I understand that seasoned travelers are accustomed to that sort of thing. There are a couple of men from Scotland Yard waiting outside on the front steps."

Humphrey looked toward the front hall. Panic and resolve flashed across his face. Then he turned, preparing to flee past Amity in an attempt to exit the kitchen door.

He stopped short when he saw that she had whipped open her fan, revealing the honed steel leaves and the sharp spokes.

But it was Benedict who spoke.

"Let him go, Amity, he's no longer our problem."

Amity stepped aside and folded the fan. Humphrey shot past her. He flung open the door and fled out into the garden—straight into the arms of Inspector Logan and a constable.

"I forgot to mention that there are also a couple of men from the Yard, waiting at the back door," Benedict said.

"You are under arrest, Mr. Nash," Logan said. He took out a pair of handcuffs.

"You don't understand," Humphrey said quickly. "Amity Doncaster is a spy. She is guilty of treason. She brought some valuable papers here today. She stole them and tried to sell them to me, if you can believe it. I was going to lock her up and summon the police."

Cornelius Stanbridge ambled into view out in the garden. "I do agree that Miss Doncaster has what it takes to make an excellent spy, including an ideal cover for traveling abroad. She is really quite talented. Nerves of steel. I am considering employing her as an agent for the Crown."

Amity blushed. "Why, thank you, Mr. Stanbridge. That is very flattering."

Benedict narrowed his eyes. "You can forget any notion of taking up a career as a spy, Amity. My nerves could never stand the strain."

She sighed. "Really, sir, must you take all the fun out of foreign travel?"

Forty-four

"Inspector Logan will disappear from my life soon," Penny said. She went to stand at the window of the study. "The case has been closed. He has no more reason to call on me."

Amity crossed the room and stopped beside Penny. Together they contemplated the garden. It was raining again. The day was gray and dreary. There was a fire on the hearth to ward off the damp chill.

"We need a plan, as Benedict is fond of saying," Amity said.

Penny gave her a watery smile. "What sort of plan do you suggest?"

"Inspector Logan may not have any reason to call on us but you could certainly give him a reason to call on you."

Penny glanced at her. "How do you suggest that I do that without being obvious?"

"What's wrong with being obvious?"

Penny sighed. "It's not the possibility I might embarrass myself that worries me. I'm afraid that being too forward would put him in a very difficult position in the event that he does not wish to continue with our acquaintance."

"Trust me, the man wishes to continue the acquaintance. I can see it in his eyes every time he looks at you."

"I fear he is overly concerned about the differences in our social and financial stations."

"Then it is up to you to convince him that you do not care a jot about those differences." Amity paused. "Unless I am mistaken and they do matter to you?"

"No." Penny turned around, her eyes wet with tears. "I don't give a bloody damn about that sort of thing."

Amity smiled and patted Penny's arm. "I didn't think so."

"But how on earth can I explain that to John?"

Amity raised her brows. "John?"

Penny flushed. "That is his given name. It is how I think of him in my private thoughts."

"Of course." Amity reflected briefly. "I have a plan."

Hope mingled with wariness in Penny's eyes. She hesitated and then curiosity got the better of her. "Well? What is it?"

"I think it would be a very good idea to invite some of the people involved in this case to tea this afternoon. It seems to me that we all have a great deal to discuss and there are some questions I would like to ask the inspector in particular."

Penny looked doubtful. "I'm not sure Inspector Logan is free to come to tea anymore. The demands of his job, you know."

"Something tells me that the inspector is quite capable of coming up with an excuse to interview the witnesses in such an important case one more time. At the moment he is something of a hero at the Yard."

"But what can I say to him that will let him know I wish to continue our association?"

"Why don't you tell him that you were happy to be of service to Scotland Yard and that you stand ready to assist in future cases that involve suspects who move in Society?"

Mrs. Houston appeared in the doorway. She cleared her throat. "I beg your pardon, ma'am, but you're welcome to tell him that I'd also be pleased to assist in future cases. Between the two of us it seems to me that we can cover everything from the kitchens to the bedrooms in Society."

Penny was nonplussed for a moment. Then, slowly, she smiled. "What an excellent notion, Mrs. Houston."

"But I'd suggest breakfast tomorrow morning rather than tea today," Mrs. Houston said.

"Why is that?" Amity asked.

"Healthy gentlemen of the sort we've been entertaining of late prefer a hearty meal," Mrs. Houston said. "Something about eggs and sausage and toast along with strong coffee puts them in a good mood."

Forty-five

They gathered again for breakfast the following morning. Penny sat at the head of the table. Amity sat at the opposite end. Benedict, Logan and Declan were arranged at varying places in between. Amity noted that the three men had very nearly emptied the trays on the sideboard. The violent activities of recent days had certainly not put the gentlemen off their food, she thought.

"We have had the most wonderful news," Penny announced with a flourish. "Mr. Galbraith, Amity's publisher, is rushing her book into print. He says that all the publicity surrounding her will ensure excellent sales for *A Lady's Guide to Globetrotting*."

Benedict looked pleased. "Excellent news, indeed."

Declan grinned. "Congratulations, Miss Doncaster."

"I shall certainly purchase a copy," Logan promised. "I hope you will sign it for me, Miss Doncaster?"

"With pleasure," Amity said. "But tell me, what will happen to Humphrey Nash?"

"In an ideal world, Nash would stand trial on all manner of charges," Logan said. "Conspiracy, treason and murder, among other things."

Amity put down her teacup. "In an ideal world?"

"What the inspector means is that there is nothing more the police can do," Benedict explained. "Nash is under arrest but he has made it clear that he is willing to make a bargain."

"What sort of bargain?" Penny asked.

"He claims he has a great deal of information to sell," Benedict explained. "And evidently Uncle Cornelius is in the market for that information."

Penny was outraged. "Do you mean to say that Nash will walk away from this a free man? That's unacceptable. He murdered both Mrs. Dunning and Lady Penhurst. He set a trap designed to murder Amity and Mr. Stanbridge. Who knows how many others he killed along the way?"

Logan put down his fork and picked up his coffee cup. "Cornelius Stanbridge has assured me that the Russians take a dim view of agents who sell their secrets to others. If Nash is released he will find it necessary to go into hiding. At the very least he will certainly be forced to take on a new identity."

"Huh." Benedict looked thoughtful. "If he assumes a new identity he will no longer be able to sell his photographs under his own name."

"In which case he will be obliged to start his career over again," Amity said.

"I wouldn't be surprised if he turns up somewhere in the West," Declan mused. "We do seem to attract a wide variety of people who are looking for new lives."

Amity smiled at him. "Speaking of the American West, what of your own plans, sir?"

Declan smiled. "Odd that you should ask. I have been doing a great deal of thinking about my future lately. I have concluded that I'm not cut out for the oil business. But I took a great deal of satisfaction assisting Inspector Logan and the rest of you in your search for the Bridegroom. I'm considering establishing a private investigation business, headquartered in San Francisco. Perhaps in time I will offer my consulting services to the police."

"Excellent notion," Logan said. "One thing I discovered in the course of this case is that there may be something to be said for the use of the science of psychology in solving crimes."

Amity looked at Declan. "What about your father?"

Declan straightened his shoulders and assumed an air of resolve. "I am going to tell him that I do not intend to take an active role in the family business and that I will be setting up my own firm instead."

Benedict looked at him across the width of the table. "If it's any comfort you will not be going home empty-handed."

Declan frowned. "What do you mean?"

"It's true that you did not manage to obtain Foxcroft's notebook, but you can assure your father it doesn't matter."

Everyone looked at Benedict.

"Why doesn't it matter that I failed?" Declan said.

"I had a long talk with Uncle Cornelius this morning," Benedict said. "It turns out that the Russians are no longer interested in the potential of solar energy."

"What on earth?" Amity exclaimed.

"There is even worse news," Benedict said. "I have been informed that the Crown is no longer interested in solar energy, either. Even the French are abandoning that area of research."

Logan frowned. "Canceled for lack of funding?"

"No," Benedict said. "Lack of interest. Evidently the British government, the Russians, France and the Americans are coming to the conclusion that the future is in petroleum." Benedict gave Declan a wry smile. "Your father may be right."

Amity was the first to recover from the shock.

"Oh, for pity's sake." She crumpled her napkin and tossed it on the table. "After all we went through?"

"Trust me, I was no more pleased to learn that news than you are," Benedict said. "But that is the way of all governments, I'm afraid. There is a strong tendency toward shortsightedness when it comes to planning for the future."

Logan regarded him from across the table. "What will become of Foxcroft's notebook?"

Benedict smiled slowly. "An interesting question. Uncle Cornelius and I discussed the subject at some length. Foxcroft gave the notebook to me to look after. With the Crown no longer interested in his work, Cornelius and I have concluded that the notebook should go into the Stanbridge family archives."

Declan looked amused. "My father will be relieved to know that no one over here intends to waste any more time investigating the potential for solar energy."

"Not now," Benedict said. "But who knows what the future holds? Today we are concerned with the prospect of running out of coal. Perhaps one day we will have the same concerns about petroleum."

Amity noticed that Logan was smiling to himself.

"Do you have something to add to the conversation, Inspector?" she asked.

Logan picked up his coffee cup. "I was just thinking that I may have made a good investment, after all, when I sank what was left of my father's money into American oil stocks." He looked at Declan. "Including Garraway Oil."

There was an acute silence as everyone stared at Logan. Penny's eyes sparkled with laughter.

"I suspect that will prove to be a brilliant move, Inspector," she said. "I have made a few investments in that area myself."

Amity smiled. "If Penny says that petroleum is a good investment, you can take that advice straight to the bank. My sister has a head for making money, Inspector."

Benedict laughed. In a moment they were all laughing, including Mrs. Houston.

Amity fixed Benedict and Declan with what she hoped was a meaningful look. "If you two gentlemen will accompany me to the drawing room, there is something I would like to say to you both."

Benedict frowned. "What?"

Declan looked bewildered. "Something wrong, Miss Doncaster?"

"I will explain in the drawing room," she said, trying to put a not-so-subtle emphasis on each word. She could tell by Benedict's expression that he was about to ask more questions. She got to her feet. "Now, if you don't mind."

At the sight of her out of the chair all three men hastily rose. She smiled benignly at Logan. "Why don't you stay here and chat with Penny while I talk to Benedict and Declan."

She whisked up the skirts of her gown and went toward the door of the morning room. Benedict and Declan obediently trooped after her.

When they reached the drawing room, she closed the door and whirled around to confront her audience of two.

"What the devil is this about, Amity?" Benedict asked.

"My sister and Inspector Logan require a few minutes alone," she said. She brushed her palms together. "The three of us have just provided that for them."

Declan's expression cleared. He chuckled and looked at Benedict.

"I believe this is about romance, sir," he explained.

Benedict stared at him. "What romance?"

"The one that is blooming between Penny and the inspector," Amity said, striving for patience.

"Ah, that romance." Benedict smiled a self-satisfied smile. "No need to worry on that front. I took care of everything."

Amity stared at him, dumbfounded. "And just how did you do that?"

"Very simple. Logan and I drank some brandy together and formulated a few plans. He is no doubt inviting Penny out for a walk in the park as we speak."

"I'm impressed," she said. "That was brilliant, Benedict."

"I thought so," he said. "Now, if Declan will excuse us, I would like to proceed with my own plans for the day."

Declan grinned and made a show of taking out his pocket watch. "Would you look at the time? I must get a telegram off to my father letting him know he need no longer worry that solar energy will be competing with oil any time soon. After that I must pack for the voyage home. Don't worry, Miss Doncaster, I'll see myself out."

"Good-bye, Mr. Garraway," Amity said.

But she did not look at him. She could not seem to take her eyes off Benedict, who was gazing at her with an intensity that riveted her senses.

Declan opened the door and moved out into the hall.

"Amity," Benedict began, "I wish to speak to you about last night."

Mrs. Houston's heavy footsteps sounded in the hall.

"Don't forget your bonnet, ma'am," Mrs. Houston said, uncharacteristically cheerful. "And a parasol. Too much sun isn't good for the complexion."

"Thank you, Mrs. Houston," Penny said.

Amity turned and saw a brightly flushed Penny and a smiling Inspector Logan.

"Where are you going?" Amity asked.

Penny's blush deepened. Happiness brightened her eyes. "John has been given the entire morning to conclude interviews with all the witnesses in the Bridegroom case. He and I are going for a walk in the park."

"Nothing like fresh air and sunshine to clarify a witness's recollections," Logan said.

Mrs. Houston opened the front door with a bit of a flourish. Penny and Logan went down the front steps and out into the sunshine.

Mrs. Houston closed the door and looked at Amity and Benedict.

"A lovely couple, don't you think?" she said. She sounded quite satisfied.

"Yes," Amity said. She smiled. "A lovely couple, indeed."

"It's about time Mrs. Marsden found a spot of happiness," Mrs. Houston said. She stopped smiling and glared at Benedict. "And what about you, sir? Are you just going to stand there like a very large frog on a log?"

Benedict blinked and then frowned. "A frog on a log?"

"I think you take my meaning, sir."

Benedict's expression cleared. "Right. As it happens, Mrs. Houston, I was just about to ask Amity to join me for a drive."

"Were you, indeed?" Amity asked.

"The day is very fine and I happen to have a carriage waiting in the street," he said. "All part of the plan, you see. Will you come with me?"

Amity caught her breath. "Yes. Yes, I would like that very much."

Mrs. Houston took Amity's bonnet off the peg. "Here you go, miss. Now, off with the both of you. I want to put my feet up for a bit. Been a busy morning."

Forty-six

He took her to his home and introduced her to Mr. Hodges and Mrs. Hodges, who greeted her with a degree of warmth that amazed Benedict.

"I read about your narrow escape in the papers," Mrs. Hodges gushed. "Thank heavens you and your sister are unharmed."

"We are great fans of your travel articles in the *Flying Intelligencer*," Mr. Hodges said, his enthusiasm genuine.

"Such an exciting life you lead," Mrs. Hodges said. "Will you and Mr. Stanbridge be doing a great deal of globetrotting after you are married?"

"Well," Amity began. She cast an uncertain look at Benedict.

"We will definitely be doing some traveling in the future," he said.

"Allow us to congratulate you on your engagement, Miss Doncaster," Mr. Hodges said with a courtly inclination of his head. "I believe that I speak for myself and my wife when I say that we are extremely pleased by the prospect of Mr. Stanbridge's upcoming nuptials."

Amity cleared her throat and smiled. Benedict got worried. Her smile was a little too bright, he concluded.

"Thank you, Mr. Hodges, but I'm afraid there is some confusion as to the matter of my engagement to Mr. Stanbridge," Amity said.

Mrs. Hodges's eyes widened in alarm. "Oh, dear."

Benedict tightened his hand on Amity's arm. "Miss Doncaster means that there is some confusion about the date of the wedding. Naturally I'd prefer to be married as soon as possible, but I am told that when it comes to weddings there is a great deal of planning to be done."

"Yes, indeed," Mrs. Hodges said. She relaxed again and beamed at Amity. "But there is always the option of a quiet little ceremony followed by a formal reception at some later date."

"Excellent idea, Mrs. Hodges," Benedict said before Amity could argue. "Now you must excuse us. I'm going to give Miss Doncaster a tour of my library and my laboratory."

Mrs. Hodges's eyes narrowed in what Benedict knew was a meaningful way. "Are you certain that is a good idea, sir? Perhaps after the wedding might be a better time to show Miss Doncaster your library and the laboratory."

"No," Benedict said. "The tour must come now."

Mrs. Hodges sighed. Mr. Hodges looked resigned. He patted his wife on the shoulder.

"It's for the best, Mrs. Hodges," he said in low tones.

Benedict whisked Amity down the hall and through the open door of the library. Behind him he heard Mrs. Hodges muttering to Mr. Hodges.

"I suppose it's only fair to the lady," Mrs. Hodges said. "Miss Doncaster deserves to see what she's getting into."

"Try not to worry, Mrs. Hodges," Mr. Hodges said. "Miss Doncaster is the adventurous sort."

Benedict closed the door and turned the key in the lock. He looked at Amity, who was examining the titles of some of the books on the shelves.

"Yes," he said. "Miss Doncaster deserves to know what she is getting into." He moved away from the door and swept out a hand to indicate the walls of dusty tomes. "This is the real me, Amity, or, I should say, this is part of me. The rest is behind that door at the top of the steps."

She glanced at the circular wooden steps at the far end of the library. Amusement sparkled in her eyes.

"How exciting, a locked chamber," she said.

He winced. "I'm afraid it's not all that thrilling."

"May I take a look?" she asked.

"Yes." He steeled himself. "That's why I brought you here today. I want you to know the real me. It's part of my plan, you see. I am not a dashing man of action, Amity. I'm just a man who, when he is not working on an engineering project for the family firm, is quite happy to putter around in his laboratory."

"And what do you do in your laboratory, sir?"

"For the most part, I conduct experiments and design devices and machines that will probably never have any practical applications."

Without a word she collected her skirts and went up the steps. He followed, a great sense of urgency flooding through him. He knew that his entire future was at stake.

At the top of the steps Amity moved out onto the balcony and stopped in front of the door. He took the key out of his pocket and inserted it into the lock.

Amity watched without saying a word as he opened the door, turned up the lamps and stood back so that she could enter the chamber.

She stood on the threshold for a moment, examining the array of instruments and tools on the workbenches.

"So this is your laboratory," she said.

"Yes."

He waited.

She walked to the telescope that stood near the window and studied it with an admiring eye. "You have a great deal of curiosity about many things."

"I'm afraid so."

"As you know, curiosity is one of my own besetting sins."

He smiled. "I am aware of that."

"It gives us something in common, wouldn't you say?"

He hesitated. "Our interests are not always the same."

"Perhaps not but it doesn't matter." She moved to a workbench and studied the static electricity machine. "It is the trait of curiosity that is important. You possess an inquiring mind. That is one of the many things that makes you so interesting, Benedict."

Interesting. He was not sure how to interpret the word.

"There are those who find me decidedly boring," he warned, just in case she had not grasped the point he was trying to make.

"It is only to be expected that those who lack curiosity about the wider world would find those who possess that particular characteristic uninteresting."

"My fiancée ran off with her lover after she saw this room."

"Face it, Benedict, your first engagement was a mistake. If you and Eleanor had gone through with the marriage, you both would have been miserable."

"I am well aware of that." He paused. "Which is why I want to be very sure that you know what you are doing if you consent to marry me."

Amity turned around to face him from the far end of the aisle. "Are you asking me to marry you?"

"I love you, Amity. I want nothing more than to marry you."

"Benedict," she whispered. "You must know how I feel about you."

"No, I don't. Not for certain. I think I know how you feel but at this point it is only a theory—unproven and founded only on hope."

She took a few steps toward him and stopped. "I fell in love with you on board the *Northern Star*. I sensed that you had some feelings for me, but I was so afraid that those feelings were inspired by the knowledge that I had saved your life."

"You did save my life. But that is not why I fell in love with you."

Her eyes brightened. "Why did you fall in love with me?"

"I have absolutely no idea."

"Oh." The glow in her eyes faded.

"I could list all the things that I admire about you—your spirit, your kindness, your loyalty, your courage and determination." He paused. "I could also add that you are a woman of great passion. Making love to you is the most thrilling sensation I have ever known."

"Really?" She flushed a vivid pink.

"Really. Those things are all admirable traits, mind you. But none of them explains why I love you." He took a few steps toward her and stopped. "That is what makes it all so fascinating, you see. Loving you is like gravity or the daily sunrise. It is a mystery that I know I will be content to explore for the rest of my life."

"Benedict." She rushed toward him and hurled herself into his arms. "That is the most beautiful, most romantic thing that any man has ever said."

"I doubt that very much." He folded her close, savoring the soaring happiness. "I'm an engineer, not a poet. But if those words make you happy, I will be glad to repeat them as often as you will let me."

She looked at him, her eyes brilliant with love. "That sounds like an excellent plan, sir."

He took the Rose Necklace out of his pocket. The rubies and diamonds blazed in his hand.

"I would take it as a great honor if you would accept this as a symbol of our love," he said.

Once again he waited.

She looked at the necklace for a long moment. When she raised her eyes he could see the sheen of tears. But she was smiling.

"Yes," she said. "I will keep it safe."

It was all she said but it was enough.

She turned around. He fastened the necklace around her throat and then he put his hands on her shoulders to turn her back to face him.

"Once upon a time I gave you a letter to keep safe," he said.

"And I made you promise that you would survive to deliver it."

"We kept our word to each other," he said.

"Yes." She put her arms around his neck. "That is how it will always be between us."

The future, lit by the promise of a lifelong love, glowed brighter than the gems in the Rose Necklace.

"Always," he said.